Praise for Carrie Laben's *A Hawk in the Woods*

"*A Hawk in the Woods* is wonderfully dark and spellbinding, mixing the road novel, family drama, time travel, cosmic horror, and maybe even a little *Heathers*. Carrie Laben is an original, compelling new voice. Consider me a fan for life."

—Paul Tremblay, author of *A Head Full of Ghosts* and *The Cabin at the End of the World*

"*A Hawk in the Woods* is a stunning, chilling masterpiece by one of the best new voices in literary horror. Searingly intelligent, gorgeously wrought, this gripping tale of two gifted, haunted sisters begins as a classic get-away story and soon unfolds into a terrifying excavation of the American dream of unbridled power. Carrie Laben writes with a ferocious grace; a master of the gothic pastoral, of the slow burn, of surprise. Carrie Laben is a monster—they don't even make writers like this anymore. You will be reading her name for decades to come."

—Cara Hoffman, Author of *Running* and *So Much Pretty*

"Ride or die sisterhood, conjured from the bones of H. P. Lovecraft."
—Molly Tanzer, author of *Vermilion* and *Creatures of Will & Temper*

"In this uncanny world, the darkest moments don't come from the supernatural horror but from the realization that the Waites' underlying dysfunction is a near and dear part of our own."
—*Foreword Reviews* (Starred Review)

"At once sly and grim, soberingly real and darkly fantastical, the story of the Waite sisters will haunt readers like an eerie old folk song."
—*Publishers Weekly* (Starred Review)

A HAWK IN THE WOODS

A HAWK IN THE WOODS

CARRIE LABEN

WORD HORDE
PETALUMA, CA

First Edition

ISBN: 978-1-939905-46-8

A Word Horde Book
www.wordhorde.com

For my family

CHAPTER ONE
Prelude

"Ab… Abihail Waite?" Abby saw the receptionist's confusion and even though it was a bit annoying, simply because it was so routine, she couldn't blame the older woman. She shot out an embarrassment-smoothing smile as she unfolded from the slightly-too-low waiting room seat.

"Abby's fine," she said, and waited, but the curiosity remained. It was gratifying. "It's an old family name and I guess no one told my mom that it would just weird everybody out."

The receptionist return-volleyed a smile, this one grateful, and entered a few brisk keystrokes into her computer—a note for later, or for whoever had to deal with Abby next. "Very good. You can go right in; Dr. Tremblay's in the first examining room on the left."

Abby saw as soon as she walked into the room, before the doctor even looked up from her chart to face her, that his thoughts were downcast and dark. When he faced her, concern poured over her, and he swept the papers up in one hand as though he was worried that she would see them, even though they were about her and in a few minutes she'd know what they said.

Well, shit.

"Please sit down," he said, gesturing to the smaller and starker of the room's two chairs with the hand that held her file. "How are you feeling?"

She was feeling better from the minute she walked in and felt herself the subject of so much worry, but that wasn't something to say out loud. "About the same. Nervous, of course. And the biopsy sites itch a bit."

"Of course. That's very normal." He said it in an abstract way. How she was feeling didn't really matter, from his point of view, compared to what was printed on those papers. And he didn't want to talk about that, although he must see bad biopsy results all the time.

"The results are in?" she prompted.

"They are. I'm afraid it's not the news that we were hoping for." He was afraid, at that. Of what? Of her reaction, she supposed. He seemed to realize then that he was holding the papers, and laid them back down on his desk. "It's cancer. And it's fairly advanced."

The words hit her even though she'd already known in her heart. She squeezed the arm of the chair but there was no padding to dig her nails into, nothing to tear a hole in. No way to escape.

"I can't say for certain without further testing exactly how far it's spread, but given the thickness and ulceration of the original tumor and the fact that we found satellite tumors, we're looking at a late stage III, at best." He locked eyes with her, and she pulled strength from that. "Now, the thing to understand is that the science of melanoma has advanced very rapidly in the past decade and although stage III sounds bad, you could still have a better than even chance to come out of this cancer-free with aggressive treatment."

This was not a dark basement full of monsters; there was no reason to put on a brave face and suppress any hitch of fear in her voice, but she did it anyway, running on instinct. "How much better than an even chance?"

"Depending on how far it's spread, maybe fifty-six, fifty-seven percent."

So not really better than even, then. Abby didn't realize that she'd stood up from the chair but maybe she was going to try to escape after all. The doctor stood too, and she was nearly eye-to-eye with him although he was not a short man.

"Please, sit down," he said, and she did, and he handed her a box of tissues even though she wasn't crying.

"You probably think I'm an idiot for not coming to see you sooner," she said, because she thought that herself.

"Oh no, oh no," he said quickly, as though his opinion would make her feel better. "That's exactly the problem. Melanoma takes healthy young people, because those are exactly the people who don't realize they're sick until it's too late."

She was almost certain that he was thinking about her funeral in that moment, about how sad it would be to see a pretty young girl go down in the dirt, which told her exactly what fifty-six percent was. She nodded slowly, to show that she understood, not that she agreed to any of this.

"We won't know for sure until we do further testing," he said, "which we'll do as soon as possible, of course. And then we can decide on a line of attack. You're lucky to be in Buffalo, really," he said, which couldn't possibly be true. "Roswell Park is running some very promising clinical trials right now, in the event that it's spread further than we'd like."

"Okay," she said, more to test her voice than anything. She sounded good. Normal. Okay.

"Myrrah at the front desk will set you up with your follow-up appointments," he said. "Do you have anyone to drive you home?"

She just stared at him blankly, giving nothing, until he got uncomfortable.

"And whatever you do, try to stay positive. People fight this thing and beat it all the time."

She made it through setting the follow-up appointments in a

daze, half-conscious that it didn't really matter when they were. She made it out to her car. She locked herself in, turned on the AC, and screamed "Motherfucker!" at the top of her lungs. It helped a little.

Then she started to think about what to do next. She'd hoped to have decades to get a plan in place before it came to this. Hell, like anyone on the uphill side of middle age, she'd secretly harbored a hope that she was unique in all the world and the day would never come for her. Grandfather hadn't had to worry about this shit until he'd crested ninety—but then again, Grandfather wasn't a good example of how to handle these things.

Well, whatever she was going to do, the next step at least was clear. The next step was to go get Martha. She needed her sister.

CHAPTER TWO

The road to Wende was dull, and got duller as you got closer to the prison. Squat buildings that housed self-storage units, auto mechanics, a pool supply store. Scrubby woodlots and fields of timothy hay. Blue chicory and goldenrod. Occasional ranch houses, their yards beginning to brown with midsummer, furnished with a rusty swing set or a driveway basketball hoop or an ATV parked out front with a For Sale sign leaned against it. Roadkill, mostly bloated woodchucks and raccoons this time of year, the occasional smeared barn cat.

The house that always had the sign out front saying "Be not deceived, God is not mocked" still did, and the Gator Bar and Grill at the crossroad a little further on was still having a special on wings and pitchers of Labatt.

The car Abby was driving was a rental, her own Miata left behind in her driveway, not up to the job without a few hundred bucks in repairs that she didn't have time for. Her impulse had been to trade up, go for a Jag or a Mustang convertible, something glamorous, something that would turn heads. Seeking anonymity didn't come naturally to her. But in the end she'd talked herself into a Jeep Grand Cherokee, dark blue, a model from a couple years back. She hadn't even bothered figuring out how to plug her iPhone in yet, so she poked at the dashboard until the radio came on.

There was supposed to be Sirius but somehow she'd gotten an old radio instead and it didn't offer much—Lite 97 and Kiss 98.5, NPR and country and a bunch of religious crap. Why did they even put this shit in newer cars? She hit Scan and let the numbers drift away to the staticky end of the dial while she imagined Martha's face, the gratitude and wonder.

Like a stab from a knife the static yielded to a clean, clear voice— a woman accompanied by something folky—a mandolin? A zither? And the singing was just chanting really, a series of nonsense syllables. *Seven years a hawk in the woods. All alone and so lonely-o.* Some college kids at GC3 pouring authenticity into the air on a weak beam that no one ever listened to.

It wasn't driving music—no beat, and the scattered lyrics she could make out didn't make her want to fly or run or fuck or anything like that, they didn't even make her mad. She hit Scan again and got nothing for her trouble but more static, then turned the radio off.

She was running late, too. Visiting hours would be almost over by the time she got there; the last thing she needed was to get stuck behind some drug addict's devoted grandma's half-broken-down Pontiac on the way out of the parking lot. The shortest jailbreak in history. It'd make a good story, but she wouldn't be tweeting about it. She stepped on the gas.

At the gates, the guard in the little box smiled and she smiled back hard and tangled his thoughts and he waved her in, no checking her ID, no hassles. He was a tall older man with a crew cut and glasses, a little pasty and a little paunchy, maybe a dad or even a grandfather if he or his kids had been a little too precocious. Far too sympathetic-looking for her to get away with running him over or shooting him with the gun she didn't have or need. People hated cop-killers, except from time to time when they turned around and loved them. She could pull that off, the folk-hero schtick, Pretty Boy Floyd or Dillinger but as a photogenic woman so even better. Hell, maybe she should have done that. Too late now. Unless she…

There, just outside that door that seemed to be clanging even when it was shut, stood Martha.

Abby waited for the woman to turn or gesture and be someone else, someone who just happened to resemble the two of them in passing, but she didn't. It wasn't possible to mistake her own eyes, even when they were set in the rough un-made-up face of a woman standing alone on the pavement. Abby had never met anyone else out in the world who looked quite like herself and her twin, tall and slightly tan even in winter, pointed noses, pointed chins— striking not cute, queens not princesses.

Martha wasn't looking very queenly right now though, leaning a little, letting the duffel bag she held rest on the ground even though there was no way it could be heavy; it slumped in on itself, half-empty. Her gaze scanned the parking lot and the fence and the world as a whole without any evidence of either desire or fear. That blank look on Martha's face always used to annoy Abby, but it wasn't worth being annoyed about now. It would change soon enough.

An elderly Hispanic woman carrying a thick black book glanced at Martha as she passed, and that evidence that her twin existed to other people too jolted Abby into action. She threw the car into neutral, leaned across to the passenger door. She could barely open it, let alone reach out and gesture, but Martha looked up and no-ticed her anyhow. Her eyes got a little wider.

Martha didn't seem to hurry, but in an instant the duffel bag was in the back and she was in the shotgun seat. As soon as Abby heard the door slam she was accelerating, lurching through the parking lot and blasting by the pillbox where the crew-cut guard waved.

The prison receded in the distance and the car reached seventy, eighty, ninety, a hundred and three miles an hour. This was the critical moment, the only time she really needed to worry about pursuit; she couldn't handle too many of them at once, not if they were focused, full of rage and bravado. Abby clutched the wheel, her shoulders up as if she could physically ward off the sirens when they came. She took a corner and felt the Cherokee wobble a little, its center of gravity nosing off the road towards the cornfields like a wayward beagle, but she didn't touch the brake. They weren't going to get Martha back, and they sure as shit weren't going to get Abby.

The sirens didn't come. She glanced in the rear-view mirror. There was no one behind her. Not a single other vehicle on the road except, in the distance, a lumbering John Deere crossing from one field to another with a wagon-load of hay.

Were they still getting their asses sorted from their elbows back there? Or had they gone ahead to set up a roadblock? If so, where? How many cars, how many men, how many guns? She glanced back again, just to make sure they weren't gaining on her.

"I knew you'd come," Martha said softly.

"I'm sorry it took so long," Abby answered, not taking her eyes off the road. She should have gone for the sports car.

"They offered to put me on a bus, but I said no, my sister will come for me."

"Of course I came... A bus?"

"When they release you they pay for a bus ticket to somewhere, in case you haven't got anyone coming for you. A lot of the girls don't. But I said, my sister will come."

Abby had the presence of mind to decelerate slowly. "I know math was never my strong subject, but it sure hasn't been thirty years."

"They gave me time off for good behavior, I guess."

"You guess? You haven't been keeping track?" She locked the rage out of her voice as best she could.

"It all gets to be one big day after a while," Martha said meekly. And then, some time later, "Can we stop at a Dairy Queen or something? I could kill for a sundae about now."

Abby's first clear memory is of…

No, actually, her first clear memory is of feeding the crusts from her sandwich to the ducks in the pond behind the next-door neighbor's house, where she wasn't supposed to go but went anyway until they gave up telling her not to. The ducks were shiny green-black with bright orange feet and sometimes when they got excited they nipped Martha with their bright orange bills. They never nipped Abby, though, because she could see in the energy and direction of their thoughts when they were getting too worked up, and she used her brain to shove them back. She'd always known how to do that, the same as she knew how to shove things with her hands.

This time she didn't see their thoughts, though, because they barely had time to think. Suddenly, the ducks were all around them, a thunder of laboring dusty wings, a mad ripple of quacking, the rich-smelling splat as the birds with full guts jettisoned the extra weight. Two that were too fat to fly were still as rocks at Abby's feet.

Martha gasped and pointed. At the far edge of the pond a huge brown bird mantled over a smaller, slower duck. The predator fixed them briefly with a single yellow eye, then decided they were far enough away to ignore and bent to rip into the duck.

"Hey!" Abby yelled out loud as she pushed at the hawk's mind. "Get out of here!" She was upset about the duck, bloody and dead now, but almost more offended. The hawk's mind, tiny and focused as hard as a walnut, did nothing but drive the beak harder into flesh and pull up a wad of red-stained feathers.

"Hey!" But she could do nothing with the hawk's mind. Finally, in spite, she picked up a good-sized rock and chucked it into the pond, creating a geyser of water and mud. The hawk flapped away, duck in talons.

Her second clear memory, then, is of Mom and Grandfather fighting. She tried to tell them not to, push them apart, but it didn't work. She thought she remembered being surprised, although that didn't make sense—Mom and Grandfather would have been too much for her, just like the hawk was. Had she known, at that age, that distraction and flared tempers should have made them more vulnerable? When would she have learned that?

Anyway, she remembered Mom throwing a can at Grandfather, hitting him in the shoulder. She can picture the label on the can, the yellow and orange of store-brand soup. She remembered Grandfather turning and raising his hand to hit Mom in turn—he was a bit taller than her, still, before the osteoporosis fully set in. She remembered tensing up as though she was the one who was about to be hit. But she doesn't remember him actually hitting her.

Was it just the normal fuzziness of a little kid's memory? Or did Martha fold that part away?

CHAPTER THREE

After the sundae, a banana split with nuts, and after their traditional spoon-duel for the last few bites of hot fudge, which Abby
won as always, most of her rage had evaporated with the adrenaline
let-down. She hated to have to rely on Martha, even accidentally,
but in some ways this was better than how she'd planned it. Abby
could keep more of her own reserves for the end of the trip. Of
course she wasn't going to tell Martha that. And it was annoying to
realize that she could have used her own car after all.

At the Batavia shopping center, while Martha stocked up on
new clothes and little necessities at a consignment shop, Abby
ducked into the liquor store and picked out a bottle of Barefoot
Pink Moscato. Basic in every sense of the word, but something they
could both enjoy. Tonight they would toast her sister's freedom.
Also it might help if Martha was a little tipsy when Abby broke
the news about her cancer—in fact, on second thought Abby put
down the bottle and selected a magnum. Then she headed out to
wait by the car.

Heat waves made the parking lot shimmer and distorted the
gulls around the McDonald's dumpster into bulbous grotesques. It
didn't help the smell much, either. She slid into the Cherokee and

turned the AC up full blast.

A moment later she looked up and Martha was loading the back seat of the Cherokee with bags. She'd changed into a new outfit already—a cotton sundress with a yellow and green fish print, brown sandals with turquoise chips along the straps. She was still too thin and her long dark hair was still frizzy with split ends, but the green of the fish echoed her eyes, made her look less sallow and worn out. For a moment Abby imagined a life that might have been, the country twin and the city twin on a road trip. In the prime of life, in the prime of summer, no shadows over them at all. Maybe Abby was making a miniseries, discovering America for one of the networks—the networks seemed to need to discover America every couple of years—or maybe Martha was moving to California to start a new job and had some time off in between, or maybe they'd decided to buy a farm and raise organic goats in Colorado, or maybe...

Abby shook her head. No point regretting what wasn't. What was would be fine, once they got to Minnesota. It would have to be.

"You look good," she said to Martha as she started the car. "A couple of weeks of decent moisturizer and a new haircut, it'll be like you never went away." That wasn't one hundred percent true, but Abby thought that most of the damage would be reversible.

"Thanks," Martha said, but she was distracted, twisted into the back seat and searching through her bags. Abby felt oddly unsatisfied and she picked up her phone out of habit. When she planned this she'd expected that half the county would be thinking about her by now, enthralled by the news of the jailbreak, feeding her their attention. Or at least that Martha would be a bit more excited to see her.

"Turn on some music," she said just to make Martha do something, and Martha, still run by old habits, dropped the bags. She turned on the radio and immediately landed on the folk station again, and after a few seconds Abby realized that she was listening to the same zithery, chanting song. The same lyric, *Seven years a hawk in the woods.* The DJ was obsessed. Or maybe it was some kind of marathon or a contest or something. She could tweet about it. She could use the juice, and the station would probably be glad of her attention.

"There's something wrong with your radio." Martha poked at the button, but the song went on, lilting across nearly an entire verse despite the numbers on the LED display skipping downward.

Great, Abby thought, half distracted. *This would happen when I can't get a refund.*

She reached across and hit the button herself, and the radio turned obedient and tuned in a car dealership commercial. She tried again. *Cellino and Barnes, The Injury Attorneys. 888-8888.* Normally she hated that fucking jingle—it was impossible to stop humming to yourself—but it was better than having that weird, creepy folk song stuck in both their heads.

"It must be you," she told Martha, half-teasing. "You must be giving off electromagnetic rays or something."

"Hmph." The commercial ended and a man with an over-worked voice discussed next season's hockey prospects, and Martha switched it off without any problem.

Back to the tweet. Was there some kind of pun she could make on the word 'folk'? Nothing jumped to the top of her mind, and sarcasm was just as effective anyway. "WGCC is really rockin' out on the cutting edge today," she typed, and scanned quickly for autocorrect stupidity before she hit send.

She looked up from the phone to find Martha staring at her. "What are you doing?"

"Tweeting. Come on, you had to at least have heard of Twitter. Even in there."

"Girls mentioned it, yeah, but I didn't really get it." She kept staring, her attention thoroughly wrapped around the iPhone in its custom dark-green leather case, with the tiny scuff on one corner that irritated Abby to death every time she saw it. "Can I get my own phone now that I'm out?"

"Can you? You'd be like an Amish person without one. I'll get you one as soon as I can." Abby rubbed the scuff with her thumb—it didn't help, any more than the last five times she did it—and put the phone back in her purse.

The replacement case she'd ordered last week—she'd never get that now. Goddammit. She'd forgotten all about it.

"You want to swing by the old homestead before dinner?" she said, trying to sound as if she might take no for an answer.

Martha turned her stare out the window and didn't answer right away. The shadows of the trees were starting to eat the fields.

"I suppose I should," she said slowly, at war with every word. "I mean, I guess I kind of have to at least see Mom, or she'll be mad..."

She caught herself, bit off the clause, but it was too late. Abby, without taking her eyes off the road, pounced on the opportunity.

"See Mom?" She arched her right eyebrow so high it hurt. She could hear Martha turn to look at her and suck in air.

"It just doesn't seem real, that's all, I haven't absorbed it yet..."

"It's been five years. And it's not like it was a big surprise when it happened."

"But I haven't been home, I didn't even get to go to the funeral, and..."

"I'd have thought you'd throw a party." She paused before cutting to the heart of it. "You've been folding time again, haven't you?"

Martha gave way immediately. "I didn't mean to. Sometimes it just happens. I'm not thinking, and then without realizing it I've done it. Like scratching my nose. You know."

"Sure. But almost two decades?" She thought she managed to

make that sound more angry than impressed.

"No, there really was some time off for good behavior too. I don't think it can have been more than ten years... twelve tops."

Okay, good, she was on the back foot. Abby put on a face partway between pissed off and concerned. "I don't care if it's twelve days. Once it unfolds, they're going to want to know where the hell you're at. And here I am walking around with you with my bare face hanging out—we're probably on half a dozen security cameras between the Dairy Queen and plaza. By this time tomorrow I'll be a fugitive."

"It's not going to unfold."

It wasn't like Martha to be overly confident, and Abby plowed over it to her predetermined conclusion. "We'll have to lay low for a bit, is all. And then pop up somewhere else with new identities, make new lives. We both should have left here years ago anyway." They drove in silence for the rest of the five minutes it took to reach their childhood home.

Maybe it was not fair to call those last two clear memories at all. Maybe her *real* first clear memory was the day in kindergarten when she made Nicole Parsons give her a birthday party invitation. Of course the teacher, who was young and eager and not a local, had helped by telling Nicole that she couldn't hand out the invitations in class if she didn't invite everyone. Still, it was a good memory, and she had every bit of it, the look on Nicole's face melting from disdain into misery, the teacher looming over them both, the stiff die-cut invitation in her hand. It was shaped like a troll doll, with purple hair and a small rhinestone glued on where the belly button would be, and it was actually addressed to Dawn DeVoto. It was probably still up in her room somewhere, in one of the boxes of things she'd put away when they got too childish but couldn't quite bring herself to part with.

Mom had been proud of her; Grandfather too. So not only had she gotten to go to the party, where Nicole's mother had hovered over her fearfully and disguised it by constantly handing her more Pepsi and cake, but the very next week she'd started lessons with the big leather-bound books that she'd always been forbidden to touch, the ones that Grandfather kept in his bedroom. Grandfather teased Mom a little, because she hadn't been able to start learning that stuff until she was seven.

Abby knew she hadn't been meant to overhear that. Grandfather's mind was all on Mom, no tentacles sneaking away to show that he knew she'd frozen just the other side of the door frame.

Martha had hung around as she studied, jealous and annoyed, and tried to peek over Abby's shoulder until Grandfather sent her out of the room. She tried to make the kids in her class give her their ice cream money or toys like Abby did, but she just couldn't. For Abby, it was the dawn of the notion that she and her sister were different people. Abby was a person who could see the lines radiating out of another person, marking where they focused their attention, their energy, their thoughts and intentions. Abby was a person who could grasp those lines and bend them into a new shape, clumsily at first and then better and better, like learning to tie her shoes. Abby, like Mom and like Grandfather, was a person who could make other people do what she wanted, which was the best kind of person to be. And Martha was not.

This realization made her feel so darn magnanimous (a word she'd learned from one of the leather-bound books) that when their classes were out together on the playground she made people do things for Martha, just for the pleasure of it. Sometimes she got a headache later in the afternoon, but it was worth it. She was usually bored by then anyway, and she could always get sent to the nurse by the sympathetic young teacher and from there get sent home, at least until the parent-teacher conference when Mom was ordered to take her in for an eye test. She managed to squeak by without glasses, but she did get a lecture about how to behave around out- siders. Martha was left on her own to deal with the snubs and the balls tossed at her head by classmates who already knew they hated the Waite girls, but not why.

CHAPTER FOUR

Since Mom died, Abby had paid their old neighbor James Bonetrager—the man who owned the ducks—to come by the house every so often and keep everything in order, plus extra in winter to get the leaves out of the gutter before it snowed and see to it that the pipes weren't allowed to freeze. So it wasn't a decrepit house. What was wrong with it went much deeper than that.

It had the appropriate setting, well back from the road and shadowed by ancient pines on the western side so that it got twilight before anyone else. It had enough heft to be menacing. It had the original gingerbread trim on the upstairs windows, grayed and chipped by time until the patterns were mere suggestive whispers. It had blackberry canes growing thick and feral around the front porch and wild roses outlining where the fence used to be in the back. Further back, it had the foundation of a collapsed, burnt-out Civil War-era barn. And, of course, it had a claim to a notorious— brutal was the word the prosecutor and the reporters had always used—murder.

But there were gothic old farm houses all over Western New York. Murders too. There were houses with reputations as haunted, houses that carloads of kids drove past hooting for Satan on midnights when they were full of booze and courage and boredom, houses that the network would send Abby to stand outside on Halloween if there happened to be no actual news to cover, back when she was just a local news girl.

Never this one.

The door didn't creak—Bonetrager had one of those old-man work ethics that ruined lives, and as much as he hated the place he did what he was paid for. There were no cobwebs lowering the ceilings, no rodents living inside the furniture. They never did have problems with vermin, living here, even after Grandfather died. It was gloaming inside, of course, but when Abby flipped the switch by the door the light poured down.

She almost turned to Martha and gestured around the room and said "Welcome home," but what she was doing was unpleasant enough, she had no desire to hurt her sister for real, her only sister, her twin—the woman that she still considered her best friend, come to that. So instead she said, "This won't take long," and headed for the stairs.

There was dust on the stairs, with Bonetrager's tracks marked coming and going, proof that he was fastidious in checking the windows and making sure that the roof hadn't sprung a leak. She could see by the drag marks what it cost him, how much he dreaded going up the stairs, getting further from the door. Abby was careful to step on each mark, twisting her feet slightly to grind him away.

The master bedroom was on the twilight end of the house. Abby always suspected that the cold and dim helped Mom die as much as the pills and self-neglect and the fact that Abby left her all alone when she took off for college. But the climate was good for the books; some of them looked as though a single strong beam of sunlight could crumble them. It was a good thing she wasn't after the oldest volumes. Those were mostly curiosities, collector's items, Grandfather's rebuttal to the idea that he was a younger son and an unimportant exile in a nothing town. No, what she needed should be robust enough to stand up to a little travel. She leaned in to examine the shelves, ran her fingers over cracked and flaking spines, careful to concentrate on her task and not let her eyes stray sideways and catch the mirror over the black walnut dresser or the shadows in the space behind the door.

She should have bought herself some luggage back at the plaza, she realized as she started pulling volumes down, but it didn't matter. There were a few sturdy shopping bags from Payless and Fashion Bug still half-unpacked in the corner of the room, things Mom had purchased for a teenage Martha who would never wear them; Abby tipped the contents out onto the bed and packed the books in their place.

She filled a bag and half of a second; several of the books she wanted were massive, with their bulky leather bindings and plates of steel-cut engravings, and each only had a relevant page or two, a chapter at most. The authors, for all their starry wisdom, had an irritating habit of thinking in rambles and spirals; to a man, they would have fallen over in fits if they'd had to to write a decent press release, let alone condense their thoughts into a tweet. And then there were Grandfather's notebooks—she probably didn't need all of them, but she did need to not leave them behind for anyone who came looking. Ninety years of scratchy notes, from the first adolescent ramblings to the pages where he finally faced the fact that he might die like any other man, and he wrote at least a few lines every week. She'd read them all. They were hers now. No one else's.

She was hefting each bag, making sure that the handles were sound—she didn't want them spilling all over the driveway of some bumfuck motel—when Martha said, "Need help with those?" from the doorway.

"Nah, they're not heavy." Obviously the place didn't bug Martha as much as Abby had thought it would. Well, that was good. That was healthy.

Martha kept her hand stretched out, and after a minute Abby handed her the lighter bag and headed back downstairs. Martha lingered for a moment, and when Abby looked back at her she was still in the doorway, staring into the room so blankly that for a moment Abby worried that there was something in the mirror after all.

"Come on!"

"Sorry!" Martha hefted the bag, which she'd let sink to the floor, and followed her back down the hall.

"I'm thirsty," she said out of nowhere as they reached the foot of the stairs.

"There's nothing in the house but tap water. I'm done here, we can go to dinner right now if you want."

"Tap water's fine."

They turned left into the kitchen, where Martha abandoned the bag on the table and started rummaging in the cupboard above the dishwasher.

There was a book of matches on the counter, neat in its place alongside the candelabra that their grandmother and later their mother used to light at dinner during the winter, and Abby picked it up. Did matches get stale? She'd never heard that they did. She'd quit smoking three years ago—didn't want to get cancer, haha—so she didn't carry a lighter anymore. She should, really, though. Never know when you might need it.

Water gurgled in the sink. Martha had chosen a Yogi Bear jam-jar glass, one of her old favorites, and for a moment Abby considered asking if her twin couldn't just fold them both all the way back to sixteen, or farther, hell. Get them a do-over, knowing then what they know now, like the saying went. But she couldn't. If she could, surely she would have done it by now. And it would unfold eventually. Martha couldn't be that strong.

"The grass grows there just fine," Martha said, looking out the window into the back yard.

"Of course it does." Abby walked over by her, and looked out, and sure enough, the grass was uniformly thick and green. Overgrown, for that matter. Bonetrager had been letting that part slide a little. "People talk a lot of crap."

Martha rinsed the empty jar in the sink and stood it alone in the dishrack. "So where are we going for dinner?" she asked as she picked the bag back up.

"I was thinking Angelo's. Does that work for you?"

"Sure!"

They headed out into what was now serious dusk to the car. Abby toyed with the idea of pulling out the matches and burning the house down behind them, but finally she decided that it would be crueler to just leave it stand. The open door would be enough.

After a little while longer it turned out that Martha took after Grandma the way Abby took after Grandfather and Mom, and so she studied with the older woman, spent evenings and weekends with her while Abby was with Grandfather. It might have come between them if Martha had been stronger-willed, because Abby took her cues from Grandfather and made fun of Grandma behind her back for being persnickety. Grandma was from Massachusetts, and never let anyone forget it. She always called it Mass, as in, "Back in Mass we always…" or "When I take you to Mass you'd better not…" Being from Mass was somehow better than being from Rhode Island like Grandfather. He never defended Rhode Island, he just struck back by accusing Grandma of being too stuck up to work with dead raccoons scraped off the side of the road or kids who had lowered their own resistance with beer or weed or, later, meth and opiates. Grandma couldn't have even if she wanted to, just like Martha, but she would never admit that, and her pride was something Grandfather felt he needed to poke at.

Of course, Grandfather equally couldn't do what Grandma did, pressing time ahead on its course or dragging it back to the past. Or doing something that was a little of both and wasn't quite either, so that the tax man, say, thought it was April 14 while the weather and the school calendar and the fact that Grandfather had finally, muttering and cursing, gotten around to mailing in their forms all said it was mid-June. This particular trick always, in Grandma's words, "unfolded" eventually, but if the check had already been cashed it no longer mattered, no one was going to follow up. She did this only when she had to and took long naps afterwards, and sometimes even threw up quietly into an old mixing bowl that she kept under the bed. This was another sign of weakness in Grandfather's reckoning. Abby had long since learned to keep her own headaches to herself, and sometimes she even forgot that her head didn't normally feel that way.

Grandfather never hesitated to demand Grandma use her powers when he stood to benefit but that didn't mean he admitted that they were any patch on his. And when Martha began to use her powers on her own, sliding away a rainy recess or giving herself twice as long as everyone else on a math drill, his pride was muted and grudging compared to the big deal he and Mom had made over Abby's troll invitation. He constantly warned Martha that he didn't want to see her folding her way out of every bit of unpleasantness she had to deal with. That was the road to weakness, not strength, despite Martha's protest that it would mean practicing her skills. There was something about the way he watched out for her manipulating time, a wary quality to his attention that Abby, at the time, just found confusing. Because Martha's skills were nothing compared to theirs. He'd said so.

At first Abby felt a bit bad, teasing and provoking Martha until she'd fold away long school days for them both and then get all the blame when they'd come home early. But it was worth it, every time. And she'd do favors for Martha every now and then, despite the headaches, to buy forgiveness. By the time they hit the fourth grade they had it worked out to where they were a pretty good team most days.

CHAPTER FIVE

Sometime over the last year and a half Angelo's finally got their liquor license back, so the Moscato stayed corked in Abby's handbag through dinner. Abby had a glass of the house red, and Martha ordered a Genny Light.

"That crap? You're going to give yourself a hangover."

"It's just one beer. Anyway, besides the ice cream sundae, that's what I missed most the entire time I was inside. A cold beer on a hot day." Martha drew a little circle on her plate with her fork; it made a repulsive squealing scrape, and she smiled sheepishly. "You know what's funny?"

"You?"

Martha stuck her tongue out, the correct traditional response. "This will be my very first legal alcoholic beverage."

That set Abby back for a moment. "Wow. Yeah, I guess it would be…"

"They don't throw very good twenty-first birthday parties at Wende."

The bread arrived, and despite the carbs and the fact that she knew it wouldn't be any good Abby tore a piece off at once and dragged cold butter over the surface, glad of the distraction. Her own twenty-first birthday she'd spent in Manhattan. She'd gone to Lucky Cheng's with a handful of sorority sisters and seen the drag show, ridden on the subway and given five dollars to a guy with an ocarina playing "My Heart Will Go On", bought a cannoli at two in the morning. It still amazed her that all that had happened on the same planet as the place where she was sitting now. And Martha had never seen any of that.

"To be fair, I hardly even noticed that it was my birthday. Every day is exactly the same. That's what made it so easy to… I didn't mean to. I promise. When I went in, I thought I'd just shave off a few days here and a few days there."

She was starting to quiver, and Abby didn't want that particular kind of scene, not before the entrees even arrived. Abby should be the understanding big sister now, thirty minutes older and so much more mature. "Who wouldn't?"

Their drinks showed up, the beer foamy and picture-perfect, the wine like a garnet. Abby sipped it. It was maybe an hour from being salad dressing. She took a picture with her cell phone and posted it with a quip about appearances being deceiving. Martha cocked her head at this, but didn't say anything.

Their waiter didn't seem to recognize them, and that irritated Abby a little. Then she was embarrassed for being irritated. The boy was at best nineteen—young kids these days, getting their news from Twitter and their opinions from YouTube when they paid attention at all, she'd had that conversation with her former co-workers so often she could recite everybody's lines, back to the days when the complaint was about Comedy Central. Most of her ex-co-workers were fossilizing, stuck in a minor market tarpit, reporting on shootings and arsons and rising home prices and city council members' drunk driving convictions. The closest any of them would ever come to a national story was Craig, who covered sports—at least he could hope for the Bills to reach the playoffs again in his lifetime, or the Sabers in a Stanley Cup chase. Abby had been the only rising star among them, the one who could afford to enjoy the blogs and laugh at Stephen Colbert and tweet and use Tumblr because she was going to burst free of the tar and soar, who might someday stand on the rock where Connie Chung or Dan Rather stood. And then she realized that that rock was sinking too and grabbed onto something better, Internet celebrity. Ever upward, no matter what.

Until she went to the damn doctor.

"You believe me, right?" Martha said when the waiter was out of earshot. "You've got to, because it's true." She was flustered. Most of the time when she got flustered she looked to Abby, let her make decisions.

"Of course I believe you. I'm sure it's easy to make a mistake like that."

They sat in silence for a bit. Martha picked up the bread and topped it with her own slab of still-cold butter, then shoved half of it into her mouth at one go. Abby bit back the remark Grandma would have made about manners and the one she herself hypocritically wanted to make about empty calories.

An older woman a few tables over was staring at them. Abby felt the familiar warm caress of power like a breeze across her face, first, and when she glanced over the lines of attention were streaming in her direction. She caught the woman's gaze and smiled at her, drawing in the energy. But the woman looked nervous, her eyebrows slightly knitted, and then her attention browned out and it seemed to Abby that it recoiled a little—was it Martha she recognized? Or was she just embarrassed to be caught staring? She dropped her eyes and turned away, to Abby's disappointment.

The entrees arrived and Abby decided that an unpleasant conversation was better than none at all.

"Was it awful?"

"Of course it was. That's sort of the point of prison."

"What were the people like? The guards, the other prisoners?"

"Did I have any hot lesbian affairs, do you mean?"

Abby pointed her fork, laden with salmon, at her sister. "You are a wicked, perverse little creature, Martha Waite, and don't think I don't know it." The imitation of their grandmother was good enough that Martha laughed and took another swig of beer.

"Anyway, they were just people. Some of them would give me a hard time because of what I did. Especially the girls who thought they were so romantic because they stuck a knife in some other girl over some guy, or stuck a knife in the guy, or set fire to his house while he was sleeping. Personally, I think you have to be way more fucked up to kill someone you actually know, right?"

"I bet that theory was popular."

"Oh, I didn't tell them that to their faces."

"So smart. You always took after me."

"Yeah. Well. But I figured out who to avoid after a while. There was only this one guard… Mostly I just kept to myself or talked to the other women in my reading group, and I was fine."

"You were in a reading group?"

"Like I said, it gets pretty boring in there."

"What did you read?"

"Books with reading guides in the back so we didn't have to come up with our own questions. Stuff about moms and daughters, mostly. And stuff about sisters." Martha raised the beer again. It seemed to be getting to her. "None of them were as cool as us."

The older woman was staring at them again, and now her husband was too. Maybe they'd recognized Martha after all—or maybe they heard her talking about prison, and put two and two together. Abby smiled. This was probably the most exciting thing that would happen to a couple of small-town coots like that for the rest of their lives. Oh, when the crimp Martha put in time unfolded they'd watch the news and call the cops—they were exactly the sort who always did, eventually, even if you'd shoved them in the other direction. But that would be later, much later. Right now, they were paying attention.

Abby directed her smile at them again, turning up the wattage just a hair, coaxing the strands of mental energy away from Martha and towards herself. Their attention was thin because they were thin-minded people, but it was better than the salmon.

"Still the same old Abby, I see." There was a touch of sulk in Martha's voice and Abby abandoned the old couple reluctantly.

"What do you mean?"

"Anything for a fix, look at you. And you were lecturing me about doing a little time-folding."

"I wasn't lecturing you. Anyway, they were listening to you babble about prison. I had to distract them."

"I say you were just doing it for fun."

"Was not." She forked her salmon viciously. It crumbled, chalky and pale-pink.

Martha shrugged and swept another bite of linguine into her mouth, then slugged some beer. She'd almost finished the beer. Abby wasn't quite sure how her sister ended up having the better evening, here. Maybe she was sicker than she thought.

Martha made no attempt to get the conversation going again. She suggested ordering dessert, though.

"We had ice cream this afternoon," Abby said.

"Aw, come on."

"Fine. But we have to get it to go. I need to open that Moscato soon or I'm going to dry out."

"I just want some tiramisu. I don't care where we eat it."

"Have you ever even had tiramisu?" She regretted saying it instantly. There was keeping Martha off-balance and there was just being mean, and she wasn't going for the latter.

"Nah," Martha said, unoffended, "but I heard it's good."

"Tiramisu it is."

Their tiramisu arrived in two small polystyrene coffins, one of which Martha opened and sniffed. "I thought there would be more chocolate."

Abby shrugged and picked up her purse. She barely even had to push the waiter to get the wine taken off the bill—she just waved it under his nose. A bit more effort got the salmon comped as well, but it wasn't worth bothering to have Martha's meal taken care of—it had been polished off.

On their way out of the restaurant, she passed close to the older couple's table, close enough that if she'd been wearing a skirt it might have brushed the woman's elbow. But she'd figured that a skirt wasn't appropriate jailbreak wear. Oh well. She could feel them both examining her face, and that was enough for right then.

Their grandmother died just before Abby and Martha's tenth birthday. She got up early one morning, made toast, and then fell forward onto it at the table.

She never took them to Mass, never went back to visit her family herself. Grandfather wouldn't have gone even if he'd been welcome, and Grandma couldn't drive or manage a bus schedule on her own, let alone something as hectic and modern as an airport. In fact none of them ever traveled except their annual summer trip to the cabin in Minnesota, which hardly counted because they did basically what they did back home but with more mosquitoes. Until she went away to college, Abby had never been to New York City, to San Francisco, to New Orleans, to Chicago. Had never gone over the border into Canada to take advantage of the differences in exchange rate or drinking age. Not even a simple jaunt to goddamn Disney World like even the trailer park kids got once or twice in their miserable lives. Grandfather and Mom had been so turned inward, so focused on keeping their dumb little secrets. They'd passed up one of the great sources of power in life, hadn't even known to look for it—although Mom at least must have had an inkling. It had hurt Abby to realize how stupid they were, but that was later.

So Grandma had died without ever getting back to Mass and the sisters who'd warned her not to marry a Waite, even if she was looking to be doomed a spinster and he was ten years younger and blessed with money and charisma. Mom had gone to bed and not gotten up for almost a month except to go to the bathroom, leaving the lights off and the curtains closed, ignoring Grandfather when he yelled through the door that she was malingering. Martha wasn't as bad as that but Abby could tell she was off. She wore the old locket that Grandma had given her every single day, tucked under her T-shirts as though no one could see the lump it made. She stared into space more than usual, wandered away just when they needed to get started cooking dinner or doing laundry or whatever, all their usual chores and Mom's too.

Martha's teacher noticed the change as well, and a note came home saying that Martha needed to see the school counselor, again, and keep at it this time. Abby forged Mom's signature on it, and Abby was the one who drilled Martha on what to say and what not to let slip. Neither Mom nor Grandfather seemed to notice what was going on, and it infuriated her, because back then she thought they were so smart, so powerful that they must be ignoring her and Martha on purpose. That they had their own drama and were at their limits was something that never occurred to her. Who knew they had limits?

Still, Abby took her cue from them and pretended not to notice things either, like when Martha gave her an appraising look and asked whether she thought Grandfather might die soon too. It wasn't like Martha to be that pointed, to want to hurt Abby just to make sure she shared the pain. It wasn't like Martha to make ingenious arguments about why it wasn't her turn to bring the clothes in off the line, not when Abby was staring her down. If Martha was going to sneak away, she'd have turned up in the old apple orchard reading Anne of Green Gables, not hunting for newts in the creek using Abby's newt bucket and searching under Abby's particular rocks. It was like she was trying to be a person who Grandma's death wouldn't hurt. Then she'd snap back to the old Martha an hour later and be bewildered and upset that her favorite shoes were muddy and act like she didn't know why Abby was being so mean.

Looking back, Mom could have taken their side. Or at least explained to Abby what was going on.

CHAPTER SIX

They drove a good bit out of town and checked into a Best Western near the Thruway. If this were a real escape, with Martha not folding up time behind them, that would be the smart thing to do. Lead the eventual searchers astray, make them think that the Waite girls headed east, bound for New York City or maybe the airport in Syracuse and a lovely, extradition-free life in Belize or something. Abby had planned it all out beforehand and Martha probably wouldn't even notice the implied vote of no confidence. She was never the one to notice, to wonder, to suspect, not the way Abby did. And in the worst-case scenario, if Martha was badly overestimating herself, there was no harm in doing a little track-covering.

By the time they got up to their room, Abby's eyes were starting to get sandy and hot. The bed looked almost as appealing as the bottle. Only almost.

As soon as they'd settled in and kicked off their shoes, she realized that of course she didn't bring a corkscrew.

The nearest Wal-Mart was largely deserted by this hour; a few wandering tweakers and bored teens, a few stockers piling merchandise into edifices, a few moms with colicky babies or a last-minute need for posterboard, a few cashiers propped against their registers. All dwarfed by the ceiling and shelves, they did little to stop the place from looking post-apocalyptic. There was plenty of stuff, though.

As Abby and Martha trekked towards Housewares, a small child started howling in the distance.

"Damn," Martha said, twisting her neck as she gazed from the display of bright blue and purple tights to the great wall of cereal boxes and back again.

Yeah, Abby didn't say, I suppose that if you just got out of prison this place doesn't look like such a dump. "I covered the grand opening," she offered instead. "It was a mob scene. And at Christmas a couple of years ago there was a stampede that killed a seventy-two-year-old lady."

Another baby's wailing voice joined the first; the sound moved through the aisles like a flash flood. Martha winced.

"Come on, it'll be over in the Kitchen Utensils aisle. Aisles." Abby turned left at the display of clever little citrus zesters, only to find that this was actually cookware, the endcap a tease. And now Martha had vanished.

She backtracked and found Martha staring up—in wonder? In dismay?—at a tower of orange and green South Beach blenders.

"Shake it. We don't have all night."

"Something moved up there."

"A pigeon probably got in, or a bat. That happens sometimes." Martha didn't move. "It looked big."

"Whatever it is, I care about my corkscrew more." Abby stared down the back of Martha's head, wishing she was impatient enough to break her own long-held rule and push her sister into obedience. Before she quite resolved to walk away, though, Martha turned to follow her.

Turning at that moment probably saved Martha's face. Abby saw the hurtling shape a moment later and ducked, pulling her sister with her into a crouch, and the hawk passed just over Martha's shoulder and circled away.

"Holy fucking shit!" Abby had never seen a bird that size that close, not where she could feel the air moving under its wings and see its pupils dilate. And yet as big as it was, it had vanished like it came.

Martha lurched upright. "What the hell was that?"

"Some kind of goddamned eagle or something."

"Where did it go?"

Abby scanned the far-away beams of the ceiling and the fluorescent lights. There was nothing up there that could possibly hide a bird the size of an English bulldog. "It must have landed somewhere…" she said, gesturing vaguely upward, trying to project unconcern so her sister would stop hyperventilating.

"We need to get out of here."

"We need the corkscrew. And forks for your tiramisu."

"A giant bird just tried to scalp me. I'll eat the tiramisu with my hands, I don't care."

A few aisles away, the crying babies started a crescendo, a note of rage entering their voices. A tantrum.

"Shut up," Abby muttered. "I wish the damn hawk would eat you."

"I'm serious, Abby. I want to go back to the hotel."

"It was probably just as freaked out as you were once it realized you aren't a mouse." Martha almost looked like she might believe it. She hadn't been facing the bird, so she hadn't seen the claws, or the implacable golden eyes. And she could never see the bizarre tangle of hate around its head.

"Come on," Abby said, after a moment, and Martha finally obeyed.

They found the corkscrews behind a display of disposable plastic martini glasses with slogans like "Golddigger" and "Bitch on

Wheels" printed on them in pink glitter. Forks were easier, and before long they were being checked out by the near-comatose cashier. The babies were still howling behind them, but that didn't seem to strike anyone else as unusual.

Abby kept one eye on the sky as they crossed the parking lot, but any birds that might have been out there stayed blended with the encroaching night.

An outside observer might have thought Grandfather was suffering from grief that summer, if any outside observer had cared.

He got skinnier, more stooped; his hair and beard thinned to wisps; his skin dried. And yes, in the nonexistent outside observer's defense, he was rarely seen outside anymore. His weekly trips to the library and the liquor store ended, and then his daily routine of front porch sitting dwindled to an hour, to fifteen minutes. He abdicated opportunities to supervise the mowing of the lawn and Abby and Martha's work in the garden.

But Abby knew better. He was still giving her lessons and lectures. He was still staying up until well after her bedtime, light shining through the space beneath his door when she took furtive trips to the bathroom or kitchen. He was still yelling at Mom, only to abruptly shut up when Abby or Martha made a noise that told him they'd come back into the house. He was still Grandfather. And Martha wasn't getting as many odd mean spells. Mom was out of bed and normal-ish again, yelling back at Grandfather, making Martha take off the locket and give it to her for safe-keeping, because Martha was so scatterbrained she'd just lose it in the creek. The family got so tantalizingly close to righting itself, for a few months.

As July fourth—when they always started the trip to Minnesota—approached, Abby started dropping hints to Mom about packing. Hints were a better bet than direct questions, when it came to

Mom and Grandfather. Direct questions opened the door to direct refusals, and refusals, unlike permissions and promises, were never reversed later.

"Your grandfather's too sick to travel right now," Mom said, louder than necessary, and that was too close to a full-fledged 'no' for Abby's comfort.

"Why do you care so much?" Martha asked her later, when she complained about it. "You always say you're bored when we're there."

"I'm bored here, too," Abby said. Martha wouldn't understand Abby's suspicions that the change in routine was a sign, like a certain smell to the milk that wasn't expired quite yet, like a hairline fracture that meant she should let Martha wash that particular plate and get the blame when it broke.

The holiday came and went. Martha and Abby watched as distant driveways along the street filled up with cars and the sweet-smelling smoke from the barbecues drifted over them. When it got dark, they walked to the top of the neighbor's hill to watch the fireworks exploding, small and muffled, above the theme park miles away. Mom and Grandfather ignored the day, going about their normal routines so hard and so silent that it was obvious they were inches from screaming in each others' faces, even if you couldn't see the little daggers of attention stabbing out at each other and then, after a moment's application of willpower, retracting.

The morning of the fifth, Abby woke up early. In a normal year, she would have been squashed against Martha or Grandma, or at worst between both. She could read in the car without getting sick, so sometimes she took the middle before Mom or Grandfather made her, to get credit for being a good girl later. These last few years Grandma had smelled funny, though, and Martha was getting big enough to elbow Abby without meaning to when she turned to look at the horses or deer or funny signs for diners along the road.

Abby had decided that once she learned to drive, she'd never, ever put up with being a passenger again.

Now she had space, and time, and she could go read her books in the old barn if she wanted to or on the front porch where Grandfather used to sit. But she didn't. She lay in bed for a long time, half-convinced that if she just waited Mom would come along and yell at her for being lazy when she knew they needed to get packed and into the car.

No trip. No stops at Dairy Queen along the road for sundae battles, no playing cows-and-cemeteries, no slugging Martha in the arm when she spotted a Volkswagen Beetle. But that wasn't why she was upset, because those things only ended in mosquitoes and mooching around outside the cabin while Mom and Grandfather worked on whatever it was they were working on. She was upset because the feeling like a bad milk smell was worse than ever.

She sat up, swung her legs out of bed. She was going to find Martha, and they were going to go catch newts all day. Out of sight, out of mind, whatever was going on that was safest.

Abby went downstairs, and to her surprise found the ground floor silent and empty. She glanced out the window, and the car was gone, and for a moment she had a pang—but no, a roast was thawing on the kitchen counter, they hadn't gone far. Someone was probably around. Certainly Martha, Mom never took her anywhere that she didn't also take Abby, and probably Grandfather behind the closed door of his always-shadowed bedroom. He was just keeping quiet.

Martha wasn't in the apple orchard. She wasn't in the garden shed. She wasn't in the big hayloft or the stalls in the old barn, which wasn't surprising—Martha hated the bloodstained floors and even though Mom and Grandfather said it was impossible, that animals didn't work like that, she insisted that she could hear the long-gone pigs and cows crying in fear.

It was impossible that Abby was hearing them now, too. She'd never heard them before. They were faint, but there were sounds of pain. She held her breath and tried to be too still to make her own noise, closed her eyes against the distraction of shadows and dust motes, and turned slowly in a circle as she tried to figure out where the sounds were coming from.

Northeast. The little grain shed built right up against the far wall. She moved towards it with short one-at-a-time steps, to stay quiet of course and not because she was afraid. The moaning never broke, but she was almost sure that there was only one of—of whatever was making the noise. She couldn't tell if it was human or not. It wasn't Martha's ghost pigs, she knew that, even though she'd never heard a pig in real life. Something alive was making that sound. Something alive and in pain. Something that still had a will, and wanted to get out.

The grain-shed door was closed, but the old, dry wood was full of knotholes and cracks she could peek through. For a moment she imagined a claw poking back to put out her eye, but she shook her head and made herself lean down. That was horror movies, not real life.

They hadn't kept grain in the grain shed since Mom was a little girl, but there were still a few old empty sacks scattered around, draped over bins, undisturbed for decades because the mice never came. Now the sacks had been pulled down and used to cover the moaning thing from head to foot, without a gap. If not for the moaning she would not have known it was alive—any movement it made was too slight to be sure of in the dusty, dim light from one small dirty window.

It could be a trick, she thought. It might not be weak at all. If I go inside, it could turn on me.

There was a pitchfork near the barn door, and she backed up in her own footsteps until she was able to reach behind her and grasp it. It was heavy, and when she tried to hold it out in front of her the tines wobbled loose on the handle, so she held it at her side where it might look more intimidating.

The moaning finally stopped as she dragged the door of the grain shed open. The bags stirred and slid away as the moaning thing reached out a hand and tried to lift its head.

It might have looked like Grandfather, if something had hollowed out Grandfather's bones and sucked the flesh from beneath his skin and somehow rusted away his will to a few weak, quivering strands. Even then, though, Abby couldn't believe that Grandfather would ever make that high, whimpering moan she'd heard. This wasn't Grandfather. It couldn't be.

She'd pointed her pitchfork at it without thinking, and it had lifted its head enough to see that she was armed. Even so, the wisps of intent focused on her. "Help," it said, still in a whiny treble. "Help me, Abby."

She wanted to step forward. She wanted to back away. She just stared at it.

"Please," it said. "It's me, it's Martha. Help me."

Abby dropped the pitchfork and ran, slamming the door behind her, not stopping until she was out of the barn and on the other side of the house in the bright sunlight.

Whatever it was, it knew her weaknesses.

CHAPTER SEVEN

Martha somehow managed to fall asleep in the passenger seat on the way back to the Best Western, and barely stumbled through the door, and then fell asleep again at once, on top of the comforter, with her shoes on. Abby put the tiramisu in the fridge, and then looked sadly at the magnum of Moscato and put it away as well.

In the morning, though, she was grateful. The room was too bright to bear. She tweeted something sardonic about mornings before she took her head off the pillow just to get the boost she needed to get out of bed. A hangover to top it off would have been too perfect.

She turned to shake Martha, but her sister was already awake, staring into space like a passive lump of meat. Great. Some things would never change with Martha, obviously.

"Tiramisu for breakfast," Abby announced, "and I call first shower. And then we need to get a move on."

"We've got plenty of time," Martha said just as Abby slammed the bathroom door.

Out in the parking lot, the car was already roasting with the sun; Abby felt the sweat start to trickle down her back as she pulled out, despite the AC turned up as high as it would go. "Find us something to listen to," she told Martha, and then remembered what the radio did yesterday, the confluence between the lyrics and last night's incident. "You can plug in my iPhone, my workout mix is on there."

Martha picked up the iPhone and looked at it for a minute as though she had no idea what to do with it. Of course she didn't. She shrugged and said, "I said I have a headache," and dropped it again without even trying. Abby, irritated, sped up.

Soon they'd moved from the area that Abby knew like the back of her hand to the area she knew more like... well, the back of her shoulder, not as well as she should, not from direct observation. It wasn't a direction that had anything interesting in it, not until you got well beyond the boundaries of the local news; even when people shot their lovers and exploded their meth labs in this neighborhood, it only merited a few minutes of coverage. No one bothered to do ground-breaking stories about children slipping through the cracks out here. The whole place was a crack, and the best thing to do was just slip on through as fast as they could.

But then Martha sat up straighter and made a little noise of distress. She choked it off immediately, but Abby couldn't have missed it if she'd tried. And the worried glance after to see if she'd noticed would have tipped her off anyway.

"What's wrong?" She looked right at Martha, long enough to make sure that she wasn't going to try to lie.

"I've been here before. I was lost here once. Please watch the road."

There was nothing in the road. Abby turned her head all the way and surveyed the roadside with renewed attention. No, she'd never seen it. Although it did look like the right sort of place; lonely, boggy, the trees half-drowned and burdened with wild grape and poison ivy. And there was a feeling that she hadn't felt in years, half-memory and half a living thing. She slammed the brakes and reversed.

"What the hell, Abby?"

"Just checking something."

There was no shoulder really, but there was a place where they could pull off far enough that they probably wouldn't get hit if someone came down the road, assuming that someone was more or less sober and traveling in the general vicinity of the speed limit. A chance they'd have to take.

She stepped out of the car, left the door hanging open behind her, not looking at Martha. Normally it would all be swamp here, but it had been a dry summer. It was walkable, though the sedge was almost up to her knees. Black flies swarmed around, and somewhere nearby she heard the drone of a horsefly.

Bug spray. She'd forgotten to fucking bring any. They'd have to pick some up.

It would be a lot easier if Martha would quit curling into a pill bug in the passenger seat and come help her. But she saw from here what Mom would have seen. The lone oak she would have put to her left hand, and... yes. Directly in her sight line, a tree that had been struck by lightning despite being shorter than the others all around it.

The horsefly closed in on the back of her neck, and she smacked it, not hard enough to kill but at least it was stunned and tumbled away. She wouldn't have time to dig deep, but Mom wouldn't have either.

But Mom would have had a shovel. Abby turned back to the car, ignored Martha and tried to think. Under the driver's seat, in the trunk... there had to be an ice scraper somewhere. She almost snapped at Martha to come help her look, but that wasn't ignoring and Martha's help was unlikely to be worth much. Anyway, she found the scraper under the spare tire (half deflated, and of course she wouldn't have a chance to get her money back for that either) in the back. It was cheap and flimsy, but it was better than scratching in the dirt with her fingernails.

As she stood up, she spotted a hawk perched on a telephone pole a few yards away. It didn't mean anything, necessarily. There were always hawks along the roads, looking for careless woodchucks and stupid mice and basking snakes, she remembered that from their drives to Minnesota all those years ago. But she closed the driver's-side door as she walked by. The hawk lifted off and flew away. It was startled by the noise. It didn't mean anything.

Heartened by the sound of the slamming door and the hawk's reaction—she was the dominant species here, not any bird—she walked towards the lightning-struck tree. The serrations on the sedge grabbed her legs and sliced her skin as she pulled free—slices that hurt, and worse, would turn into red itchy welts in a little while. She lengthened her stride, trying to get across as quickly as possible, jumped over the remaining puddle at the center of the marsh, sank into the rot-smelling mud on the other side and sent a few terrified frogs scattering. But then she'd reached her goal.

Even looming above her, the tree was objectively shrimpy. A black mark ran down one side of the trunk where the heavens burned the old life out of it. Woodpeckers had been at it, and the bark had flaked away. She reached out and touched the gray, weathered-smooth wood; she could feel a tingle, like static on a dress coming out of the dryer. She couldn't miss it any more than she could miss the smell of her mother's face cream or the timbre of her grandfather's voice. If anyone had actually been paying attention, if anyone wasn't too damn dumb to notice, they might have wondered why a dead tree kept growing.

It only took a few steps to circle the corpse of the tree, but she walked it slowly, treading down the sedge with care, looking for any clue. There were a half-dozen places that seemed disturbed, the sedge not as thick, the earth looser, but those weren't what she needed. She made a complete circle, counterclockwise, without seeing what she was looking for, but on the second transit a root caught her eye. It was humped up out of the ground like the root of a very old tree, a tree that has battled rocks and erosion for a century. But this tree died young.

She squatted and pulled up a few tufts of sedge on either side of the root, ignoring the pain in her hands. Clumps of dark mud full of half-rotted leaves came up with each bunch, shiny beetles and centipedes fled the sudden light. The damned sedge was tickling the bare insides of her thighs now that she was so near the ground. She shifted carefully, only to be brushed by another stem, and then she shifted not carefully and got a welt she wouldn't be able to scratch in public. Fuck it. She tore sedge out of the ground by the handful and began to gouge dirt from under the root with the ice scraper.

It wasn't long before she hit something that sounded too hollow for a rock; a little bit more digging and she saw it. The bone was dull and the seams were loose. It would take finesse to get it out. She breathed deep, let her burning hand clutch the scraper so tight it dug into her flesh, then slowly, consciously relaxed.

The root had grown over the skull, but not into it. She supposed it hadn't had enough time, though what did she know about how fast roots grow? No more than Mom, and Mom obviously didn't know enough or she would have buried the old man deeper. Too deep for Abby to ever find.

She worked the scraper down until it hit a pebble. Pried the pebble out and threw it aside. And again. And again. If the summer had been a little drier, if the ground right here wasn't soft, it would have been impossible. As it was, there were an awful damn lot of pebbles for such swampy ground. Every one she hit with the scraper jarred her arm and slowed her down. Chunks of quartz, mostly, some granite, even a fossil clam. She stuck a few in her shirt pocket, just in case. She was so close—one side of the skull was completely free, and if she could just get it loose on the other side it was hers.

She found a piece of slate, the kind laced with iron oxide, in her way. Sweat trickled down the back of her neck as she worked the blade of the scraper under it, pried hard—and then fell back, her hand stinging and the snapped-off handle slipping out of her grasp.

"Damnit!" She would have sucked her finger—it was bleeding where the sharp edge of the plastic caught it—but that seemed like a good way to catch worms. The blade of the scraper stuck out of the mud, taunting her. She pulled it out and threw it as far as she could.

Her nails wouldn't have to be nice when this was over, but the habit of taking care of them was hard to break now. She shuddered as she pushed her fingers into the dirt, but she did it. Shuddered and scraped at the slate until she found the edge and pulled it loose. Shuddered and worked her way beneath the skull.

Her efforts must have loosened it; it came up right away. She rocked back, but didn't fall this time, and it was in her hands. The right incisor was missing, as it should be.

It seemed like the thing to do would be to wipe it clean and see the bone glint white, but she didn't have anything to do that with but the hem of her shirt and she'd made enough of a mess of herself. Grandfather had been muddy a long damn time, he could put up with it a bit longer.

The marsh didn't seem anywhere near as wide going back as it did coming across, although the grass still sliced her and the bugs still droned around her head. A wave of triumph washed her—the universe loved her, and she could do anything; she never needed to be afraid. Things always worked out right for her, didn't they? The humidity, the little bit of breeze, made the air feel like a caress.

The hawk screamed again, but when she glanced up, it was too high to see.

Martha was still huddled in the passenger seat, but at some point she'd rolled the windows all the way up. Abby considered holding the skull up like a mask and rapping on the window to get her attention. That's what she'd have done when they were both twelve. But they had a long drive ahead of them.

Martha saw the skull when Abby climbed into the car anyway. But she just rolled her eyes and stared out the window in silence as Abby pulled the car back onto the road and accelerated away.

She had to get Grandfather, he would know what to do, but she didn't want to. Her pride pricked at running away and needing help, but even more than that, she didn't want to look at him after seeing the thing in his form. But she couldn't figure any way out of it. At least he'd know what it was, where it had come from, how to get rid of it.

Inside the house she felt safer—things like that didn't come inside the house, Grandfather wouldn't let them. She needed to get composed before she went upstairs. She went to the bathroom first, splashed her face with cold water and slapped the dust off her T-shirt. She tried to feel for Mom's footprints on the clean dark wood of the stairs, in case there was leftover strength in them, but she didn't get much.

At Grandfather's bedroom door she hesitated one more time, trying to think of any solution that didn't involve knocking. Then she knocked.

There was no answer, and she hesitated again, since the right course of action now depended on whether Grandfather didn't hear or was pretending not to hear. But she didn't have much choice; she knocked again, longer and louder.

There was still no answer, and when she tried the doorknob—something that only imagining how Grandfather would react if she didn't tell him about the thing wearing his face could drive her to do—it turned. She pushed the door open and stepped inside.

Grandfather wasn't at his desk. He wasn't sitting at the window where the light was closest to good. He wasn't in bed, snoring quietly but never, never really asleep—or at least that was what he claimed.

Abby stepped further inside. It was a trick of some kind, he was hiding, testing her.

The other possibility was that they'd actually all left. That she was alone here with that thing.

But she was safe inside the house. And safer than anywhere else in the house here in this room. All she had to do was wait it out. All she had to do was put up with feeling helpless and unable to do anything, anything useful, for who knew how long.

She looked out the window, but all she could see were the branches of the old pines wobbling in the breeze, and a lone car—not Mom's—coming up Route 20 in the distance.

She wasn't going to watch and wait all day like a dog on TV. It wasn't fair—even thinking about the fact that they'd all left her made tears of anger start irritating her eyes. But if she cried, that was worse because when they got back they'd think she was sad.

She unclenched her fists, looked around. At least the anger was driving the fear out. Her eyes went back to Grandfather's desk, the books he'd left out after her last lesson.

She was still too young to dream of challenging Grandfather head-on, but she no longer believed that looking at his books without him beside her would mean instant madness and death, any more than she believed in Santa or the ghouls. At worst she'd just find some words she couldn't translate. There had never been a chance this wide-open to look at the books Grandfather said were not for little girls.

But there were gaps in the shelf, and those gaps corresponded with nearly all of the books she wanted to read. The big flaking *De Vermis*, the one she thought Grandfather himself might never have read because it looked like it would crumble if it was handled.

The three brown-edged volumes by Nicodemus of Antwerp. The slender blue-backed volumes of Bible-thin paper that Grandfather used for making notes.

She was scared again, and this time was worse, because she didn't know what she was scared of.

It felt like hours before the slam of a car door told her she needed to come out and pretend she'd never been in Grandfather's room to begin with. It couldn't have been that long, though, because she'd only managed to read a dozen pages of the book she'd settled for… but then, she'd been distracted, and the book was mostly about astronomy. It was as bad as homework.

Abby put everything just as it had been, to the inch, to the precise tilt of the gaps where the missing books were, and shut the door in silence even though they'd never hear her from outside. By the time she got to her own bedroom window, Mom and Martha were out of the car, focused on the barn. Mom was holding a shopping bag that looked big and heavy enough for the missing books, and she had the stiff gait that she adopted when she was angry and drawing herself up tall. But Grandfather wasn't with them.

Martha was inside the barn before Mom even got to the shadow of the building. She didn't creep or dart, didn't hesitate or glance back when she got to the door. If she heard the moaning she didn't give any of the usual signs of fear that the Martha Abby knew showed almost all the time.

Abby thought *If I run down as fast as I can I can warn Mom, at least.* But she didn't move and the thought passed. Mom disappeared through the heavy-beamed doorway.

They were inside long enough for her to take ten deep breaths, the kind that kept her from crying. And then they emerged. Mom first, no longer holding the bag, gripping Martha's hand instead. Martha, looking pale now and dragging her feet as though she was exhausted. And Grandfather was with them. Grandfather looking more robust than he had in weeks, the opposite of the sick parody in the barn. Grandfather swinging the bag that Mom had held so heavily. Grandfather, his clothes smooth and his face smiling. Grandfather, with one stray piece of oat straw stuck unnoticed in the thinning crown of his white hair, where only someone looking down on him from above would be able to see.

That afternoon Mom pulled her aside and said, "Abby, hon, have you noticed Martha acting weird lately?"

It was only years later that it occurred to Abby to be grateful that her first instinct was always to lie to her mother, that she shook her head so sincerely before she even thought.

Mom frowned, disappointed. "Well, could you try to keep an eye on her? She tried to run away this morning, that's why we were gone when you woke up, I had to go get her." Her hands were flexing as she talked, curling into fists and out again. "If she talks about leaving again, or actually leaves when she's supposed to be with you, you need to come get me right away. Don't chase after her yourself, and don't go get your grandfather. Just come find me. Okay?"

"Okay."

"It's important," Mom continued as though Abby hadn't just agreed with her. "She could get really hurt, if she goes off on her own. You stay with her, okay? Look out for her."

"I always do, Mom. I promise."

And she'd kept that promise, hadn't she? She'd never put much stock in promises but she'd kept that one.

CHAPTER EIGHT

In Columbus Abby stopped in a gas station parking lot long enough to check the news—nothing miserable had happened to their hometown yet, more was the pity—and to update Facebook and Twitter with vague witticisms. It would have been better if she'd had a picture for Instagram, but she had nothing to pose with, unless she wanted to show the whole world Grandfather's skull. No one wanted to see a goddamn Subway sandwich. There was nothing here. How did people even live? They'd passed twenty-seven red-tailed hawks since they entered Ohio, she'd been counting, so she tweeted about that. Immediately some little know-it-all with the handle @birdingdude responded that they were one of the most common raptors in North America. There wasn't much energy in the response, because he was mostly thinking about himself and birds, not her, but it was something.

She didn't post about how each hawk had risen from its perch on their approach and flown above the car for a quarter-mile or so before falling back and disappearing. Hard to miss after the fifth or sixth bird did the exact same thing. She also didn't post about how each time that happened, the radio would turn on and that weird song would come through as barely audible mumbling. She didn't want to risk directing more attention to it. It—if it was who she thought it might be—shouldn't be able to use it but there were a lot of things that a hawk shouldn't be able to do that he was doing. She should have known this might happen.

The main thing was to keep Martha from noticing, lest she get distracted and panicky. She'd fallen into a sulk after their unscheduled stop and then gone to sleep, snoring lightly in the passenger seat, and thankfully stayed that way through Ohio. Now she was awake and alert, though, especially since she'd devoured an entire footlong and was gurgling the last sips of a Coke through her straw. Abby put the phone back down and plugged in the charger, then started punching up her workout mix. Better not to even give Martha the chance to touch the radio. But as soon as she tried to turn up the volume she heard, not her bouncy Rihanna or a driving Adele track, but that god-damn folk song again. *And there she had two pretty babes born. All alone and so lonely-o.* The lyrics made Abby grit her teeth. He was threatening her. Threatening Martha, yes. But that was the same thing.

She yanked out the cord but Martha had already caught it—she didn't say anything but she frowned in a way that suggested she suspected more than an annoying electrical failure.

Now it was doubly important that she not notice the birds.

"Okay, hotshot, it's time you learned to drive."

"Do you think that's a good idea?"

"It's a better idea than me falling asleep at the wheel while you lay over there like a pretty princess."

"You didn't say I shouldn't sleep."

"It's fine." A slight pause, as though she was going to let it go. "But I need to sleep too."

"I know, I wasn't trying to…"

"And we can't risk any more hotels for a little while, until we're sure they're off our trail." She knew by now that whatever Martha did to time back there was going to stick, as impossible as it seemed, but she wasn't going to let Martha know that. She didn't want her getting a big head about it.

"You could just pull over and sleep."

"Waste of time. And suppose someone tries to rob us, or rape us? It's not like we can call 911."

"Sure we could. I told you I…"

Abby cut her off. "You should be excited about this. Driving is fun."

"No it isn't. It's scary."

"You'll get over it. Here, come around to the driver's side."

Martha hesitated, but when Abby opened her door and got out of the car her sister followed suit. Abby glanced up. No hawks in sight, not here. Hardly even any trees.

Martha got to the driver's side eventually, and once there she slid back inside and set her hands on the wheel, her fingers curling in a tight clutch like a kid pantomiming control of a race car.

"Not there," Abby said, reaching over to move Martha's hands to the ten and two positions. She tried to reach back to her own driver's ed days. They weren't that long ago really. "Like this. Go ahead and turn it on."

Martha stared at the steering column for a moment, then said, "You haven't given me the key?"

"You don't need one any more. Keyless ignition. Step on the brake and press the start button, there."

"Okay. Which one is the brake?"

"Seriously?"

"How would I know?"

"Muscle memory?"

Martha winced. "It doesn't work like that."

That was good to know, actually. "Okay, it's the one on the left. And don't put both feet on the pedals, just use one foot and switch back and forth."

"Why?"

"Too easy to screw up and press down with the wrong foot."

"Isn't it just as easy to press down with the right foot in the wrong place?"

"No."

Martha turned the car on. Abby watched her press on the brake with exaggerated care, depressing it firmly before she even lifted her hand to hit the button. When the engine came to life Martha flinched a little, even though the cabin was quiet enough.

"Okay. Now let your foot off the brake."

"Where should I steer?"

"Nowhere. We're still in park. And when you put it in gear it might start creeping forward a little but you'll have plenty of time to figure your shit out."

"This isn't my shit."

By mile three Abby was almost ready to say "fuck it" and take the driving back over herself, but if she did that, Martha would just give up in frustration and declare driving too hard forever. Which wouldn't even matter except for these next couple of days, but now Abby's stubbornness was engaged, and she wasn't going to let her sister off the hook without a fight.

Especially not when she'd just lost two hours.

She stared at Martha, who was staring at the road, her eyes scanning the pattern Abby described without variation, like a robot. At least she was holding her lane.

"Faster."

"I'm going the speed limit."

"You should be doing five over."

"But what if we get stopped?"

"No one ever gets stopped for five over, unless you're in a school zone or black or something. Going too slow looks suspicious. Like you have something to hide."

"I don't want to get stopped."

"If we get pulled over, just start crying and I'll do all the talking." In truth, getting pulled over would be a huge pain, with Grandfather in the back and all. She could handle it, but she was already tired and fucked off. So it was crucial that Martha stop driving like a stoner.

Abby looked at the clock and it was fifteen minutes later. Did Martha even know she was doing that? Her excuse, when caught, was always that she did it without thinking, that in fact it took a lot of effort not to warp all the time in her vicinity when she was distressed or bored. And it was Martha, so maybe that was even true. She didn't seem to do things on purpose usually.

"Stop it," Abby said anyway.

Martha stomped on the brakes, but there was no one in the rear-view mirror. Still, it could have been a disaster, which pissed Abby off more.

"Not the car. Stop folding."

"I wasn't..." Martha hesitated, sighed. The numbers on the clock jumped down. "Sorry."

It seemed sincere enough.

It surprised Abby how long Martha didn't talk to her. She stayed in bed for two weeks, while the air filled with the smell of cut hay outside and the newt creek shrank to a series of shallow pools between damp rocks. Most of the time she seemed to be really asleep, not like Mom's sulking, but even when her eyes were open she turned them away from Abby, the strands of her attention shrinking into a tight clump of just one desire: leave me alone. When Abby tried to tease out a strand and pull it towards herself, Martha curled up physically and dragged the covers over her head. When Mom saw them like that she snapped at Abby to leave your sister be, she's sick.

Abby might have been another five years figuring it out if Grandfather hadn't gotten careless with his books. Maybe he'd always been careless, but being denied the chance to read them had been enough to make Abby decide that reading them was her goal for the rest of the summer. And it kept her out of her bedroom, away from Martha's inexplicable accusing silence.

It wasn't that hard to map out the comings and goings of an old man. His morning occupation of the bathroom gave her at least half an hour all by itself. And he'd started sitting on the porch again in the afternoon. It was like he didn't even consider, anymore, that she might do something he didn't want her to—or like he didn't think it mattered. Mom was the one she had to watch out for, the one who would come up to check on Martha and stick her head in the door and demand to know what Abby was reading and had she weeded the zucchini yet?

Abby soon realized that it was a huge waste of time to bother with the books themselves. It took so long to decode them that she could get at best a few sentences a day. On the other hand, she knew Grandfather's handwriting like her own, knew his habits of abbreviation and allusion, could usually see where he was going with a thought by the time the sentence reached its first verb. Maybe it was because great minds thought alike and maybe it was because she'd listened to him mutter to himself for so long. She was a fast reader, too, and she knew how to skip the boring parts.

The first notebook she read was from when he first came to Alden, just after he'd married Grandma, and it mentioned some things that made her giggle—doing "the act" during certain phases of the moon, and so forth. After the first few mentions it got weird, though, and she started skimming. Not until three months later did she find the sentence about how his plan had worked and Grandma was crying all the time. It made her worry, somehow, even though she'd never liked Grandma much. All the crowing about what a genius he'd be if the plan worked made Grandfather sound like a cartoon villain on TV.

She hoped that, like a cartoon villain on TV, he'd just explain the whole plan soon. She'd gone back and back over the first few pages of this notebook, and she knew it continued on from one before, one that wasn't on the shelf. If everything was explained in that one, she had a long hunt ahead of her.

The notebook entries got more sporadic for a while, those nine months… only a few entries here and there about how impossible it was to raise livestock when the animals panicked constantly and would do anything to get away from Grandfather's touch. Apparently his father hadn't had that problem, so it wasn't just the powers that they hated. Hay and corn and soybeans couldn't run away, though, and so he sold off the cows when Grandma was too far along to do all the milking and concentrated on field crops, and a few hogs for personal use. The ones that Martha claimed to hear.

Then the baby was born, and there was a long, howling rant about how everything had gone wrong and what good was a girl? He'd have to try again.

Then more phases of the moon, and a hopeful note that Grandma was pregnant again, but nine months later, silence, no baby. And again. And again.

Meanwhile, the baby—Mom—had to be getting bigger, though Grandfather didn't write down anything about that. It wasn't magic and it wasn't anything to do with him so what did he care? Until, one day when she would have been six, Grandfather told her to snub a neighbor girl she'd been playing with and she'd batted back at his intentions like a kitten. It didn't sound like it had worked for her—at least, the neighbor girl was never mentioned again—but Grandfather was amazed that a daughter could do that. It made Abby want to yell at him—not Grandfather out on the porch, that was impossible, but the person writing the words. It was the first time she'd realized you could fight with a book.

Still, he was happy to give the credit to his own cleverness, his good genes and his phases of the moon. He started Mom studying. It was all just like Abby remembered from her own training—except that Grandfather was trying to teach Mom to fold time too.

At first he tried all by himself, with the help of books, and then he threw up his hands in frustration and allowed that Grandma might have a role to play in this. But even Grandma couldn't get Mom to fold time. Mom didn't have that power. And neither did Grandfather. But Grandfather had wanted it for his belatedly beloved daughter.

Abby had to put the notebook down, then, and go back to the astrology texts she'd been assigned, because it was almost lunchtime and Mom would be up soon. But it stuck in her head, how disappointed Grandfather's words were when he realized Mom couldn't fold.

It didn't make sense, she thought as she ate her grilled cheese sandwich and stared at Martha's forehead across the table. Mom and Grandfather both acted like folding was boring at best, at worst a weakness and an excuse when Martha used it to avoid something unpleasant. How could Mom's lack of ability to perform a stupid little stunt like that have upset Grandfather so much?

She looked sideways at Grandfather, who had pried open his grilled cheese and was spreading more deviled ham inside. It wasn't like she didn't know he could lie, but the thought that he could have fooled her so long and so thoroughly made her angry. Now she looked like the stupid one for going along with him, making fun of Martha and Grandma.

Grandfather's awful sometimes. It shocked her, looking back, that it took that long for her to think it for the first time.

Between this new information and the way it was getting hard to sleep in the same room as Martha when she wouldn't even speak,

Abby decided it was time to do something. She couldn't just make this go away, not if Martha wouldn't look at her.

It was Martha's turn to wash up from lunch—Mom's concern didn't go as far as letting her out of chores—but Abby got up as soon as she was done eating and started helping clear the plates. Martha looked at her, brief and cautious, and went to the sink. When Abby had all the plates and forks she took a spot alongside Martha, their gazes parallel, not a threat.

It took several tries that got caught silent somewhere at the bottom of her throat before she actually managed to speak. "You're mad at me," she said as she scraped a lump of deviled ham off Grandfather's plate to disappear beneath the soap. "Why?"

"You'll think I'm dumb."

"No I won't."

"You already think I'm dumb."

"Then telling me won't hurt."

Martha seemed to consider this as an insult for a moment, but then she spoke again.

"I had… I think it was a nightmare. But it felt real. And in the nightmare I was trapped in the barn, and you wouldn't help me."

Abby didn't move, didn't look over, didn't squeeze the glass she was now rinsing so hard it squeaked, even managed to put a little teasing—but not too much, she was supposed to be apologizing—into her voice when she said, "You're mad at me because of a dream?"

Martha took the glass from her, and it did squeak, but that was because neither of them wanted to drop it and get Mom's attention, not now. "It felt really real. And ever since I've just felt sick, and weak. And scared. Like it'll happen again. You were right, Abby. You were right." She let the glass sink into the soapy water and turned and hugged Abby tight, her face buried against her sister's neck. "Something terrible is going to happen, and that's why we didn't go to Minnesota this summer."

As apologies went, it had worked out very well for Abby, but she couldn't enjoy it. Her stomach was burning as though the grilled cheese was too much all of a sudden.

It wasn't kindness, exactly, that made her hug Martha tighter and keep the knowledge that it hadn't been a dream to herself. She just hadn't decided what to do yet, and keeping secrets was always the best choice when in doubt.

"It'll be okay," she whispered.

Martha sensed the uncertainty in that sentence, or shared it. She pulled back and finally looked Abby in the face. "Will it?" Her eyes, red-rimmed and tearful, looked even more prominent than usual. Abby almost felt as though Martha wanted to be pushed, to be made to believe.

CHAPTER NINE

Martha drove without complaint into the evening, and Abby didn't lose any more time, unless she counted time spent in an Arby's drive-through as lost, which was more of a philosophical question. Even the continued misbehavior of the radio didn't seem to get to Martha, although just to be on the safe side Abby stopped tweeting and struck up another round of chit-chat about her old job or Martha's book club books or any damn thing whenever she spotted a hawk by the margins of the road.

That was harder than it seemed because she was distracted. There was a Silver Alert for old James Bonetrager and it was not burning up the social media, at least not anywhere but the local Facebook group she only lurked in—but drifting around with a desultory #FindJimB hashtag that some wiseass had already made a whiskey joke about. Even that was better than her stupid bird tweet so she jumped on it and was getting periodic sips of attention in return. It bothered her a little though—the wards shouldn't have given out that quickly with just the door open. True, Mom had been weak at the end, but still…

So even though she knew she should take the driving over again before it got truly dark, she kept putting it off. She was tired, too, more tired than she had any right to be considering that she'd been sitting on her butt most of the day. That was another distraction, another worry, because she didn't think it meant anything good for her health. And the bites and scratches from her adventure retrieving Grandfather itched more and more the harder she tried not to think about them. She wanted a hot shower, a soft bed, and to use a restroom without asking a bored clerk with a ponytail for a key. But they needed to make their distance today; the sooner they hit Minneopa, the sooner she'd feel better. She could have everything she wanted later, if she could just grit her teeth and scratch her thigh discreetly right now.

She only knew she'd nodded off because she was so startled when her head smacked against the passenger-side window, waking her up. There was a horrible metallic scraping in her ears, and Martha was shrieking, and the entire car was jouncing like a cheap carnival ride for a moment before it stopped moving entirely. Abby had ridden on enough dirt roads to recognize the feeling of leaving pavement.

"What the fuck!" She didn't mean to yell, but she was as loud as Martha, still shrieking. It hurt her head. More.

Martha sucked in a breath and held it for a moment, as though she was trying to craft words out of the scream that still wanted to escape. Then she started crying and lunged sideways, trying to hug Abby even though they were both still buckled in. Behind her sister's head Abby could see branches pressed against the driver's-side window.

She patted Martha's arm and massaged the edge of her thoughts until she was calmer, not pushing but only soothing. She so desperately did not want her to start screaming again. They were right-way up and the windshield wasn't broken, but that was all the good news she could see from inside the car. She unfastened her seatbelt.

Martha grabbed Abby's shoulder as Abby started to pull the door handle. "Don't. It's probably still out there."

"What is?"

"You didn't see it?"

"I was asleep."

"The giant bird, the one from the store. It flew down and started attacking the car."

"Oh, for fuck's sake." Clumsy unsubtle little bastard.

"I couldn't see anything! I just couldn't see!"

"Martha, shh, it's okay, I'm not mad at you." Abby twisted, looking around the car for anything she could use as a weapon. There was the skull, but that wouldn't give her much range. Shopping bags full of clothes were too light to be effective. Shopping bags full of books were probably too heavy to swing accurately, and the handles would break. She should have bought a goddamn gun, they were right at Wal-Mart, it would have been easy.

Wait. The Moscato bottle. A little heavy, but if she used two hands and all the adrenaline that was pumping through her system, it might work. She pulled it from the narrow paper bag and hefted it. Okay. Not great, it hurt her wrists, but okay.

"I'll be right back. See if the car will start."

"Don't leave me!"

"Martha, I said I'll be right back."

"Please, Abby. If it gets you…"

Abby opened the door and Martha flinched away, crossing her arms over her face. No screech echoed from the sky, and no talons descended to rip at her as she swiveled around and got out, so she risked a look around. The road was deserted, woods on one side, lumpy brown fields on the other with the glow of last daylight over them. The car looked battered but not even a headlight was broken.

"Okay," she yelled up at the sky. "If you're dumb enough to want this fight, come and get it." Not the most original line… but then again, he wouldn't know, would he? It would be new to him.

Behind her, the engine started and the headlights came on. She startled but caught herself immediately. Don't show weakness now. Don't show weakness ever, but especially not now. It wasn't great to be standing in what amounted to a spotlight in the growing dark, so she stepped out of the beams, closer to the woods.

The first strike missed her because she was in motion, and she heard the rush of wings in time to lengthen her stride. She raised the bottle—it was heavier than it had seemed when she picked it up, somehow, and harder to grip, the neck too short, the glass slippery. Her first swing was a miss too, not even a feather clipped. The dark intent radiating off this bird was weaving, dancing, impossible to hold—the best she could do was rattle it a little, confuse it, bat the ends of the lines around and tangle them. The damn thing was tough.

But she was tougher, and even confusion was useful. The bird rose a few feet, wavered on laboring wings as though torn between retreat and attack, and by the time it circled back around on her she had a solid shot lined up. She hardly had to swing—it all but knocked itself on the head, a sound like a broken potato chip followed by an unceremonious flop to the ground, a few twitches. A little blood trickled from one nostril.

Martha hadn't moved the car at all. Abby beckoned to her, though she couldn't see her through the headlights. Then she stooped down and picked the dead hawk up by one wing, lifted it high enough that Martha would be able to see.

After what felt like several minutes—at least long enough for her heart to slow down to only pounding—Martha opened the driver's side door and got out, scanning the now-dark sky as she came despite the dead bird in Abby's grasp.

"Relax," Abby told her. "He won't be able to find another host this fast. Nothing easy. Everything is asleep right now." It occurred to her that this maybe wasn't true, owls existed, and coyotes and bats, but he—it—whatever or whoever it was seemed stuck on hawks. Anyway she was trying to calm Martha down, not make herself paranoid.

"The hawk in the Wal-Mart wasn't."

"He didn't find that hawk in the Wal-Mart. That would be too weird a coincidence." It was an unpleasant thought, how long they'd been followed without noticing… from the point when Abby had gotten near the prison and heard that song for the first time, at least. "He'd probably been following you from the prison gates. Might even have been watching before. That's all he has to do. It's probably all he knows to do. Not like he has an attachment anywhere else."

"You think it's one of them, then."

"Who else has a grudge out for you?"

"It could be Mom."

"No. Mom's dead and in the ground where she belongs."

Martha's silence was full of doubt.

"I made certain of it myself."

"They were supposed to be dead too."

"We got careless. We were young, we didn't know." It was a little unfair to say 'we' here, Martha couldn't have done anything about it… but on the other hand, if they'd stayed buried it might all have worked out, and that part was definitely Martha's fault.

"But if it is one of them…" Martha reached Abby's side, frowned, picked up the other wing so they were holding the corpse between them like the loose string of a tin-can telephone. "Where has he been all this time?"

"Maybe he can fold time too." Wouldn't that be a kick in the ass for Grandfather, for the whole lot of them. "Or maybe he was satisfied as long as you were in jail."

Martha seemed to roll the idea around. "I wouldn't have been."

"It's not like you to be vengeful."

"Well, no, I guess not. But they weren't like me, were they? They were like you."

The hawk's head lolled, and more blood ran down its beak, enough to drip off and puddle on the ground. It seemed like a lot of blood for the damage the bottle inflicted. Abby moved her shoe out of the way.

"Should we bury it?"

"It won't help. He's out. He split as soon as I hit this poor bastard."

Martha nodded and dropped her wing. Abby felt an unexpected reluctance to drop hers.

"But get my phone from the car and take my picture with it."

"Really?"

"When will I ever kill a hawk with nothing but a wine bottle again? Might as well remember the moment."

Martha shook her head. "I mean, how do I take pictures with the phone?"

"Go get it, I'll show you."

Martha walked back to the car. Her shoulders were still hunched against the sky a little bit, but she didn't look up.

Abby wished she were wearing a fifties dress and driving a fifties car. She could envision the shot, leaning on the hood, one knee bent up, the hawk spread between her hands and her face above, staring dead at the camera. Bright red lipstick, obviously. Maybe a hat. Smirking like a gangster moll. Run it through one of those old-timey Instagram filters. Beautiful. If only she'd had what she needed.

Oh well, she'd make it work anyway. Share it everywhere, get people arguing over whether she's a monster or just posing with a fake bird to prove some obscure point. Attention for days, and always the chance that some wanna-be activist would take it viral.

Martha reappeared then, holding the phone. "Is it the button with the picture of a camera on it?"

Abby nodded. "See, you got it."

"Okay, where do I look through?"

"Just look at the screen."

"How do I… okay, I see."

Abby hoisted up the dead bird and smiled, all teeth. A smirk in this outfit would be too subtle.

There was a flash, and the artificial shutter sound that the phone made. She dropped her prey and took a step forward.

"Wait, pick it up. I want to take another one. My hands were shaking."

Martha took a second shot, then a third. "Fuck it," Abby said after that, and strode across to grab the phone. She flicked through the photos with a practiced finger and eye. The light could have been a lot better, she looked half-dead. Maybe she'd take it lo-fi, make it look like a Polaroid from the 80s. "Good enough." She leaned up against the hood—there was a set of three ugly-looking scratches and a small dent. Her signal was weak and the photo took a long time to upload. Martha hovered at her elbow the whole time.

"Can you drive?" she asked as Abby put her hand on the passenger-side door handle.

Abby's impulse was to say no, to make Martha get back on the horse as the saying went. But it was dark and Martha was still shaking. Besides, Abby would be awake forever. "Sure, not a problem."

She got back into the car and dropped the blood-smeared bottle into the back seat. How long would it be now before it was safe to open without fizzing everywhere? Not that she'd be doing any drinking tonight, so it hardly mattered.

But she showed him, it, whatever the right thing was to call this thing. She couldn't ignore that. Her mood was suddenly fizzy, no doubt the result of the first few clicks and confused comments and indignant shares of her picture by west-coast dwellers and insomniacs. "It's a good thing we killed them," she said, as she worked the car back up onto the road. "Imagine what they'd be like by now if they'd been alive all these years."

Martha said nothing, and by now it was too dark to see her expression.

It got so bad for a little while that Abby would wake up and, if Martha wasn't in bed, she would immediately mix two glasses of chocolate milk. The jam jars that year had Flintstones characters on them, and Martha's favorite was Pebbles, and on days like that Abby always let her have that one. She'd carry the glasses to the barn along with a couple of books—whatever baby crap Martha was reading and one of Grandfather's notebooks. Abby was getting to hate the barn as much as Martha did.

Her first thought, obviously, had been to just take Martha/Grandfather back into the house, get her calmed down and cleaned up, maybe let her sleep through it. But it turned out that under the burlap sacks, Grandfather had tethered her—himself—to the floor with a chain and padlocked her down. Abby was never sure if this was supposed to delay Mom in her attempts to get Grandfather back in the right body, if it was supposed to keep Martha from trying to follow him, or if it was just mean.

Martha/Grandfather could feel when her body was coming back, and warned Abby, and she'd take the books and empty glasses and pretend that she had no idea what was happening. At times they'd return like they had that first day, with Mom angry and determined, but other days she seemed cowed, or even conspiratorial. Sometimes Abby couldn't read who was manipulating who at all, they were so tangled up.

Neither Mom nor Grandfather ever offered any more explanation or excuse for their absences, and sometimes Abby wondered if she was making them suspicious by not asking, but the whole subject was now like a tomato left on the counter too long and rotting inside. She couldn't bring herself to touch it, so she kept pretending that the normal-looking skin was fooling her, even though she knew it was only going to get worse. She just didn't know if it would collapse or explode.

One of the things getting worse was Martha's health. She barely had time to recover from one morning in the barn before she was subjected to the next, and even on days when it didn't happen, worrying about the next time was sapping her. They only ever took her out in the morning, and Abby could tell as each afternoon dwindled to evening how she got more and more nervous. She started ignoring bedtime until Mom scolded, and even once they were in bed she'd stay awake in the dark, whispering to a half-asleep Abby. Days started feeling longer, even though the solstice was well past. Then Grandfather would give Martha a sharp look and dark would come on faster than it should.

"Can't you fight it?" Abby whispered back to her one night. "It's your body. Can't you just hold onto it and push him back out somehow?"

It was a stupid question. Obviously Martha couldn't fight Grandfather—no one could. But Abby didn't like listening to Martha suffer without trying to solve the problem.

Martha didn't answer. She'd fallen asleep, despite her struggles. And during the day she was tired. She didn't eat much, and she was starting to look as though something of Grandfather's age was creeping into her. Her hair was brittle and fell out when she brushed it, leaving tangles on the bathroom floor. She bruised easily.

Abby didn't think that Grandfather would kill Martha on purpose, but she was starting to worry that he was careless enough to kill her by accident.

It was early August, and once school started again he'd have to stop using Martha for whatever he was doing, at least on weekdays. But that might not be soon enough.

CHAPTER TEN

The beginnings of Abby's good mood evaporated as soon as they were back on the road and she tried to accelerate. As the car reached thirty-five miles an hour, it was obvious that something was wrong. It felt like the back end was a whole separate beast, trying to overtake and pass the front end. If it were winter she'd have been convinced that she was hitting black ice, over and over—a sensation that brought on a clench of terror for anyone who grew up in the Snow Belt. She couldn't hold a line until she slowed back down to a crawl.

"What are you doing?" Martha's voice, sleepy and almost disembodied, came from the passenger seat after Abby had taken the vehicle through a dozen iterations of go slow—get frustrated—speed up in hopes that the problem would somehow cure itself—swerve and stamp the brakes just in time to keep from putting the car in the ditch again.

"Something is wrong. The accident must have screwed up an axle, I don't know."

"Is it safe to drive like this?"

The hint of a whine in Martha's voice made Abby snap, "Of course it is," but the truth was, it probably wasn't. At any rate, it wasn't safe to drive at highway speeds. And they couldn't very well crawl to Minnesota that way. She guided the car to the shoulder.

She put her hand out for her phone, but even as she did she realized how stupid it was to expect it to solve their problem this time. No one had driven by this way. There wasn't even the light of a farmhouse anywhere in sight. There wouldn't be an Uber driver in a hundred miles of here. What did people do in this situation? They called Triple A, or highway patrol. That might not be so bad, get a friendly officer to drop them at a hotel, get a new car in the morning. But that's if she had a signal, and would she?

She didn't. Fucking Martha must have gotten them lost.

Even as she thought it she saw a gray-pink stain of light above the trees in what must have been the east. She whipped around to face Martha, who to her surprise was already facing her.

"Why won't you ever let me help?" her sister said angrily. "You make me do things I'm not good at but when I actually do something I am good at you get all mad."

"I'm not mad," Abby said, and to her surprise it was the truth. It had been long years since she spent the night in a car and she would've hated to repeat the experience. Maybe there was no harm in letting Martha have the satisfaction for once. Giving her a sense of… not power exactly, what was the word the shrinks on TV used? Agency. That sounded right.

She didn't form a plan for any of it; if she had, she would have seen that it wouldn't solve the real problem. She just picked up a pack of matches one afternoon in the kitchen and thought, *I can burn the barn down. Then they can't chain Martha up in the barn.*

That said, when she looked back years later she still thought she had been clever for a first-time arsonist. She checked that Mom, Grandfather, Martha were all safely in the house. She took the matches to the back of the barn so they wouldn't spot the fire until it was too late to stop it. She'd thought it would catch easily because the wood was so old, but the first match just charred a quarter-sized spot on the beam she held it to. There wasn't much straw left, and it was rotted to almost nothing, went up so fast that it wouldn't start the beams either. It was the burlap sacks that finally did the trick.

She watched over the flames until they were strong enough to survive on their own. Leaving the barn, she skirted around the little grove of trees so she couldn't be seen from the house, slipped away up the hill. She threw the matches in the creek, with some vague idea that they might have her fingerprints on them, and then immediately regretted it.

There was no way to tell time except guessing by the sun, but it felt like a long wait before she heard the sirens come tearing out from the direction of Alden. Then another set came tearing out from the direction of Corfu and Batavia. Then more sirens from the east. It occurred to Abby that they might put it out before the grain shed went up. Then what?

She wanted to go and watch, be sure one way or the other. She thought she could do it, probably, without her thoughts giving her away. All she had to do was concentrate.

She skirted around through the neighbor's fields, through her own yard in billows of black smoke that stank more than it had a right to. There were seven fire trucks in the driveway, men in bulky grimy rubber suits everywhere. Hoses were pouring out arcs of water onto the barn but there was obviously no hope for it. They were wetting down the house, too, and although it wasn't on fire she could see now that it was too close. There was wind. Flames were reaching out, trees were catching. She hadn't thought of that.

She slipped through the side door. She had to save Grandfather's notebooks. A few years later she'd pretend that she knew she'd need them to help Martha, but she just wanted them, didn't want the fire to stop her from finding out.

She was too late. The fire wasn't there yet, but Grandfather was. He was standing in the doorway of his bedroom, arguing with a firefighter who looked a bit cleaner and more commanding than the men she'd seen outside, the two of them leaning in so they could shout at each other without raising their voices. Their wills were so thick around them that at first she was afraid that the cloud was smoke, but she couldn't smell it. She knelt down behind the banister where the stairs turned into the landing.

"You don't seem to understand. This is an order. You have to leave now."

"Order? This is my home. I'm not leaving while I can still save something." Grandfather's voice wasn't loud, but he was using a tone that Abby knew enough to be afraid of even if the fire chief didn't.

"That's our job, Mr. Waite. You need to come with me."

The fire chief was determined. But Grandfather was determined and powerful. He pushed and the other man backed up a step, probably without even realizing he'd done so.

Grandfather was determined and powerful. But as Abby watched, she realized why he wasn't as powerful as usual, why the argument had gone on even this long, why he was letting himself get pissed off. By Grandfather's side was an old black hard-sided bag, the one he used for their trips, and it was bulging full, and the bookshelves behind him were empty. But something was still distracting him, tugging his attention away.

It didn't have to be the rest of his notebooks, but whatever it was, it was important to Grandfather, and that meant it was important. She crept forward, trying to see where those stray thoughts were pointing.

She wasn't sure who spotted her first, but it was the fire chief who stepped forward, his instincts telling him to protect her. "Is this the girl you couldn't find?"

"Abby," Grandfather said with the fake warmth he would put on sometimes for the public. "There you are."

"Your mother's having a fit," the fire chief said. "This isn't a good place to hide, you're not safe here." He grabbed her hand as soon as he reached her, his intent so focused that it almost hurt. He was glad without knowing it for the excuse to get away. As he pulled her back down the stairs, Abby was able to glance back just long enough to see Grandfather turn and bend toward the big dresser that sat beside the bed.

The fire chief dragged her out the front door and onto the lawn, where Mom and Martha were waiting. Mom gave Abby a look that made Abby think she suspected, and then she grabbed her and hugged her so that it was hard to breathe, and Abby could tell she was feeling her pockets. Good thing she'd thrown the matches away after all.

But that reminded her of all the things she had to pretend not to know. "What happened?"

"The barn's on fire! Where have you been?"

"I was reading and I fell asleep." It wasn't a where but it sounded like an answer.

"Well, you scared the life out of us." The fact that Mom said "life" instead of "shit" made Abby even more nervous.

Mom didn't keep the act up very long, though, before she went back around the house to watch the progress of the flames and left Abby alone with Martha. Now she could relax for a second and actually think about what she'd done.

"Are you okay?" Martha said. She seemed not very okay herself, pale and sweaty.

"Of course I am. So long as Mom doesn't figure out..." She looked around. There were no firefighters nearby. "At least you'll never have to go in there again. You should be happy."

Martha stared at her for a moment, squinting even though the sun wasn't that bright. "But what if everything else in there can come out now?"

"I don't think that's how it works," Abby said, but in fact it hadn't occurred to her. She hadn't given Martha's boogiemen much thought one way or the other. Certainly there were things that could be trapped by a building and then bust loose when the building was destroyed, but those were things that were scary, not the psychic leftovers of some old pigs.

"Grandfather's sure it was the Davis kids and their friends," Martha said. Abby nodded, relieved. If that was what Grandfather had decided, then Mom would end up agreeing with him eventually, no matter what she suspected now. "He's upset."

"I saw him inside, I thought he was pissed off because the fire chief was telling him what to do."

"He's pissed off about that too. He's pissed that volunteer firefighters are crawling all over the place, but he can't exactly make them leave, I guess. Or the house will burn down." Martha shivered, even though it was warm. Over her shoulder, Abby could see the sun starting to set, hours early.

"What does he think they're going to see? They're too busy to read his books. If they even can read," Abby said, trying to mimic Grandfather's voice and make Martha laugh. It fell on stones.

"I don't know. I don't know if you should have done this, Abby. If he ever figures out that it was you…" Martha closed her eyes and lunged in at Abby for a hug. It had been a long time since she'd done that. Not since June.

Abby's jaw tightened, and she realized when Martha squeezed her that her stomach had started to feel sick. She wasn't going to get caught! She shouldn't have to do all the work of comforting Martha too.

"I did it for you," she muttered as she leaned in towards Martha's ear. "So if Grandfather catches me, it's your fault."

Martha sobbed, and a firefighter on her way to the trucks stopped to wipe sweat from her forehead and pity them. "It'll be okay," she said, "we'll save the house." Then she kept on going.

They did save the house. The barn collapsed, though, and Grandfather was given a summons for failing to obey the lawful orders of an officer, which the fire chief, as it turned out, technically was. The Darien fire company, the closest one, stayed late into the evening hosing down the rubble while Grandfather and Mom watched; they sent Abby and Martha to bed but neither girl went to sleep. They crouched by the window and watched until the firefighters coiled up their hoses and drove away, well after moonrise. Looking down at Grandfather from above this time made Abby feel as though everything had come full circle, as though she had fixed everything, but she didn't say anything about it to Martha.

CHAPTER ELEVEN

Abby had to pee, suddenly… But of course not suddenly. She had to pee as though she was just waking up.

The trees were not thick, and she didn't love the idea of squatting with her skirt hitched up and her panties down concealed only by a few birch stems, but she needed to go. She wouldn't even be able to think what to do next until she was more comfortable; bad enough that she was hungry and stiff and a little bit chilly in the damp morning air, for all that it was July. She nodded at Martha, who she would have sworn smirked, but only for a moment. Then she moved heavy-footed into the woods, stomping down brush rather than going around it—counterproductive, since that just gave the twigs and brambles more chances to cut at her, but she wanted them to pay, wanted to feel them snap.

It took perhaps five minutes to get far enough into the woods that she felt safe from random eyes, locate a good spot with the right slope, scan it for poison ivy. Only after she had her panties down did it occur to her that they could send another hawk at her now, when she was comically vulnerable. There was no real way to hurry while peeing, but she tried.

After she'd stood up and reassembled herself she took advantage of the slender privacy to check her shoulder too. It didn't feel any different, but it hadn't felt any different before she went to the doctor either and that hadn't been any protection. She could use her phone, take a picture over her shoulder, but she'd have to take her top off to get a clear shot and if Martha noticed that and asked why… this wasn't the time or the place for that conversation, not after the night they'd had. Or hadn't had. She'd just have to wait until they got to a hotel.

She wasn't quite in view of the car again when she heard a man's voice.

"Hey Miss. Hey! Are you okay there?"

Well shit.

She didn't let herself run, didn't let herself stomp any more bushes despite her frustration. In fact she stopped for a minute, rearranged her dress and her face. She could have swept in and all but tackled him, if she wanted to, but it would be easier if he stayed calm and thought she was pleasant, welcoming.

The man approaching Martha was young, not a teen but definitely younger than Abby, though he was several inches taller. His brown hair was just a little on the short side of shaggy, and he was wearing a polo shirt that was a bit too big across the shoulders. His attention was focused and not duplicitous, there was nothing in his voice but concern, and Martha wasn't freaking out, just staring at him mutely while her thoughts tried to decide what to do about him.

"Hi!" Abby said, loud and confident, as she stepped from the tree line. "Sorry"—she wasn't, why would she be, but saying that disarmed them and made them comfortable—"We're okay. Just some car trouble. I hope we didn't scare you."

"Oh!" He looked up, and as he saw her his general air of concern and confusion focused in on her face, became lighter, more hopeful. He was worrying about what to do too, was someone hurt, should he call the cops. Now he wouldn't have to make a decision either.

For her part, Abby's smile felt more genuine already. She could work with this guy. As she reached him she tilted her face up and made sure to lock in his eyes—hazel, wide-set, in a slightly ruddy face that suggested Irish blood and time outdoors even though he was dressed for school or a casual office.

Even as she made the assessment, though, his frown half-returned. He'd noticed how rumpled she looked, her sedge-torn skirt and muddy shoes. Straight guys always noticed shoes, in spite of the stereotypes—they just didn't notice themselves noticing. Now he was worried that she was some kind of trouble, that she might have something to do with why Martha was so silent.

"Sorry," she said again, to get back on the right track, and pressed. "Is this your land? We had problems with the car and I thought it would be safer to just wait it out until it was light."

"Yeah," he said. "Well, my dad's land. It's no big deal. You're not hurting anything." He looked into the car briefly but Abby took another step towards him and he shifted his attention back, let it rest on her. She didn't feel hungry anymore. He couldn't see Grandfather, or this would all be a lot harder.

"What kind of car trouble?" he asked after a moment, stepping back from the window and surveying the whole machine.

"We hit something in the dark. Some kind of big bird. It startled me so bad I went off the road." Taking the blame for Martha's fuckup was annoying but letting him know that she was the driver here was important. "After that it wouldn't steer right when I tried to accelerate. I get some speed and the back end wobbles."

"Want me to take a look at it?" He was already bending down, and Abby slid over beside Martha, nudged her. She couldn't stand there like a mute.

"That'd be great, thanks!" Martha sounded exaggeratedly bright to Abby's ears, and nodded too deeply, but it was good enough.

"I'm sorry," Martha added all on her own after a moment, as if a spell was broken. "I didn't catch your name."

"Ryan." He'd bent himself down almost under the car, but now he extracted himself and straightened up, dusted off his hands as though he'd actually fixed something.

"Abby." She extended her hand; he looked pleasantly surprised as he took it. His handshake was middling firm. "And this is my twin sister Martha."

"Nice to meet you." He looked over her shoulder just long enough to smile at Martha, who stayed well behind her. "I don't know for sure but it looks like you might have bent the tie rod. The rear wheel is sort of toeing out."

"Can you fix it?"

"Oh no," he said, and he had this grin like he was tickled that she was so dumb. She made herself hold her own smile. "You'll need to take it into a shop."

She looked past Ryan and saw his truck just up the shoulder; a red Ford with a crew cab, nothing flashy about it but it was new-ish and it looked well-maintained.

"Well darn. We're not from around here. Do you know a good place?"

"Absolutely. I can give you their number." Abby reached out and poked his intentions gently. "Or, you know, I'm driving right by there on my way into town, I could give you ladies a lift."

"That would be perfect! Then we could grab some breakfast, too, if you know a good place. I'm starved." She turned to Martha. "What about you? Hungry?"

Martha gave her a look before nodding and saying, "Yeah, starved. I'm starved too."

If Ryan noticed the lack of enthusiasm he gave no sign. "Well, hop on in the truck then, there's plenty of room."

Abby didn't see the dog until she walked around to the passenger side. It was a black-furred, brown-eyed floppy-eared thing, mostly

Labrador she thought. Unlike Grandfather, who'd been universally hated by every living thing not a Waite, Abby was okay with about fifty percent of dogs and nearly all cats—but occasionally an animal would see her and go berserk. She wanted to make him leave it behind, it wasn't worth the risk, but he'd balk hard at that, and she still didn't feel a hundred percent… The dog hung its head out the open window and she braced for the barking to start, but it just sniffed twice and then sneezed.

"That's Buddy," Ryan said as Abby wiped the mist of dog-snot off onto her skirt. "He's harmless." He snapped his fingers at the dog. "Make room, you."

Buddy clambered over the seat-back, and Ryan pulled open the door. "Sorry about the mess. If I'd've known I was going to have two pretty ladies in my car, I would have cleaned it up."

Abby didn't have to look back to see Martha look askance at that one… but no, from behind her she actually heard a giggle. Martha had woken up enough to play along then. Good.

"Oh wait!" She made it sound like she'd just thought of it. "My bags, I don't want to leave them here."

"They'll be safe. Hardly no one comes along this road, and anyway, people around here don't break into locked cars. Or unlocked cars, even."

She grabbed a sluggish strand and tugged. Not hard, it didn't have to be hard. "It just makes me nervous. Humor me."

"Well. Okay, I guess." They always got so confused the first few times she pushed and pulled at them. And he seemed like the easily confused type to begin with.

Back at the car she consolidated most of Martha's new clothes into a bag with Grandfather and the books, hiding him completely. She managed to grab all the books, her own bag, and the rest of Martha's purchases, but she left the prison-issue duffel bag behind. If Martha wanted anything in it, she should have said something.

She was a little surprised that Ryan hadn't come over to help her with the bags, but when she looked back, she saw that he and Martha were already in the truck, talking. Martha was holding her hand out for the dog to sniff, it looked like.

So she lugged the bags herself, and Ryan did at least have the good manners to look embarrassed as she slung them into the back seat with the dog. She'd planned to sit next to him—if she couldn't hold his eyes, having a little bit of contact with his elbow or leg would be the next-best thing—but it would look weird to tell Martha to move, far too overt. She wouldn't need to push him while he was driving, anyway.

"What about my bag?" Martha said, and Abby would snap at her if it wouldn't ruin the illusion of pleasant harmless girliness.

"I'll get it," Ryan said, and said it fast. That was better. He returned with the near-empty duffel bag and Martha pulled it onto her lap as though it were precious cargo.

"So, where are you ladies headed?" he asked as they pulled away. Abby was distracted, staring at the Jeep and wondering if she forgot anything, and before she could rouse herself to deliver a lie Martha said, "Minnesota. Our family has a cabin there."

Abby pinched Martha's leg, even though she could fix this. Martha flinched away but she knew better than to make a noise. That was what she got for insisting that Abby not push her.

"Minnesota? I've never been, but I've heard it's real nice. They've got good hunting there, right?"

"Absolutely," Abby said before Martha could talk again, and rattled off the list of reasons why people, in their ignorance, rented the cabin. "Deer, turkey, geese, black bears. Good trout fishing too. You hunt?"

"Just deer, for the freezer. Wouldn't mind going bear hunting some time. I bet that would make a great story."

"We saw a bear at the cabin once. When we were kids." Martha smiled. Abby hadn't noticed until now how yellow and awful her teeth had gotten. "It was just looking for berries or something across the river. Our grandfather yelled and scared it away."

"They've gotten a lot bolder around here, lately. In people's chicken coops, in their garbage cans. This old boy ran one off from our back yard last fall." Ryan reached back and ruffled Buddy's ears.

"Brave dog!" Martha said.

Abby was about to speak when she was distracted; a red-tailed hawk rose from the margin of the road and flew directly into their path. Ryan spotted it and hit the brakes; Martha gasped, but Abby pinched her again before she could start shrieking.

Then the hawk flapped hard and rose steeply across the windshield. It seemed like it had to be too late, but no, the bird cleared the top of the truck and continued away into the trees to the east. Abby watched it glide to the top of the tallest birch and settle. It made no move to follow them, didn't even turn its head.

"That was a close one," Ryan said. "Didn't you say that you hit a bird last night, too?"

"Yes," Martha said, her voice a little cracked, but Abby talked over her. "Yeah, and it was at least that big. Are we too close to their nest or something?"

"Red-tails are everywhere out here. Could be they're fledging, I guess. They're pretty clumsy when they're first learning how to fly."

Abby managed to drop the smile and arrange her face into concern. "Oh! I hope we didn't hit a baby."

Martha pinched her back, but she ignored it.

The morning after the fire Abby woke up at first light and checked Martha's bed as she'd gotten into the habit of doing. Martha was asleep, her face calm and normal.

She looked out the window and saw the hills that used to be hidden by the barn and the view took her harder than she'd expected, as though she'd banged her chest against the windowsill. Of course the barn wasn't there anymore. That was why she'd done it. But somehow, *the barn isn't there anymore* was different when it came in through her eyes. A couple of white-tailed deer craned necks and twitched ears in the pink space where the hilltop met the sky. They'd get this close, no closer. If the barn had been there she'd never have seen them.

But Abby had underestimated how much the fire would upset the adults. They weren't just put out by not having a place to stash Martha when they stole her body. Grandfather couldn't seem to get over the insult of being ordered around by a volunteer firefighter. He seethed and muttered and stopped bothering with Abby's lessons or any of what remained of his old routine. Mom was nervous and Abby was nervous around her and she couldn't tell which was the cause and which was the effect. Martha started having nightmares, waking Abby up with the same sort of noises she'd been used to hearing in the barn. And Abby herself spent the rest of the summer just trying to keep out of the way, hiding out in the orchard or by the creek. She felt uneasy indoors even when Mom wasn't around, and the creeping feeling that she was about to be caught kept her from even trying to look further at Grandfather's notebooks.

It was almost a relief when school started. Through some kind of clerical error, they'd even put Martha in Abby's class for the fifth grade. Since Martha seemed to share Abby's paranoia about talking in the house since the fire, Abby had begun to feel as though her sister was somewhere else, unavailable—and though Martha wasn't much use in a situation like this, Abby still hated it. So having her around every day at school, where the most threatening forces were jealous kids and stupid rules, would be a relief.

Relief, and the fun of wearing new clothes and a new bracelet and carrying a fresh notebook, made her heedless. Looking back, she should have noticed the whispering and the way even the older kids went tense when she and Martha walked up the aisle of the school bus. But the driver was a big, serious Mohawk woman from the rez and no one started fights on her bus, not even with a Waite girl, not ever.

Maybe they wouldn't have started a fight that first day anyhow. No one did in Mrs. Grant's room before the bell. They just stood around, looking somber. Some of the girls sniffled in a way that struck Abby as ostentatious and irritating.

Mrs. Grant came in wearing black, and when she sniffled too, Abby decided that she'd been wrong and she was going to hate this school year after all. She tried to catch Mrs. Grant's eye, or anyone's eye, and force them to stop making the awful noise. None of them looked up.

"I have some very bad news," Mrs. Grant said, as though that wasn't obvious enough. "As some of you..." She paused when Nicole broke out in an actual sob, and didn't tell her to hush up. "As some of you already know, Jeremy Davis and his brothers Justin and Jeffrey were killed last night. Carbon monoxide poisoning. There will be a counselor meeting with the class today, once we've taken roll. In the meantime, please join me in a moment of silence."

The moment dragged on until Abby was fidgeting with her bracelet, rubbing her fingers across the faceted beads. She didn't even notice Mrs. Grant until the shadow bent over her.

"Give that to me." Mrs. Grant was whispering but Abby could tell she was furious.

"Why?" A risky question, but the bracelet was purple and it was brand new and Abby didn't want to explain to Mom that she'd lost it.

"You're being disrespectful," Mrs. Grant said, and Abby saw that the old fat teacher was roiling, that she could barely keep her hand from slapping, that she hated Abby. It was so unexpected that for a moment Abby was scared, and when she pushed back it was too late. Mrs. Grant had her hand out and she wouldn't back down now, not in front of the class.

She rolled the bracelet off her wrist so quickly that the rough edges of the plastic beads scraped her wrist. As she dropped it into Mrs. Grant's palm she was hot with hatred and the unfairness of it, but she knew those feelings. It was the confusion that was overwhelming her. She couldn't understand why Mrs. Grant was so angry, and if she didn't know, how could she do anything to stop it?

"I'm sorry," she muttered, as much as it galled her, since that was always a good fall-back option.

"Are you?" Mrs. Grant curled her fingers around the bracelet. Abby would never see it again. "Good. Show us you're sorry. Say a prayer for those poor boys."

The fact that a teacher was willing to break the rules so openly scared Abby even more than it made her mad. Suddenly everything she relied on was erased by Mrs. Grant's anger. Abby didn't see how she was going to get out of it, and she didn't know how to say a prayer.

Everyone was staring at her, too many to push or persuade that they were seeing anything except the stuck-up girl they all hated getting put in her place.

Her mind felt as though it was moving extra fast in those moments, as though she were a hero in a cartoon. Later, looking back, she would wonder what might have happened if she'd realized that that was the energy pushing her from behind, and turned and learned to use it then. But how could a fifth grader have done that, in the moment, without help?

Martha twitched next to her, and that reminded Abby's racing mind of something that had happened a long time ago, before they'd gone to kindergarten for the first time. Grandma had corralled them on the living room couch and warned them about the danger of religious zealots, and made them recite the Lord's Prayer over and over again, trying to get them to memorize it.

Mom had broken it up after only a few repetitions though. "They don't set people on fire for that bullshit any more," she'd said with a laugh. "Stop scaring the girls."

"They didn't set us on fire," Grandma said. "They hanged us. And pressed us. And you never know when they might start again."

Now Abby struggled to remember, and felt pressed. "Our Father," she said, then hesitated. The next bit had sounded old-fashioned, she remembered that. "You art in heaven. Hello. Be thy name." Some of the kids were starting to laugh, and Mrs. Grant was getting madder. The next bit was something, something, kingdom come, she was pretty sure.

But before she could figure it out, Mrs. Grant grabbed her by the shoulder. "You're in a lot of trouble, young lady."

"Mrs. Grant! Mrs. Grant!" Nicole sounded so eager that only her red eyes showed how miserable she'd been acting a minute ago. "Let me say a real prayer, Mrs. Grant!"

"Of course, Nicole. I know you and Jeremy were friends."

"Dear Jesus, I just…" Nicole hesitated. Abby noticed that Mrs. Grant didn't turn mad at her. "I just want to thank you for your love and grace and just ask you to take Jeremy into your arms in heaven and Justin and Jeffrey too, and help Jessica and Mrs. Davis get better in the hospital. And I just want to thank you for saving Jessica and Mrs. Davis, and for sending the firefighters and just, uh, just help them not be sad, Lord. And please make sure Jeremy can still watch football in heaven. He was really excited about the next season." Nicole looked over at Abby and smiled broadly. "And make sure they catch whoever blocked up the dryer vent and then put him in jail for a long time. Amen."

The simultaneous amens from the other students surrounded

Abby and almost drowned out the fact that Martha had started crying.

CHAPTER TWELVE

The influx of energy Abby felt when she got into the truck peaked and rolled back before she was even half satisfied. It wasn't hard to see why; Ryan's attention was getting as far as Martha, jammed in tight between them, and no further. It kept drifting from Martha's face to her cleavage and jerking back up again, although there was nothing particularly predatory about the thoughts themselves, they were just warm and wanting. Abby was the thirdest of third wheels, completely extraneous.

There was no accounting for taste, it could even be as simple as the fact that they were touching. It could be that he saw Martha first. The why didn't really matter. Martha had just better not screw things up. Abby didn't have the patience right now to be the fixer.

She could have just grabbed at his mind and straight-up stolen him back from Martha, but she decided it would be smarter to conserve her strength for later if this weak shit was all the attention she was going to get. A man like that would probably kick at being separated from his truck just as hard as he'd fight ditching his dog, maybe harder. Attention he wasn't freely giving would be the opposite of what she needed, a drain and not a fountain.

And more than any of that she shouldn't have to, god dammit. He should be able to figure out which sister was the better deal on his own.

The radio turned itself on, but before she could hear the first notes of the song Ryan slapped at it without any apparent thought and it shut off again.

Her welts itched and she clenched her hands around the handles of the last shopping bag to stop from scratching. Martha giggled again—giggled! for real!—as Buddy sniffed at her from the back seat, and Ryan tried to conceal a grin. The dog was another idiot, then, because Martha had to be at least as ripe as Abby felt, a full stressful day since their last shower.

"There you go," Ryan said, with a laugh in his voice. "Now I know you're not escaped bank robbers or something. Buddy is an excellent judge of character."

Abby turned to stare out the window. No use dwelling on the spectacle Martha was making out of herself when she wasn't getting anything out of it. The landscape wasn't that much different than what she was used to—more vines and rhododendrons in the woodlots, fewer cars on the road, but the same sort of disappointed houses and hayfields she knew from childhood. She wondered, not for the first time, how anyone could stand to stay in such a place very long once they had a choice. She knew that someone like Ryan here, for instance, actually did stay on purpose, that he wasn't secretly yearning to be free, but she couldn't understand how that could be so. It really was like these people were a different species or something.

A hawk sat on a speed limit sign, unmoving, hunched, and neither Martha nor Ryan noticed. Abby couldn't miss it, though. Its yellow eyes were full of rage. She ground her teeth and tried to will her share of anger back onto the bird as well, but it didn't work—one tiny bird mind couldn't hold that much.

Choke on it, she thought to the bird. *You get none of her, not now and not ever, you get none of anything that's mine.*

Looking back, Abby could see that the right strategy for her fifth-grade year would have been to seek out other outcasts and bring them under her sway—even the special ed kids and that one girl who kept dead birds in her desk would have been of some use. She didn't have that sort of perception back then, though. She still bought into Grandfather's view, the world and all the people in it as things to be crushed, not to be used. All she could see was that this flock of people surrounding her had decided that she and Martha needed to pay for what had happened to Jeremy, Justin, and Jeffrey, even though they weren't Grandfather, even though there was no proof that Grandfather had done anything, even though there wasn't even proof anyone had done anything—the official verdict was a starling nest in the dryer vent, to the class's palpable disappointment.

Without Martha's talent, that year would have been an even worse hell. Abby could stave off actual attacks, when they were one-on-one, or even a few-on-one. But she couldn't do anything about being ganged up on. She couldn't do anything about the weird constant keep-away game of being ostracized when peoples' intentions flew all in tangles not really ignoring them. Martha could at least make the days slip by.

At home things were tense and fearful. Not only did Martha still have nightmares, but Abby started waking up with a feeling of being watched. One morning while she was brushing her teeth, the steam on the bathroom mirror began to shift, melting away faster than it should, creating patches that almost looked like they would have formed a face if Abby hadn't swiped at them with her sleeve before she bolted out of the room and called for Grandfather.

"This is your fault," Mom said, after they'd covered every mirror in the house with dark cloth. Abby flinched but Mom was facing Grandfather, who was ignoring her, bent over one of the forbidden books that he'd brought down from the bedroom to the well-lit, mirror-free kitchen. He grunted at the accusation but didn't lift his head.

"Honestly, it would have taken about two seconds to bind it when it was first awake and confused. But no, you need to get revenge on those little idiots over on Harlow Road, who you don't even know for sure if they did it…"

"Of course they did it," Grandfather said, and his voice sounded dangerous to Abby, but Mom went on.

"Even if they did, aren't there a million better ways to deal with it than letting something like that run loose? You know it's going to come back here eventually, to someone with Waite blood. You know you can't control it if it gets too strong. You can risk yourself if you like, but I live here too, and my children. How dare you put us in danger."

"You'll be in more danger if you don't let me read," Grandfather said, and Abby grabbed Martha's hand and pulled her from the room.

That September was rainy and cold, so they were stuck inside most of the time, with Grandfather burning gross-smelling powders and chanting at things that didn't seem to respond. The mirrors stayed covered and that wasn't so bad, except when Abby was trying to do her hair, but they had to be careful of butter knives and the metal garbage can and dishwater in the sink, and they left the TV on all the time, and when it got dark outside the windows were dangerous.

Abby tried to get Grandfather to explain what was going on. She said she wanted to learn and help, and that was true, but more than that she wanted to be able to handle it on her own. It wasn't just pride, it wasn't just knowing what he'd done to Martha. It wasn't just Mom's "you can't control it if it gets too strong." She didn't want to have to run and get Grandfather again.

He told her it was something she'd learn when she was older.

She should have tried harder to find out, but she let it go. The problems at school were worse than some ghost-creature trying to talk to her through mirrors; they were fifth grade kids and they hated her. After what Mrs. Grant had done they could tell it was open season. Her pens disappeared, starting with the fancy glittery one with ten different colors of ink, but eventually even the boring clear Bics and the ones Mom took from the bank would vanish if she turned her back. Then she got in trouble for coming to class unprepared. Meanwhile, in the coat closet, someone kept stuffing plastic crosses and comic books about Jesus into her jacket pockets. Spit balls hit her in the back of the head.

It was worse for Martha. Martha would cry when someone upset her, and when she tried not to she would slowly turn red and the tears would build up in her eyes and her nose would go snotty. The other kids thought this was hilarious.

Finally Abby told her to just go ahead and tell Mom, breaking all their rules about their secrets. At least Mom outranked stupid Mrs. Grant.

Mom looked at Martha and then over at Abby. "Is this true?"

Abby nodded, and wondered what would make Mom think they'd lie about something like this. Lying was for making yourself look better, not worse.

"Well, you need to look out for your sister, then. You know that's your job." She turned back to her cooking. "You two can't come running to me with every little problem that you have all of your lives."

Abby was almost out of ideas. She could try punching someone, she supposed. Girls who did that usually got sent to the counselor, and with the counselor one-on-one maybe she could get herself and Martha moved to a different class, one where the teacher didn't hate them even if the students did. But Mrs. Grant had already decided she was a bad kid, and boys and bad kids got sent to the principal, not the counselor.

She racked her brain for something else for weeks, but they were short weeks, because Martha was folding time tighter and tighter in her misery, and Abby couldn't very well tell her to stop even once it got annoying. Nothing came to her. And so one afternoon on the playground she found herself standing by the tall slide, curling her fingers and getting ready to take a swing at Amelia Matthias. Amelia wasn't a popular girl, and if she'd been trying to accomplish something in that direction by picking on Martha she'd failed. Firstly pushing Martha into a mud puddle was not that impressive. Secondly no one was watching, not even in a sideways ostracizing way.

Still, Abby couldn't ignore it and she was just about ready to give up and get in all the trouble there was anyway. She didn't even know if it was possible to get kicked out of school in fifth grade, that was something she'd only heard of happening to high school kids, but she might as well try.

She put up her fists like Bugs Bunny did in cartoons, and Amelia got a funny look on her face and her mind went funny too, like she hadn't expected that at all. The tendrils of her thoughts were slow and lazy, like the creek gone muddy in the summertime, and Abby didn't even bother to try to push or block them. It didn't matter what this stupid girl did at this point, so it wasn't worth trying to change her mind. The thoughts were going to touch her, and it would feel gross, and then she'd punch Amelia in the nose as hard as she could.

As they touched her, Abby felt the unpleasant buzz and almost did push back just out of habit. Then she realized what it felt like. It felt like the neighbors' electric fence.

Just to see what would happen, she let the feeling linger for a moment. Amelia's brain was so slow! And her intentions didn't jump around or grow or shrink or sway; it was like they were barely alive. After she got used to it they almost weren't even unpleasant, slightly warm, still buzzing. And Abby felt ever so slightly better, as though she'd gotten a good night's sleep.

She pushed back at Amelia, making her drop her fists and turn away. It came easy, like jumping from the top of the swing's arc. Amelia wasn't even looking at her anymore when Abby stopped her, made her turn to Martha and pull her up and apologize.

Martha, shocked, moved to Abby's side. They could have held hands, but everyone knew that was for babies now.

By the next day, Abby had a plan for what she supposed Grandfather would have called an experiment. Mrs. Grant didn't like Amelia either so antagonizing her wasn't as dangerous as it might have been. All morning, Abby stared at her and poked at her mind to make sure she noticed—completely deniable, not actually an offense, but she could tell that it bothered the other girl. A couple of times, when she felt she could risk it, she threw little wads of paper at her, but they never connected. She crossed her eyes. When they stood near each other in the line for the water fountain, she hummed very, very quietly.

By the time they reached the cafeteria for lunch, Abby was so warm with the tingling energy that she was actually beginning to sweat a little.

Someone always started something at lunch. It wasn't always the same someone—usually it was her own classmates, especially Nicole or Robert, but other kids would get in on the act too. Jeremy's cousin Troy had actually tried to pick Martha up and stuff her in the garbage can once, which turned out to be beyond the limit of what the lunch ladies would tolerate. But today everyone was leaving them alone. It was like they knew she'd powered up.

"What's going on?" Martha whispered over the top of her fruit cup. "What did you do?"

Abby just smiled at her, because she never admitted to Martha when she didn't know.

CHAPTER THIRTEEN

The cafe Ryan took them to was the kind of place that could parlay its relentless mediocrity into a Food Network publicity binge of road-trip nostalgia, but it didn't have to because it was the only non-McMuffin game in town. There were fifteen kinds of jam, four kinds of sausage, and only one kind of sweetener for the one kind of coffee. The option to get your omelet made with egg whites was penciled in at the bottom of the breakfast menu, a recent concession to not killing the customers.

Abby got a rush as soon as they stepped around the corner that separated the entrance from the main dining area. The curiosity of the old-timers washed over her, not the thin trickle of attention that you got from people who expect to deal with strangers daily, but thick like lotion, with an almost living warmth. Just as she'd suspected—they must have wandered pretty far from the highway. It was amazing, that there were still places where it could get this good, that it ever was this good. For a moment she was reminded of an aspiring travel writer she'd known in college, a girl who would gush about the trout streams in Montana or the stars over Joshua Tree until Abby finally told her to just get a dildo and shut up, already. They'd never spoken again, and Abby still didn't regret that, but she understood the impulse to gloat now.

She ducked into the bathroom even before they were seated. After a long satisfying scratching of her thighs she scrubbed her hands and splashed cool water on her face. It helped. It helped enough that even when she came out to see Ryan and Martha leaning in to talk, she just absorbed the curiosity of the rest of the restaurant and let it go.

They sat in a booth towards the back, Ryan on one side and Abby and Martha together on the other. A pair of old men sitting nearby nodded to Ryan, who nodded back. There was a certain similarity that made Abby think they might be related, but in truth everyone in here looked the same—not just the same race and class but all light-hued, much of a height, a similar cast of features, with retiring eyes and dry mouths that were soft-set but not necessarily generous. She and Martha stuck out here. And yet the flickers of curiosity that came their way were also dry now that the first rush was over, now that everyone was satisfied that Ryan was handling it and they didn't need to do anything about her.

She could almost understand why Grandfather thought it was a good idea to settle in a town so like this, isolated, vulnerable. She might make the same mistake herself if she hadn't already lived with the results. The things people could learn to ignore and live with in places like this were amazing. And even if someone came looking for you in a place they didn't know even existed, they'd be outsiders too, with the same handicaps.

"Excuse me," Martha said, and made off in the direction pointed out by the restroom sign. Abby directed her attention to Ryan and turned the smile back on before his eyes finished tracking Martha's ass out of sight.

"Thanks again for rescuing us," she said. "I don't know what we would have done. Heck, we were so turned around before all this happened, I don't even know where we are."

"Welcome to scenic Daines, West Virginia," Ryan said. "Stay awhile. Try the pancakes."

"West Virginia?" *Well shit.* "Shoot. We were lost!"

Ryan chuckled. "Yeah, I figured as much when I saw the New York plates and then your sister said you were going to Minnesota."

Ah yes. Martha's big mouth. "Well…" Abby leaned in. "Look, can I tell you something?"

"Sure." Ryan's smile faded a little and he leaned in in turn.

"Well, you might have noticed that my sister, well… she's kind of sweet but she's not very smart sometimes."

Ryan nodded, although intellectually Abby would guess he couldn't touch Martha's hem.

"In fact, she's not 100% all there." Abby dropped her eyes to the table, tried to look sorry to have to say it. "That cabin she thinks we're going to, Daddy sold it back in 1996. So if she says stuff that sounds weird, sounds off, don't worry about it too much, okay?"

Ryan nodded, and glanced uncomfortably in the direction of the restrooms.

"She's totally harmless," Abby said, and reached out to pat his hand. "I just didn't want you to not know."

"Thanks for telling me," he said. Abby felt a small part of his attention dart towards the door as though he was considering ditching them right then and there, but as she'd hoped, he was more scared of being rude than he was of a maybe-crazy girl.

Martha came back to the table a moment later, and didn't seem to notice the change in mood. Abby smiled broadly at her until Ryan got the message and smiled too.

"What's good?" Martha asked, and that spiraled into a discussion of the four kinds of sausage, the fifteen kinds of jam. Ryan went from acting like nothing was wrong to really relaxing in short order.

They'd gotten lucky, really. She should be happy.

Abby ordered an egg-white omelet, and then reconsidered and

changed her order to a regular one. Martha got the French toast and didn't change her order even when Abby pinched her again. The temptation to push her popped up out of nowhere but Abby pushed it away, annoyed with herself—one meal wasn't worth it. And by the time Abby had the argument in her head the waitress had taken Ryan's order too, and was gone.

It was while watching the waitress disappear that Abby noticed the television above the counter. It was tuned to Fox, and though she couldn't hear a word the blond anchor was saying, Abby could see the way the old men in their Carharts stared up at her. Even people who insisted they didn't care a bit about the news would stop what they were doing and watch the flickering life on a screen. Even people who claimed to 'never watch TV.' Especially people who 'never watch TV.' You couldn't ignore movement and colors at the edge of your vision—humans weren't built that way.

Martha noticed her line of sight and smirked at her. "Must be driving you crazy," she said.

"What's that?" Ryan said.

"Oh, Abby is a news junkie," Martha said lightly. Under the table Abby could tell that she was rubbing the spot on her leg where Abby had been pinching. "Whenever we go on vacation she gets crabby because she's away from the boob tube and the Internet."

Who even said boob tube anymore?

Ryan laughed. "I never watch that stuff. It doesn't mean anything for regular people, anyway."

"Yeah, that's what I think too." Martha smiled harder. It suddenly occurred to Abby, with forehead-smacking clarity, that it had been a long time since Martha had interacted with a man who wasn't telling her what to do or when to go back to her cell or worse. She hadn't had the opportunities Abby had to grow jaded about nice boys with nice eyes, wearing nice clean baseball caps. And Ryan was thick with nice.

"Well, someone has to pay attention to what's going on," she rejoined, but with a smile, a little duck of the head, telling them that she was on their side still and willing to take a bit of gentle ribbing. She didn't want to argue, not now; she needed to concentrate. She'd just seen the name "Bonetrager" scroll by in the crawler.

"I promise the world will still be terrible when we get back," Martha said.

"Ah, the world's not terrible," Ryan said. "A few people are, that's all. If we didn't watch the news, most of us wouldn't even know that serial killers exist, or wars, or anything."

God, what a holy fucking innocent. Abby started reassessing how lucky they were to find this guy. He might annoy her to death before she could get the truck off of him. And that's if it wasn't a cover for something worse, which niceness so often was.

The waitress came by with coffee in a carafe from a cheap drip machine. Ryan put cream and sugar in his and now, suddenly, Martha did too. More useless calories. Abby didn't even bother pinching her this time, it was obviously making her contrary. Instead, she kept her attention on the screen, but tried not to make it too obvious. A mere silver alert wouldn't have made the news all the way out here. Bonetrager wasn't a cute kid or a pretty blond woman.

The waitress blocked her view bringing the food and she missed the crawler the first time it repeated, but it came around again soon enough. Three dead, no names, Bonetrager and his teenage grandson missing.

Abby lost what little appetite she had. She didn't give a damn about Bonetrager or any of the neighbors, and she'd known this would happen eventually, but it shouldn't be happening this fast. She'd miscalculated something, overlooked something. And that suggested that she might be wrong about the birds too, and worse forces were in play than she'd thought. It didn't line up, not the way she understood it.

Or this was a coincidence, the kid had snapped and annihilated his family over some real or perceived abuse, and the world was just continuing to be the normal amount of terrible despite what Ryan said. She made herself chew and swallow a small bite of omelet. Either way, she needed to keep up her strength. The waitress wandered by with more coffee and a diffident "Everything okay?" and Martha's sincere-sounding "wonderful!" covered for Abby's lack of enthusiasm.

By the time breakfast was over, Martha had devoured not only every single bite of the French toast soaked in cheap fake syrup, but two refills of the cream-and-sugared coffee. She even managed to snag several bites of Ryan's home fries. Whether that was flirting or greed, it was deftly done. Ryan seemed flattered and paid their bill without prompting. Abby, nagged by worry and by the need to wave off the waitress's repeated offers of a box for the abandoned half of her omelet, had to wonder if it was her own damn fault— some guys thought broken and crazy was just a more interesting form of cute and helpless. She'd assumed he was too salt-of-the-earth for that.

As they went back to the car she made sure to walk a little faster so she could take the seat between the lovebirds.

She'd never asked Grandfather about her new-found power, this ability to absorb energy from others. He was too busy, too angry, too besieged. Besides, she'd find out more about it in his notebooks, she was sure. That was the good thing about the shadow over their home that autumn, it meant that she was able to raid Grandfather's room in peace while he and Mom shouted in the basement and threw salt around in the attic. She hadn't found the secret stash yet, but there were still a lot of his more recent notebooks to get through.

In his notebooks, he lost interest in things every few years. He'd lost interest in Mom when she was eight or so, changed his focus to his money worries. Then he'd gone back to Mass, to Salem, though he didn't take Grandma with him. He was very successful there, he wrote, coming back with several trunks full of material for his experiments. A few months after that Grandma came into an inheritance that let him buy a John Deere and several more books that he'd had his eye on. And a very promising piece of property in Minnesota.

It got so bad that Abby resorted to skimming before very long. Grandfather had project after project after project, most of them dull or elusive in his hints, pointless meanderings about the positions of the stars, occasional entertaining obsessions, and again and again schemes to raise more money or ghosts or ghosts who knew where money was hidden. He almost seemed to see power as a way of getting money sometimes, and not just as something that you wanted for itself.

Abby slowed down only when she caught a reference to Mom—"S. starting to show Akashik shielding", "S. reported dream about sunken city last night"—or the barn, or anything that hinted at moving body to body, invading, stealing, draining energy one to the other.

One spring when, by Abby's count, Mom would have been twelve or maybe just thirteen, she found the line "Tried transference on S. Satisfactory. Fem. brain structure not as limiting as I feared. She kicks a bit though—would have to, wouldn't she, that's my girl."

It was all true, then. Of course she'd already known, but he'd written it down, it was truly, truly, true and not a bad dream.

She cracked down. No more skimming. Every word of Grandfather's ancient nattering, despite the need for secrecy, despite meals, despite Mom's haphazard attempts at keeping up normalcy through lessons and chores, despite Grandfather in the flesh still carrying on at war with the thing in the mirrors. If she'd been coming home from school ground down from the hostility instead of glutted on the energy she was now absorbing—a few times it made her almost sick to her stomach like too much sponge candy—she'd never have been able to do it.

Three days later she was reading a page where Grandfather noted that Elaine—Grandma—knew, that he was almost sure she was helping Mom shake him off, to spite him. He had a test planned to see if that was the case. But before she could get through his astronomical notes to find out what that test was, Martha came dashing through the half-closed door.

Abby slammed the notebook shut and shoved it under her desk, angry with the awareness that she'd been too slow, too wrapped up in her reading. If that had been Mom or Grandfather she would have been caught.

Martha was panting, and her voice came out squeaky. "Mom says you have to come right away." Abby didn't ask questions, just got up and followed her sister—but she didn't run, either.

By the time they got down to the basement Grandfather was gurgling and bluish, worse than his body had looked even with Martha trapped inside. Mom was standing over him with hair all wild and her arms thrown up, screaming words that Abby knew. Not the words Grandfather had been yelling for weeks, but a more elaborate variation of them.

In the corner behind the hot water heater, the dark had gone solid and was sending out tendrils of intention as thick and material as Abby's leg. Most of them lashed blindly in empty space, but one had found Grandfather's ankle, and that one had grown what looked like a mouth or a suction cup full of teeth on the end.

Mom didn't take her eyes off the dark, but gestured toward Abby. "Get down here. Don't let it touch you. Martha, you go back upstairs."

The sentence had barely ended when the cellar door slammed,

with Martha on the other side.

Abby eyed the tentacles. They were reaching out close to the bottom of the stairs; she'd have to step over them. She wasn't going to risk it. She pushed at one but it was immovable and icy-cold, something she'd never felt before.

"Hurry up!"

She jumped. Mom caught her by the arm as she was landing and she stumbled, but away from the darkness.

Mom continued to grip her arm, and in that moment for the first time she felt the pressure at the edges of her mind. Startled, she resisted by instinct, but Mom squeezed and twisted her arm and she was distracted by pain, her vision doubled—she was Abby and she was looking at Abby, who looked small with big cartoony eyes; she was Mom and she was looking at Mom, glaring with concentration.

Both mouths took up the chant again, and Abby could feel two throats burn from screaming but she was powerless to stop either of them.

The dark tendrils slowed their sweeping, then fell still. The volume and pitch of the chanting rose, frantic, the pain increased. Abby pushed at the mind behind the eyes that saw Mom, scrabbling to get back into her own place. Her grip on her arm grew tighter, and Abby saw the tendril at Grandfather's leg detach and flop back, and stopped struggling, because the tentacles were everywhere falling back but also because the mark the thing had left on Grandfather's bare ankle was so ugly she couldn't look at or think of anything else, the edge of the wound shredded and the inside like raw meat already growing rotten, sheened with iridescence.

As soon as she stopped resisting their voices got even louder, firmer, and the darkness retreated faster and that in turn made the voices get louder still and it was like a thin sheet of ice melting away in the sun.

When there was no darkness but the legitimate shadow of the water heater, Mom dropped her arm. Abby felt her mind snap back into place, her vision clear, but she stood stunned and unmoving while Mom lurched forward to grab the dropped cane at Grandfather's side.

Her whole body was tingling like a foot that had gone to sleep. Mom was using the end of the cane to scratch in the dirt on the floor.

"Okay," Mom snapped, before Abby was sure that she could move again. "Help me get him up the stairs."

Abby wasn't tall enough to do much, and the stairs were too narrow for the three of them to go up at once anyway, so Mom ended up dragging Grandfather by the shoulders while Abby made a token attempt to help by holding up his feet. She kept her fingers away from the wound, which looked even more rotten up close and smelled that way too. She tried to feel her way into her body again, stretching, letting the tingle fade.

Martha was sitting slumped against the wall at the top of the stairs. She'd obviously been listening and she didn't even try to hide it. Abby didn't meet her eyes.

They laid Grandfather on the couch. He was still lying there three hours later when Martha came into the kitchen, where Abby was drinking a Coke and still trying to shake off what had happened, and tugged nervously on her sleeve.

"He's not breathing."

Abby stood and wobbled into the living room. Martha was right. Grandfather was not breathing. His face was gray, and his mouth open, a thin trickle of drool hanging down onto the couch-arm where they'd propped his head. And the smell of rot was stronger.

Reluctantly, Abby reached out and let her hand hover over his wrist as though she were touching him. Martha looked at her. Abby shrugged.

"Should we tell Mom?"

"She'll be angry if we wake her up."

"But I think he's dead."

"There's nothing Mom can do about that." This was a place, she had to admit later, where her instinct for secrecy led her wrong. Mom could have done a few things to make sure he was dead. Mom had only just then showed she could do something that Grandfather couldn't.

With Abby's help. And Abby didn't want to be grabbed and split and trapped in the back of her own mind again, any more than she wanted to wake Mom up and get yelled at.

Martha looked at her for a moment, as though expecting Abby to solve the problem right there. Then she left. In a moment she was back with a blanket from the hall closet, which she tucked over Grandfather's still form.

Then they went upstairs to do their homework.

CHAPTER FOURTEEN

Abby let Ryan get out of sight of the diner, make a few turns, before she started pressing his attention. All she wanted in the world was just to pull out her phone and get more details about what was going on back in Alden but she needed to take care of this first.

"Hey, are you ladies in a hurry?" he asked after only a few seconds' effort.

Martha glanced anxiously at Abby, who was already saying, "Not at all. Why?"

"I was thinking you might like to see the World's Largest Concrete Duck," he said, pronouncing the capitals. "It's pretty much the only thing around here that tourists might like to see."

"That sounds neat," Abby said, even though it sounded horrible. The Martha thing wasn't all bad. He thought he was coming up with reasons to spend more time with them on his own.

They made another left, and it wasn't very long before the storefronts turned to houses, the yards got bigger. Garages looked more and more like barns, until they passed one with a horse grazing on the parched lawn outside of it. Cornfields began.

"It's not that far now," Ryan said. "They built it back in the fifties—it used to have a burger restaurant inside but now they just sell T-shirts and stuff, when Bob is around to open it up."

"Sounds neat," Martha repeated before Abby could come up with something that wouldn't sound sarcastic. "Why a duck?"

"Bob's grandfather liked ducks, and he was the one that built the place. People used to use this road a lot more before the Interstate was built."

"Sort of like Route 66?"

"Exactly. But no one ever wrote a song about us."

Why would they, Abby thought irritably. She wanted to press him to shut up, but making him uncomfortable would be counterproductive.

The dog nuzzled the back of her neck, and it felt comforting despite being cold and damp. Not a bad dog, really. It hadn't made much noise and unlike Martha it didn't smell too awful. Sometimes Abby was still a little angry at Grandfather for never letting them have pets growing up, even though it would have been impossible. She could have gotten a cat when she moved back to Buffalo, or even while she was in college. But it was just as well she didn't.

"Okay," Ryan said. "If you look over there at about eleven o'clock you can see the head just up above the trees now."

"Eleven o'clock?" Martha tapped the clock on the dashboard. "It's only like nine-thirty."

"No," Ryan said, and chuckled. "I mean if the world were a clock and straight ahead was noon, the duck's right over…" He squinted, and Abby followed his gaze. A fingernail clipping of white concrete was visible over the tree line. "There. Not far now."

Abby couldn't help but wonder what kind of idiot Bob's grandfather was. The whole point of a roadside attraction was to be visible from a long way off. The trees had wrecked any chance of success for him well before the Interstate could have.

Then again, it was a duck. Even if people could see it, why would they care? Only these local people, who were almost like ducks themselves, would think it was special.

They didn't get a good view of the duck, two stories tall and decorated with a structurally improbable blue bow around its concrete neck, until they'd pulled into the parking lot. There were spaces for at least a dozen cars, most with strands of dry brown grass in the cracks of the pavement. Ryan pulled into the spot closest to the door and they climbed out of the truck. It was already a lot warmer than it had been when Abby woke up, but still just as humid. A shitty day to not be in a nice new air-conditioned vehicle.

Ryan gestured up at the sun-faded, crackled curve of the duck's breast and neck. "It was in Ripley's Believe It or Not once," he said, and Abby ignored the rest of what was coming out of his mouth because a hawk soared over as he spoke.

It wasn't likely to try anything physical in front of an outsider. But that meant it might start thinking of other strategies instead. Time to act.

Ryan was smiling at Martha and she at him. Not paying any attention to Abby at all, again, which would normally be the rudest thing in the world, and would normally ruin everything. But she moved in his peripheral vision, just enough to make him notice her, and that was all she needed with someone this soft after having her fill of the diner.

She pushed at the strands of his attention, pulled and stretched and wove them. His smile widened and so did his eyes. He was ready.

"Hey, I have an idea," Abby said, and Martha looked over at her and the smile disappeared from her face like smoke. "How about you give us your truck and you keep our car?"

"What? That's crazy?" His hand started moving towards his pocket while she was speaking, but he managed to stop it. "Why would I want to…"

"It would make perfect sense, though," Abby said without letting him finish a thought. "We're already fifteen minutes out in this direction and backtracking would be stupid."

"But…"

Martha was shaking her head, mouthing the word "no", but Abby had it in the bag now. The words didn't even have to be particularly plausible, not with this guy. In a moment—she pressed him harder, just to make sure—in a moment he'd think it was his own idea.

He pulled out the keys and held them close to his chest for a moment, obviously struggling. Martha grabbed Abby's wrist. A little distraction like that didn't matter now, though. That sad bastard of a diner had nourished her in a way that fifteen kinds of jam could never touch.

He handed the keys to Abby, and the smile returned to his face. "Here, take these. I don't want to hold you guys up anymore."

"Thank you," Abby said, and then, because Martha was squeezing her wrist so hard it hurt, she leaned forward and kissed him on the cheek. "This is a huge help."

She backed away from him, towards the truck, keeping her eyes on him for as long as possible. Fumbled with the key fob until she heard the beep and click of the door unlocking. The sounds tugged on Ryan for a moment and she had to steady his resolve.

"Get in," she said to Martha, but her sister didn't move. God dammit. Even if Abby was willing to push her, she wouldn't want to divide her attention until she'd got the truck in gear and was ready to pull away.

"Get in!"

Martha still didn't move.

Then, before she even had time to wonder what the hell she was going to do with this bitch masquerading as her sister, a hawk screamed high above. Martha flinched and dropped Abby's wrist, rushed to climb into the cab.

"Nice work, asshole. Thanks." Abby knew it couldn't hear her but she couldn't resist saying it out loud. Ryan looked baffled, but that was good too, he wasn't thinking about fighting her anymore. She turned her back and climbed into the truck.

About ten miles down the road, she finally deigned to speak to Martha. "I don't know what you're so mad about. At least we got to keep the dog, didn't we?"

"His name is Buddy," Martha said angrily, but when he was invoked he stuck his head over the seat and leaned into her ear and she softened. "He is neat, isn't he?"

"Yeah. Don't you remember how bad you used to want a dog?"

Martha nodded. "I wanted to keep Ryan, too. He was cute."

"It would have been too much. People would look for him."

"He's going to say you stole the truck, when he gets back to himself. We'll have the cops after us for real."

"No he won't. He was inspired by God to an act of charity."

"You're sure? Even after it wears off?"

"I've been practicing." It sounded more impressive than *he'll never be able to admit that two girls stole his truck without a gun or anything.*

Martha nodded. "That's really good, actually." She rubbed Buddy's ears for a moment, and seemed mournful, but she'd had to adjust herself to much bigger disappointments. "Can we really keep him?"

"For sure."

"I'm sorry about back there. I was worried you were going to hurt him or something."

"It's okay," Abby said, and it almost was. It was a bit gratifying, really, when Martha apologized, gratifying when she tried to resist Abby and failed without having to be pushed at all.

Abby was deep in an exhausted sleep, despite the Coke, when Mom discovered Grandfather's body. She woke briefly to high-pitched yelling and Martha's whimpers, turned over and drifted off again.

Later, when she was properly awake, she wandered downstairs to find Mom and Martha in the kitchen, working on a batch of brownies. It was such an unlikely, TV-like scene—Mom hardly ever let them have dessert, and the way she was hovering over Martha, touching her shoulder, paying close attention… Abby stepped off the bottom step with a thud that made both of them glance up.

"Hey," Mom said. "Come here for a second. I've got some good news and some bad news."

"The good news is the brownies?" Abby meant it to sound guarded and maybe a little sarcastic, like a kid on TV, but Mom's voice sounded warm and enthused and that batter dripping over the edge of the bowl looked delicious. She crossed the room to stand next to Martha without thinking.

"A-plus!" Mom said with a laugh, and patted Abby's shoulder too. "You woke up in time to get a vote on whether we put peanut butter in, or cream cheese."

"Peanut butter," Abby said without hesitating. Grandfather liked cream cheese in the brownies. No one else did.

"Then it's unanimous."

"So what's the bad news?"

"Your grandfather had to go to the hospital. When he fell down the basement steps, it was too much for him."

Fell down the basement steps…? Mom had never been as flamboyant about her powers as Grandfather was, had never threatened or hissed at people in public, but since when did they pretend here at home?

On the other hand, the brownie batter looked super good. And from here she could smell it.

"Are we going to bring him brownies? In the hospital?"

Mom frowned for a moment as though that was the wrong answer, but then her face cleared. "Oh! No, not right now. We might be able to visit him soon but the doctors just don't know."

Abby nodded and held her face steady.

She was able to corner Martha and get the whole story from her later. Grandfather was in the burned-out foundation of the barn, covered loosely with cinders. The shopping trip to town had mostly been about buying garden lime and a shovel—the brownie mix was to make things look more normal. Yes, Martha thought Mom was acting weird, too.

"But it's kind of nice, isn't it?" Martha said after a moment.

"I guess. I don't think she's going to make brownies all the time though."

"No, I mean, maybe if she's pretending we're normal she won't push us around anymore."

It was so stupid it had to be a joke, but Martha hardly ever made jokes, and especially not sarcastic ones. Abby sliced herself another brownie from the middle of the pan.

"Hey, why do I get stuck with all the edge pieces?"

"Because I'm faster."

Martha opened her mouth and shut it again, and took a piece from the less-burnt side.

Of course. Martha didn't even know what having power was. She wouldn't understand that you'd never let go once you had it.

With all the sugar and caffeine and the mid-day nap, Abby was in no mood to sleep at bedtime. Still, Mom's new jovial mood struck her as a thing not to lean too hard on. So she'd been flat on her back in the dark for what felt like hours when she heard their bedroom door open.

She let her eyelids open just enough that she could get a flickering glimpse, through her lashes and out of the very corner of her eye, of the door and the backlit form standing there.

It looked like Mom, and Abby was surprised at how relieved she felt. She'd never felt that way about Mom before.

Mom didn't say anything, just stood in the doorway watching them. She was still there, watching, leaning to one side or the other slightly every few minutes, when Abby finally fell asleep.

The next morning Mom didn't wake them. The school bus cruised by without stopping while they were in the kitchen eating Frosted Flakes.

Martha glanced up in dismay and then got very quiet. A moment later, the yellow bus rolled by again. Martha looked as though she might cry.

Mom grinned, or at least bared her teeth. "No school today, girls. We all deserve a break, don't we? With your grandfather in the hospital and the fire and everything else, it's been a pretty stressful school year so far."

A week ago, that would have been the best news Abby had ever heard. Had Mom actually, somehow, finally, felt bad about sending them off to be pecked to death by ducks?

At least it was clear, finally, cloudless and warm for September. After breakfast Abby pulled her Lurlene McDaniel book—with one of Grandfather's notebooks hidden inside—from her book bag and headed for the door, planning to go up to the apple orchard where Mom's odd hovering wouldn't interfere with her reading.

"Where do you think you're going, Missy? We're having a family day."

"Okay." The concept of 'family day' had never come up before and Abby wasn't quite sure of the parameters.

"I was thinking we could rent some movies and make popcorn."

Abby nodded. The popcorn maker usually only got hauled out about once a year, so this family day concept seemed worth getting behind.

And once they were actually eating the popcorn, watching the movie—it had Steve Martin in it and Abby wasn't sure why most of it was funny, although the dog was pretty great—she had to admit it felt good. The three of them on the couch together, Mom between Abby and Martha, snuggled so close their sides were touching. The popcorn slightly soggy from butter and very salty, the way Abby liked it best. Mom smiling, snorting at the film, even laughing out loud. It was like they were in a commercial for Sony.

But eventually the popcorn bowl held nothing but greasy, unpopped kernels. And a little while after that, the movie was over. Abby looked up at Mom, hoping for a clue about what came next, but she didn't get one.

Mom was staring at Martha, who seemed dozy, confused.

"Hey." Mom poked Martha in the arm, not gently. "Wake up, there."

Martha lurched forward a little bit and then righted herself, shook her head like a dog and seemed to focus.

"Family day's not over yet," Mom said. "We're going to make some more popcorn, and play Trivial Pursuit." She stood up so fast that Martha almost listed into Abby.

Abby couldn't remember the last time they'd played Trivial Pursuit; the dust clung gray and furry to her fingers as she opened the box. Mom grabbed the cards and shuffled them haphazardly; Abby picked at the yellow game piece, which had a pink segment stuck in it the wrong way around. When she looked up, she saw Martha staring at her in an odd sharp way. Abby stuck out her tongue, and Martha didn't giggle and break eye contact. She just kept staring.

"Okay." Mom set down the cards and reached for the green piece. "Let's go."

Martha grabbed the blue piece.

"Hey, I want that one." Abby didn't exactly like blue, but Martha always let her pick first.

"You can have the brown one," Martha said, squeezing her fingers shut around her prize.

"Brown is stupid."

"Girls!" Mom reached over and pried the contested piece from Martha's hand. It took her several seconds. "Just for that, I'm going to take blue. You can have green, Abby."

Abby shrugged. You didn't defy Mom when that tone came out, and she didn't even like blue anyway. Martha stared at Mom for a moment, that same weird stare, and then took the orange piece without a word.

"You can go first, Martha," Mom said, not conciliatory exactly—more like it was a test. Martha scooped up the die and shook it in her cupped palms, frowning. She rolled a six and moved her piece to a brown square.

Mom squinted at the card. "In the Yogi Bear series, what is the name of Yogi's sidekick?"

"That's..." Mom placed a hand on Abby's ankle before she could finish the thought, and Abby shut up. But it was obviously the pink question.

Martha's frown deepened, but instead of objecting, she hesitated a moment and said "Swami?"

The hand vanished from Abby's leg, and before she could see what was happening Mom had tackled Martha and pinned her to the living-room floor, one hand clamped over her mouth and the other around her throat.

"Abby," Mom said. "I need you to go outside to the barn pit. Don't be frightened. Get Martha back into the house."

Martha—Grandfather, obviously—twisted under Mom's hands. But the body was still a little girl's. He couldn't get away.

As soon as Abby opened the back door, she heard the wailing. It barely sounded like Martha at all, too wheezy, too weak, even for her. The sun was high and bright and warm, and the smell reached her on the stir of breeze only a moment after the sound did.

Martha had managed to crawl out of the pit, god knows how, since Grandfather's hands were barely holding together. He only died yesterday, Abby thought when she saw how the skin had slipped from his face, but then she remembered the rotting wound that the creature in the basement had left on him. Those things didn't understand time; they didn't have to.

While she thought these things she looked everywhere but right at Martha, only letting her eyes skim over the corpse and see one detail at at time, the last few clinging strands of hair or the way the hands looked like old work gloves left out in a field, but she didn't have to look to know that her sister was out of her mind with fear and intent on crawling back to the house.

That's what Mom wanted. Martha back at the house. Abby didn't have to do anything, didn't have to get closer or touch. But she was taking so long, the body uncoordinated and weak, barely able to make forward progress. And it might... she felt sick, but the thought wouldn't go away once she'd had it... the body might fall apart before Martha got there, and how would they get Martha back then?

Abby came to a decision and stepped backwards through the still-open door. Martha's cries rose in pitch for a moment, but she couldn't keep it up, not if she wanted to keep crawling too, and it only took a moment anyway to grab Grandfather's old work jacket from the hook.

Carrying the jacket, Abby stepped into the back yard. Martha, reeking, desperate, still crying through rotting lips, was only a few yards away. It seemed like the kind of situation where people fainted. But Abby had never fainted and didn't know what it would feel like if she was about to now.

The last few feet as she got closer to Martha she had to look away completely, up towards the hills and the apple orchard beyond where she could have been right now, reading in peace. She felt something snag at the hem of her pants and if it was rotting fingers, Martha reaching out for her, she didn't want to know. She dropped the coat over the whole mess and only then knelt down beside it.

"Martha, you need to get up to the house." Abby inhaled through her mouth. She could look at Martha now, or at least at the coat, but she still needed to not look at the crushed damp grass where she'd crawled. "I'm gonna help. Try not to flop around too much, okay?"

She decided that the slurred answer was "Yes." What else would Martha say? She put her hand on what seemed like the coat's shoulder, and grabbed enough fabric to hold it steady. "Can you get your arms into the sleeves?"

Once Martha was firmly wrapped in the coat, it was just a matter of dragging and not thinking. She was light, much lighter than Grandfather had been when they'd carried him up the basement stairs. Abby found herself wondering if maybe it was Martha's spirit that was lighter than Grandfather's somehow.

In the living room, Mom still had Grandfather pinned. "No," she was saying, as angry as Abby had ever heard her. "She's my daughter. Not yours." Grandfather had arched Martha's body rigid, like he was throwing a tantrum, and gripped a thick chunk of Mom's hair, bending her head to one side.

Abby dropped Martha and ran to Mom, grabbing Grandfather/Martha's wrist and squeezing hard with her nails. The twisted face of her twin turned towards her and Grandfather lunged in to bite at her hand. He'd just gotten his teeth in her when Mom slapped him; they tore the skin of Abby's wrist as his head rocked back.

Mom slapped him again on the backstroke, and again, and again, until the body in front of them whimpered in Martha's voice. Abby heard it clearly, but Mom slapped Martha a few more times before she realized. Abby grabbed the real Martha by the shoulders and dragged her away.

Mom was breathing heavily, not even acting like she noticed the smell. For a minute, she just crouched there. Then she stood up, unsteadily, but her voice was very even when she spoke. "Abby, Martha, go on up to the orchard or back to the creek—anywhere you like, but out of the house. He won't be able to pull that off again any time soon." Martha, despite her flushed red face and snotty nose, almost sprang towards the coat room and the back door. Abby hesitated a little longer, just long enough to see Mom return from the kitchen with the biggest meat cleaver. Then she scurried, before Mom had to repeat herself.

When they came back to the house at dusk, Grandfather's body was gone, again. No one said anything more about it. They never had a family day again.

CHAPTER FIFTEEN

Even out of the corner of her eye, Abby could tell that Martha had struggled over the issue for a while before speaking up again. "I think we're going the wrong way. Shouldn't we be heading sort of northwest?"

"We would be, if we were going straight through to Minnesota anymore."

"But we're not." Martha sounded satisfied. Like, at least she hadn't been wrong even if she hadn't caught Abby being wrong either.

"Not yet. Just in case. Wouldn't want to be followed."

Martha nodded, and that seemed to settle it for a moment, so cleanly that Abby let it go and started to worry whether the song would come back first or the damn hawks. But then Martha spoke again. "You're not worried about Ryan following us, or any of them from back there. You told the truth the first time, they're not the problem."

Abby kept her eyes on the road. There was a hawk on the roadside power lines up ahead, but it didn't rise or even turn its head as they passed.

"You're worried about the house. The thing that killed Grandfather. I saw that you left the door open."

"And you didn't tell me not to."

"I didn't." Martha sat for a moment. "But I saw the news in the diner, too. You knew it would come for Waite blood, eventually. That's the same mistake Grandfather made."

"I didn't know that and you don't know it either." Since when did Martha get to have opinions about things like this? "It might not be the blood. It might be the land. It might stay put and just kill whoever is stupid enough to come poking around. That's all we know so far."

"But you're worried now."

"I'm just being careful. Which Grandfather never was."

Behind them Buddy whined, smelling an argument Abby supposed. Martha turned to pet him and the tension in the truck eased perceptibly. She'd done right to bring him along after all.

"We're just going to stick to the back roads for a while," she told Martha, taking a left that looked promising. "Just do me a favor, please. Stop drifting."

But how was she going to stop Martha from drifting when she couldn't stop drifting herself?

Her last tweets and updates were only a few hours ago, just after they'd gotten the truck. She shouldn't have been tired. Was she sicker than she thought? Sicker than the doctor thought? She could go inside gas stations instead of paying at the pump, stop at real hotels where the desk clerk would look her in the eye and smile and push energy at her because it was his job. But she shouldn't have to. Martha should never know how close to true she'd been with that little "addict" jab in the restaurant the other night, shouldn't suspect what was keeping her alive.

When she was a kid, she'd happily spent entire summer vacations with nothing but her family for company. But she didn't know what she was missing back then. She thought being weak was normal.

She'd need to be sure that she had all her wits about her once they hit Minnesota. She'd need a plan.

"Why were we going to Minnesota anyway?" Martha said, but there was less sharpness and more sulk to it now. It wasn't the voice of someone who was afraid or angry, just the voice of someone who'd remembered a few million squashed mosquitoes.

"It's just a place I know how to get to where no one will recognize us."

"We could go anywhere else in the entire U.S., Abby. I don't think they abolished cheap motels while I was in the pen."

"We can't stay on the east coast, it's too obvious. And any place within a hundred miles of either border is out, Border Patrol can stop whoever they like." She was spitballing excuses—Border Patrol stopped very specific people who didn't look much like Waites— but how the hell would Martha know that?

"I told you we're safe. They're not looking for us. I took care of it."

"We're not taking the risk. You make one mistake and we're both fucked for life."

"Abby…"

"No coasts. No borders."

"That still leaves so many places! Literally hundreds of places!"

"Calm down." It wasn't easy, but Abby refused a laugh at "literally hundreds" or at how flustered Martha was getting. She forced herself to look solemn, a little vulnerable, instead. "It's just… didn't you ever think that after we stopped going there, that's when everything started going wrong for us?"

"It wasn't the cabin, though. It was Grandma dying and Mom and Grandfather fighting and everything that happened because of that."

Fighting over you. No. That was too blunt a dagger for right now.

"I just thought it would make me feel better, okay? You have to admit, there are some good memories there. No one hassled us there. And what we need now is to not be hassled. Just for a little while. Once we're done there, we can go wherever you want. Name it."

"Whatever, Abby. You're just going to do what you want, like you always do."

"I'm serious. Name a place. Anyplace. If you want to go there, we'll go there once it's safe."

Martha was silent for a minute, eyes on the road, doubt pinging through her thoughts, and then a little hope. "One of the girls in my book group had a grandma in Phoenix. She said it was way nicer than Buffalo. Warmer."

Abby almost opened her mouth to argue—Phoenix, ugh, full of old people—but she did just all but give her word, and she needed Martha to trust her. Besides, Phoenix might not be so bad. Full of old people, and old people still watched the news on TV. If she ever found herself caught truly short she could get her old job back. To say nothing of the Facebook possibilities. Everyone's grandmother was on Facebook now.

And it was true, the weather was nicer than Buffalo's. She'd never again have to figure out what to wear to stay warm without looking puffy, or how much heel she could risk on the ice. She'd just have to be religious with the sunscreen. Which, obviously, she should have been anyway.

"I've never been to Phoenix," she said, letting the smile inflect her voice. "That should be interesting. We could get a house with a swimming pool and swim all year."

"Yeah," Martha said, warming up in turn. "And Kelly said that her grandma had an orange tree in her back yard with the best oranges she ever tasted."

"We can have orange trees. We can have lemon trees and lime trees and grapefruit trees. We can have a kumquat tree, what the hell. An orchard. Fresh juice every morning."

"I've never even seen a kumquat. I thought they were, like, a made-up Doctor Seuss thing."

"They're little. Think of an orange the size of a grape. But they taste different."

"Cool. I'll sit by the pool and eat kumquats and drink beer and work on my tan all day."

"Tanning's out of style," Abby said quickly, although she wasn't exactly sure that was true in Phoenix. "Gives you wrinkles. Cool girls are pale now, and they dye their hair red."

"Well, we're screwed on being cool, then."

"Hair dye has come a long way since we were playing with Manic Panic in the bathroom. If you paid for it, you could be a blonde and nobody would know the difference from the real thing."

"Really?"

"Yeah, and you might have to be. Just to make sure no one's going to recognize us."

"Being blonde would be weird."

"It doesn't actually feel any different. I was blonde for six months in my sophomore year of college, but it got to be too much of a hassle to keep up with the roots." And it had turned out that it made her hard to recognize. She knew by then that she didn't want to go unrecognized.

"I'm sorry I snapped at you before," Martha said. "I shouldn't have said that stuff."

"It's okay, it's not a big deal."

"I just... I shouldn't treat you like you're Grandfather or Mom, you know? I know you're not. But it's hard to believe anything anyone says after dealing with those two."

"Oh trust me, I know."

Mom kept up the fiction that Grandfather was in the hospital for a few days, and then he died a third time, the official time. There couldn't be a death certificate or a funeral, of course, but no one was interested in those things. The Advertiser ran a brief obituary, a notice with just enough beloveds and suddens to not look out of place. At school, even Mrs. Grant didn't have the combination of gall and decorum needed to offer condolences; she took the note that Abby handed her and made a noise that might have been a cough, or a grunt. The kids didn't make anything of it either, except Nicole, who said something cheerful about praying for them. Abby pushed her until she was so confused she walked into a desk and dropped her books everywhere. It wasn't very satisfying, though Robert and Tabby Schmidt laughed.

Mom moved into Grandfather's old bedroom, and let Abby move into hers. Mom also got a job at the Erie County Home. It was a shock—they weren't hurting for money, Grandfather had had enough successful treasure-hunting expeditions to keep them comfortable for decades. Abby didn't know all the details but if what he'd written about his plans in the notebooks was what he'd actually done, they had enough money for him to live on through Mom's lifetime and Abby and Martha's and their eventual children's too, without him ever having to dirty his hands with anything as mundane as trying to grow or make or sell.

"He wasn't good at work, so he thought it was beneath him," Mom had said when she announced that they'd be coming home to an empty house after school from now on. She didn't say "Don't be like that," but Abby could hear it fine. "Don't be like Grandfather" was the message in everything that had changed, from the new portable TVs in the girls' bedrooms to the pale-green curtains that had replaced the light-blocking drapes in the living room.

Being latchkey kids seemed exciting at first too. What could be better than unsupervised access to Grandfather's books and a bedroom of her own to read them in for hours if she chose? She'd learn everything. She wouldn't be like Grandfather because she'd be better than him, the best, unstoppable.

Sure enough, Grandfather had laid it all out at the beginning, in language as if he was copying words from one of the big leather-bound books that Mom had hidden—how he got inside of Mom as a little girl, the same way he must have done to Martha and where he'd been going. There were places and times, marked by star alignments, by stones and trees and natural wells, where you could make the transfer more easily, hold the new body longer, strengthen the bond. Depending on the place, the time, and your own strength, you could make it permanent. And then you left whatever sickness or weakness or old age your old body was weighing you down with behind, and ran off new and fresh.

Grandfather, looking at secret maps and charting the stars, had predicted that there was a place out in Minnesota where ley lines converged and making the transfer was so easy it barely required any power at all. On the strength of that prediction he'd bought a tract of land and built a cabin, and he'd been right. He celebrated being right for pages, as though he actually admitted the possibility that he could have been wrong. It barely sounded like the Grandfather she knew. He'd even gotten so cocky that he decided not to make it permanent with Mom—he still didn't want to be stuck a girl—but to instead wait and see if she had any sons he could use when he got old.

It made Abby feel weird, sad, to see this evidence that he'd been young once, the same crawling feeling she got inside when she'd found some old black-and-white photos of Grandma smiling before her wedding, holding up a fish she'd caught, looking alive despite her high lace collar and the heavy old-fashioned locket she was wearing even at the seashore. Those young people must have felt so trapped inside the papery, brittle grandparents she'd known. If she wasn't careful, that could happen to her too.

CHAPTER SIXTEEN

As the sun passed the arc of the sky Abby pulled over and told Martha to have another go at driving. Martha whined about it less this time, and actually smiled as she accelerated down the first significant hill. Buddy barked, a happy sound even if it echoed uncomfortably in the cab. Abby pulled out her phone.

They'd found Bonetrager's body. He'd been submerged in the pond. He'd been submerged in the pond for a week or more, the coroner said, even though he'd only been reported missing yesterday. The grandson was still missing, and there was a picture of him for the scrutiny of strangers—greasy-haired and wearing a nose stud, but smiling with baby-round cheeks. Criminal? Victim? The world had yet to decide between the two polar options.

There had been times when Abby had daydreamed, without the slightest sense of shame, about going missing, because if she wasn't incapacitated immediately she'd more or less come back as Wonder Woman from all that public hysteria. This wasn't one of those times, though. She tweeted a sweet-solemn condolence message under #justiceforJimB and retweeted the grandson's picture with #findCaiden and scrolled through the responses to the hawk photo—a self-sustaining mixture of "you'll get bird flu" and "I hope someone breaks YOUR neck" and "no you don't get it, it's art" that could go on for days—and waited for relief to come, but it didn't. Slowly she realized that this was because she wasn't tired or low-energy at all, she was fretful, anxious, and that was completely different. It was like that diet tip about eating too much when you were actually thirsty. She closed Twitter and just as she was about to put the phone down altogether she noticed a new news alert.

"Mystery body at site of Bonetrager slayings," it said, and when she tapped it she learned that of the three bodies in the Bonetragers' house, only two had in fact been Bonetragers. The third was a white man estimated between seventy and ninety years of age, cause of death indeterminate, known to no one on the local police force, carrying no ID—no wallet at all—and with no tattoos or scars or other distinctive marks that gave hope of tracking him down. Out of respect for the dead a sketch artist had created a portrait to use instead of a photo with this new story.

Abby opened the sketch and then enlarged it. She was able to stop herself from gasping but the cringe was unavoidable and for a moment she was surprised that Martha didn't notice just as she'd noticed Martha doing the same thing on the back roads in New York. She wanted Martha to notice and care and be worried with her. Not that there was anything to stop for, anything to find here. The problem now wasn't something buried in the mud, it was something criss-crossing the air on beams and zipping through wires over half the U.S. and maybe more.

The picture wasn't Grandfather—he had Grandfather's dark wicked eyes and high cheekbones and the same odd pouched skin on his neck, but the ears were less flared and the nose was just a touch broader, the chin a touch weaker. Still, it was nearer than an actor would have needed to be to play Grandfather in a TV re-enactment, nearer than some sub-Alex-Jones conspiracy theorist would need to 'prove' to the satisfaction of thousands that Grandfather was still alive. Or had been up until yesterday when the body had been found on the floor of a bedroom in the Bonetrager home, dead with old Bonetrager's daughter and son-in-law dead on the kitchen floor downstairs and Bonetrager himself dead and rotting faster than he had a right to in the pond. Abby didn't need to know this man to know that she would have feared him if she'd seen him in life.

"Are you hungry?" Martha asked, breaking Abby's horrified contemplation of the black-and-white face on her screen.

"What?" Abby pushed the power button to wipe the face away and lock the phone again. "Of course not, we had that huge breakfast."

"Hours ago. It's pushing three already. Lunch places will be closing, and you said yourself that you don't want any more fast food if we can help it."

Maybe it was being shaken that made Abby decide to be agreeable or maybe she was hungry after all, a little bit. She'd pushed Ryan hard and she'd barely touched her omelet. Or maybe it was looking up again and seeing another hawk soaring over, one that looked larger than the last few—or else lower than she thought. Maybe it was wanting to show Martha the picture after all, and not wanting to do it in a moving car where Martha's freak-out could kill them both.

"Okay. Next exit that goes to a real town and not a rest stop, then."

She watched Martha check the mirrors. Like a person who'd been driving forever, not a terrified automaton. Good. Excellent. So why did it worry her?

Well, because of things like that, she thought as they cut across two lanes and a cop's lights started spinning in the distance. Coming closer. Obviously aiming for them. And not a big deal, really, in the grand scheme of things except that Martha had already started hyperventilating.

"It's okay," she whispered even though she didn't need to whisper. "Just pull over, it's okay, I've got this. I'll take care of it."

"You'll take care of it?" Martha demanded this at a volume that they don't need, not after Abby whispered.

"I will fucking well take care of it."

The cop that got out of the cop car was so short and so butch it would be an offensive caricature if she wasn't real. She could have been wearing a little Napoleon hat, had one hand tucked into her shirt like in the cartoons. She marched up to the truck with full Napoleonic force, ready to face down whatever bro was inside, and instead she got a crumpled Martha.

"You didn't signal," she said officiously and Martha was just a bit of wrack in her hands, but she didn't seem satisfied. This annoyed Abby, who had seen Martha break a thousand times and knew that her current state was both real and extreme. This bitch was being uppity. Asking for too much already.

"What seems to be the problem," she said like she wasn't just a passenger but a person who was being driven.

"You didn't signal." The cop put her chin up as she repeated this bit of trivia, and Martha seemed to rot down further somehow. "And there's an APB out for this truck. Stolen. You're coming with me, girls."

Motherfucker.

But Abby was not going to give as willingly as that.

"Really?" she said, and she pushed. And it should have worked. But it didn't. The cop's mind was a hard little dehydrated walnut like she hadn't seen since…

Shit.

"You girls are coming down to the station." This woman liked to repeat herself a lot, Abby thought irritably.

Anyway, so they were.

After a little while—it felt like a month, maybe, but who could say—it turned out that Grandfather's third death was going to occasion some paperwork after all. Mom had brazened and pushed her way through the lack of a death certificate, sure, but the old bastard (that's what Abby heard Mom call him once, just after hanging up the telephone, but at this point it didn't surprise her or even make her giggle anymore) had had a legal last will and testament on file with his attorney and it left all of his money and property to Martha in an elaborate trust that Mom couldn't touch. Even though in the end an attorney that Grandfather could push and bluff was an attorney that Mom could push and bluff too, Martha had to sign some papers which meant that she and Abby both had to sit in a dark office where the carpet smelled vaguely smokey and the walls were lined with books that had cloth bindings and gold stamped titles—not as fun as a V. C. Andrews paperback but not really important like Grandfather's books either.

It was all horribly dull and took forever, so while they sat Abby watched Mom work on the lawyer. Mom wasn't better than Grandfather in the sense that she was stronger when she pushed, though she was just about as strong. She was better because instead of yelling and huffing like Grandfather did she smiled and flattered while she pushed. This seemed to make the lawyer's brain softer, and sometimes she barely had to poke him at all brain-wise.

Abby wondered why Grandfather had never done that and then she tried to imagine him complimenting this red-faced bald man—complimenting anyone really, or laughing at any joke he hadn't made himself—and then she did giggle, but mostly on the inside.

Once it was over, Abby expected Mom to quit the Erie County Home job but she didn't. She took as many hours as she could and sometimes was at the Home, wasn't back at their home, until after the girls' bedtime. When she was gone Abby still kept the curtains closed and the mirrors covered—it made her more comfortable—but she uncovered them when Mom got home, because Mom insisted they didn't need to do that, there was nothing left to be afraid of.

"Maybe she really meant it, about not being too good to work," Martha said when Abby mentioned it as they boiled pasta together on a school night around eight. Between them they hadn't quite figured out how to stop between crunchy and mushy yet, but they were getting closer.

"No way," Abby said. "If it was about that she could do something more interesting, cooler." She wasn't sure what but she was sure there must be cooler things than a job that meant you smelled like mothballs and piss when you came home. People were on TV, they went to offices, they wore suits and bright-red dresses.

For that matter, just working hard didn't make anyone different from Grandfather. What Grandfather had done had been work, a lot of work, a lot of star charts and a lot of digging and a lot of running away when things got sketchy, too, in the early days. Just because he'd enjoyed it didn't mean he hadn't nearly killed himself doing it.

In retrospect, of course, Abby had wondered for a time if Mom had discovered the secret of using other peoples' minds like a battery too, and not been able to tap into it as effectively for some reason. But there was no evidence of that. Mom came home from work tired out, not stronger. She often hit snooze two or three times before getting out of bed in the morning, and lingered in the shower until there wasn't enough hot water left for Abby and Martha before school. She hated her job just like any good American, but she clung to it anyway just like any good American.

The best Abby could ever figure out afterward was that deep down, Mom really honestly kind of wanted to be normal. And that was the weirdest thought of all.

CHAPTER SEVENTEEN

They'd been sitting at the police station, sans police officer, for twenty minutes. Martha hadn't said anything sarcastic about Abby 'taking care of it' yet. Martha was just sobbing messily and hyper-ventilating. She'd tapered off a few times only to start again, but now it seemed like she was getting control of herself for real. All that was... not good, exactly, but at least reassuring in Abby's book, because it meant that not every single thing in the world had suddenly stopped working the way it was supposed to, even though small-town boys and small-town cops definitely had.

It wasn't that this cop was so set on doing her job right, although there was a current of that deep down under the walnut shell where her actual personality was lurking. She hadn't searched the truck or seen the skull, although for all Abby knew she might be doing that right now. She hadn't mentioned their rights. She'd locked them up in the same room—not a holding cell but an interrogation room with a window and a table—and left them alone together, and she hadn't cuffed them or demanded their ID or searched them for weapons with more than a desultory pat. (The pat-down was when Martha had started crying and breathing like a soap opera widow, which worried Abby a lot in a there-was-someone-she-might-have-to-go-back-and-find-at-Wende-and-kill-later kind of way.) She hadn't even taken Abby's phone.

There wasn't much chance that Ryan's tale of car and dog theft—she should have known bringing the damn dog was a mistake, she'd gotten soft—would have made the news yet. It was strictly police-blotter-in-a-tiny-weekly-paper fare. But she looked anyway; if this was, somehow, nothing more than what it seemed, and if by chance there was some chatter out there on it out there already, it might help her put together the story that would get them out of this despite the cop's bizarre recalcitrance. It was a forlorn hope and she knew it, but she wasn't just going to sit here and listen to Martha snuffle. She had tried to comfort her sister a couple of times but that only led to fresh gushes of "I'm sorry, I'm sorry, I shouldn't have done it in the first place, I should have just stayed home," which Abby could tell were only half-aimed at the here and now.

It turned out that there were headlines from Daines, West Virginia, all right, all over CNN and Yahoo! and Fox, with a hashtag on Twitter and a page on Facebook where people could check in. All of this had nothing to do with a stolen truck and a missing dog. There was, in fact, no goddamn way in hell that anyone in Daines was worrying about one truck and one dog right now.

A freight train with a full payload of crude-oil tankers had rolled through downtown Daines about an hour or ninety minutes after they'd left Ryan and the concrete duck behind. Not unusual, except that this train hadn't braked or steered. The runaway had jumped the tracks at the first small bend, right at Main Street, not far from the fifteen kinds of jam and the four kinds of sausage; from the early reporting it looked like that was all gone now, along with everything else for half a mile around. Which would be, by Abby's reckoning, basically all of poor old Daines. Blurry bystander videos of an unrecognizable mass of flames topped articles that were being updated by the minute. There was wild speculation about the engineer, since a dead man's switch should have stopped the train if he'd fallen ill or forgotten to set the brakes while he stepped out for a piss, but it didn't look like there would be any identifiable fragments of him left to ask.

She wondered if showing the CNN story to Martha would distract her, maybe even cheer her up—look, we got lucky! But before she could decide whether to put that thought into action or not the cop returned. Ryan was behind her, wearing an anger on his face that looked all wrong against his thoughts, like play-acting. And next to him was #findCaiden, his hair still greasy, cheeks thinner now—more so than a few days on the road would accommodate—but unmistakable. And wearing the same Cannibal Corpse T-shirt he'd had on in the picture for that matter.

Martha jumped to her feet, driven to move towards Ryan and away from the cop at the same time. Instead she stood still and, through a last sob, said, "It's okay. We have Buddy. He's still in the truck!" And Abby felt a surge of protectiveness—both because Martha, even scared, had tried to come up with a strategy and because that was all she'd managed to think of.

"The dog? I took him to Animal Control," the cop said. The decision hadn't been hers but the words were spoken with deliberate maliciousness that was all her own. Martha gasped. Ryan smiled. The smile was the last piece of evidence that Abby needed that that wasn't really Ryan, any more than #findCaiden was really a high school junior from Alden whose relatives were worried sick because he was the youngest kid in the family and he'd never spent the night away from his parents before.

"Come with us," the cop said. You couldn't not see #findCaiden pushing her, not if you had that kind of eyes. Were they so stupid they didn't know that? Never, not if they were smart enough to be here. So they were confident that it wouldn't matter now. That was a little worrisome.

But people did overestimate themselves, all the time. Grandfather had. Mom had in the end too. Abby stood up and, with her left hand just behind her and out of their sight, gestured to Martha to stay close.

"Come on," Ryan said harshly, in a much more gravelly voice than he'd had this morning. Maybe a person might think he'd inhaled a lot of smoke.

Abby followed the three of them into the darkened corridor with Martha close on her heels. The window to the interrogation room they'd just left made itself a mirror as the cop lingered to turn out the light. Abby spotted the coil of a tentacle, the moist slit of a mouth. *The gang's all here*, she thought, but she was only pretending to herself that she wasn't afraid. But for whatever reason, the thing didn't slip into the real world and grab them yet.

Things didn't settle quite all the way down even after Mom had had the trust dissolved. It seemed like they had for another few months, although the lawyer blabbed all over town and a few kids tried teasing Martha about being rich for a while. It didn't take long for even the dimmest of them to realize that that wasn't something you could make fun of a person for, not when Mom started sending Abby and Martha both to school with brand-new clothes and real haircuts not done in someone's aunt's bathroom, or even at Fantastic Sam's, but at a salon over in Lancaster. Nicole made a few passes at calling them 'stuck-up' but she actually seemed a little brokenhearted about it, underneath, and Abby could have outright started dancing when she realized that.

At first Abby was irritated by all the shopping and primping and whatnot, strangers' hands in her hair and Mom deciding what her new favorite colors were. But it didn't take long to learn how to do it right and the way it drew peoples' eyes in was amazing. And once you had their eyes you could tap into their brains easily enough.

Going to school was something she'd started to look forward to. Even her grades went up. Martha's did too, although not as much, just from not being harassed nonstop any more. This in turn made Mom all the more pleased with them. It was an upward spiral, ever upward.

It was in that spirit that she took the pop-eyed young man staring through the playground fence at her—and, if she was being honest, at Martha too—as just so much more fodder. But when she reached out to draw from him, despite his hungry eyes, she hit a wall.

"Gross," Nicole said, noticing the man. "Looks like you've got a boyfriend."

"Never seen him before," Abby answered, and tossed her head, letting her smooth, conditioned hair fly around her shoulders. "I can't help it that I'm magnetic." Magnetic seemed like a better word than pretty, especially since the word boyfriend had curdled her amusement a little bit.

One of the teachers on playground monitor duty—the same one Abby and Martha had had for kindergarten, no longer quite so young and eager but still not a local by a long shot and thus still trying to do her job—saw the man and went over to the fence. After a second two other teachers, Mrs. Grant and Mr. Berman from the other fifth-grade room, realized that the man was a stranger and went to back her play. Abby never saw the man turn, but he must have run to be out of sight by the time she looked back.

She'd almost forgotten about the man by Wednesday, Mom's next working-late night. She remembered in a hurry, though, when something tapped the southern window in the living room, the one that looked out onto the front porch. She pretended it wasn't real the first time, but the second, about thirty seconds later, Martha said "what's that?" and Abby couldn't pretend anymore. It sounded like branches, light and stiff, but there were no trees with branches that could reach that window.

If she wanted to know what it was she would have to turn out the lights and open the curtains and look out into the dark and let whatever was out there look in at her too. There was nothing she wanted to do less. Except, maybe, hanging around in here not knowing what it was or what it was doing out there. She wasn't quite sure. As the tapping came again she glanced at Martha, who was staring at the window, frozen in place with the same conflicting urges.

They couldn't both stay frozen. Abby took three big steps to the light switch and threw the room into darkness, then darted back across the room before whatever was out there could realize what happened. For good measure she flicked on the porch light by the door too, and jerked the curtain open with her other hand. As fast as she was she only just saw the young man's back as he leapt from the porch and ran west into the dark towards the tree line.

CHAPTER EIGHTEEN

#findCaiden let up on the cop once they were out in the sunny parking lot and the thing couldn't scare her into balking, but the shell stayed up around her mind and there was no chance Abby could turn her; any probing for a crack would be spotted immediately. Abby had searched and searched in Grandfather's notebooks and his ancient tomes for every useful trick and weapon, for years, but she'd never seen mention of shields like this let alone instructions on how to put them up or knock them down again. Apparently she wasn't the only member of the family who'd come up with new techniques along the way.

So the cop, of her own accord, herded them toward a transport van. Ryan had slipped behind them and #findCaiden to one side. Abby spotted the truck on the other side of the parking lot and let her mind wander in the direction of making a break for it, though she knew that it would never work. So they were going with a kidnapper to a third location, and no one would know and therefore no one would get excited about it and give her strength.

She glanced back at Martha, who was following close just like Abby had told her. She seemed amazingly calm, considering. So at least they had that going for them—not panicking. Abby hoped that would do them any good at all.

They loaded into the van, the cop driving and #findCaiden in the passenger seat and Abby and Martha on the middle bench and Ryan behind them. They weren't far from the door but there wasn't a handle on the inside. Ryan took out a handgun and aimed it at the back of Martha's head. "I can see what you're thinking," he rasped quietly.

Abby turned her thoughts inward to more abstract questions than the door. If she wasn't thinking about anything concrete, he could watch all he liked. These guys—not #findCaiden and Ryan but whoever was inside their bodies now—didn't have Grandfather's skull, at least not with them, and they didn't have the books, either. So what were they after?

"Where to, Enoch?" #findCaiden said over his shoulder to Ryan. Ryan—Enoch now, apparently—shut his eyes, cocked his head and then rocked it back and forth until it seemed to stabilize of its own accord. Opening his eyes again, he said, "East. And a little north."

The cop nodded and rolled up back onto the highway on-ramp. A sign above said Slanesville, 31 miles, Martinsburg, 78 miles. They could be anywhere. They could end up anywhere. This was why you never went with a criminal to a third location.

She didn't want to pull out her phone now—if they saw it, they might take it from her. So how was she going to figure this out?

Well, there was always the oldest, simplest journalistic technique of all.

"Where are we headed?" she asked, trying to sound younger than herself and less confident, but at the same time not really scared. Let them think she was too dumb to fully realize the trouble she and Martha were in.

"Wouldn't you like to know," Enoch said, but #findCaiden laughed a high school kid's laugh. "Shepherdstown, missy. We're going straight to Shepherdstown and you're going to stay there a good long time." The cop's mind twitched a bit under the shell at the word "missy".

"Briggs!"

"Be calm, Enoch. It's not going to matter a bit, and don't you want someone to know how clever we are?"

They can't be that stupid, Abby thought. Enoch agreed, apparently, because he moved the muzzle of the gun to cover the back of Briggs' head instead. "Shut up, Briggs, or you're moving out of that bag of meat prematurely and you can just fight it out with one of these bitches until we get there."

"Calm yourself, nephew. We killed fifty people back there; I have energy to fight a dozen hard-water Waites from here to the Pacific if need be."

"Braggart." Enoch didn't move the pistol. "You've gloated to me about your cleverness five thousand times since we left Providence, is that not enough for you?"

"Killjoy," Briggs said.

Abby knew she'd heard of Shepherdstown before, and quickly remembered why. Grandfather had considered a spot between there and Sharpsburg, Maryland, along the Potomac River as one of a handful of potential places, before he'd settled on Minnesota for his summer base. He'd passed on fifty acres there, at half the price of the Minnesota land. Shepherdstown was weak, he'd said in his journals, weak and unreliable. So either they didn't know about Minnesota or they didn't think they could make it there. She was hoping for the former. Because they were getting out of this, and they were getting to Minnesota. She was not giving up her body, cancer and disappointment and fugitive status and all, to the third and fourth removed collateral cousins Grandfather had left behind in Rhode Island.

"Hard-water Waites?" She kept up the ingénue voice and leaned forward a little bit, out of the line of Enoch's terrible muzzle control.

"The fools and weaklings who couldn't hack it at home and ran away inland. Weaklings like your grandfather, and fools like his descendants."

They would have seen her anger flare at that, but what did it matter? Ignoring people like this, contrary to legend, never worked. Anyway, the thing was that their attention—even their scorn—was delicious. Briggs was speaking the truth about being powered up from the deaths they'd left behind them (an interesting technique, one that Grandfather would have appreciated, but it struck Abby as incredibly wasteful—you could only kill a person once) and he didn't even seem to notice her drawing him down bit by bit.

"Didn't you realize that setting the shoggoth loose would draw us from wherever we were?"

"Like it did last time," Martha said, and there was a note of re- proach in her voice.

"Nathaniel wasn't ready to make use of the opportunity," Briggs said. "He took too long."

"Or his messenger did," Enoch said quickly. "Or he decided you and your halfbreed mother weren't what he wanted at the time.

"The point is," Enoch said firmly, "we knew what we wanted and we were waiting."

"Don't you have any cousins closer to home?"

Both Enoch and Briggs looked sour at this, and neither respond- ed. After a few seconds of silence Enoch sighed and aimed the pistol back at Martha. "Hold your tongues," he said to Abby and Martha both. "The last thing I want to hear is you squawking for the next hour."

Twenty minutes, Abby thought. *I'll let it rest for twenty minutes or half an hour and then I'll get Briggs going again and wind them both up.* She glanced in the rear-view mirror, saw the imprint of a sucker there, and put her eyes back on the road ahead.

Neither Abby nor Martha said anything to Mom about the weird pop-eyed young man when she got home from work; that went without saying. Mom didn't like to be bothered with problems when she came home from work, even if she made it while they were still up. Over breakfast the next morning, though, Abby still intended to keep silent. She didn't say anything to Martha. She thought that the rightness of it would be obvious.

"There was a guy staring in the windows last night," Martha blurted as Mom sipped coffee and Abby had her mouth full of Frosted Flakes. At least, Abby thought as she swallowed frantically, Martha had the presence of mind to make it sound like they'd had the curtains open.

"A perv?" Mom said, with an odd note to her voice. She didn't sound mad at least.

"He didn't have his thingy out or anything like that," Abby said. "He just tapped on the windows a couple of times and then ran away when I turned the porch light on."

"Around what time?"

"A little after dark. Eight-thirty? Maybe nine?" They were supposed to be in bed by nine-fifteen but Mom seemed okay with them breaking that rule when she wasn't around to see it.

Mom nodded firmly and didn't say anything else except "Hurry up, you're going to be late."

That day Mom came home early, or maybe she called in sick and never went in to work at all. At any rate, she was home when Abby and Martha got off the school bus, drinking a glass of wine in the living room with the curtains wide open.

"Nothing yet, girls, but we'll get him." She smiled. She sounded pretty excited about getting him, actually.

Abby had to admit that it was nice to have Mom cook dinner again for a change, something that wasn't just spaghetti and sauce from a jar, but it was annoying not to be able to go read in her room when dinner was over. Mom insisted that they stay downstairs with her, curtains wide open, night pressing in outside.

"Don't stare," Mom scolded when Abby snuck nervous glances at the reflecting windows. "We don't want to tip him off." Abby was more worried about him not tipping them off, not until it was too late. She wasn't sure why but since yesterday his pop-eyes had grown in her mind, and being looked at by them seemed more and more dangerous. She tried to concentrate on the TV show Mom had picked but it was stupid and didn't make sense; invisible people laughed at the wrong times and the family acted like no family ever, the kids telling the parents their secrets without even being threatened and the parents responding like Muppets or cartoons, all smiles.

During the third commercial break he tapped at the window again. Mom looked up and Abby could see she was pushing him; her eyes went a little wider when she hit the shell. *I could have told you that it wouldn't work*, Abby thought. But Mom adjusted quickly, standing up and smiling, her eyes locked on his creepier ones as she moved to the door.

To Abby's surprise he didn't run this time, although he looked like he wanted to. When Mom opened the door he just stood swaying slightly until she gestured at him to come inside. Then he obeyed, straight into the living room and through to the kitchen where Mom poured him a glass of water without a word. He drank it down and held out his hand for another, and Mom gave it to him as though there was nothing odd about this about it at all.

After the third glass of water he began to pant, hands to his knees, and Mom dropped the glass into the sink with a clank. And then he straightened out.

"You only had girls," he said, like he was someone and wasn't half fainting in their kitchen. "You thought that would protect you."

Mom gave him a look of the most perfect scorn, and Abby had

never loved or admired her more than in that moment, and would never again. "That's not what's protecting me," she said, and her tone matched her face. "But yes. I have two beautiful girls, and they're mine."

Behind Abby, Martha crept into her shadow, as though she could disappear and they could become one.

"It's not 1937. We can use girls."

"So you can. But not if I don't let you, so you might as well go crawl back home."

He glared at her, his eyes looking like they'd come out and fly around the room if they could, tiny UFOs. His whole neck was heaving with his breath and he licked his lips until Abby wanted to offer him chapstick. "Give them to me. My master has need of them."

"The hell with you and the hell with your master. Do you think you'll compel me?"

He stopped a moment then and Abby saw his thoughts reach out towards her mother and then draw back in disarray.

"The shoggoth's locked in its place," Mom said mockingly. "The ground is mine, the house is mine, the girls are mine. You have nothing. No crack through which to creep to me, and no lever by which to compel."

The pop-eyed man, who was the pop-eyed boy in Abby's eyes now, seemed to crumple in on himself. He looked longingly at the sink and the glass.

"I gave you water already," Mom said. "You can't say I treated you with anything less than perfect hospitality."

"I cannot," he rasped.

"You might as well go," she said, letting the repetition hang.

"I might as well." He began to walk back to the front door, and Abby and Martha shifted out of his way. He never made it out of the kitchen.

Mom bent over him where he lay on the linoleum. "They didn't give you very much to go on, did they? Was it worth it?"

His voice came out a sob. "What choice did I have? There aren't Waites to spare, and Uncle Nathaniel is growing old."

"You could tell them no. As base a man as my father did." There was something in Mom's voice then, a species of regret. She ran her fingers across the pop-eyed boy's forehead as he gasped on the floor.

"You say that as though it's easy."

He died on the kitchen floor in the night, and Mom brought the cleaver out again in the morning. There was no further trouble with him.

CHAPTER NINETEEN

Twenty-two minutes later, out of an abundance of caution, Abby started talking again. "So," she said casually. "What relation are you to our uncle Nathaniel?"

Enoch started laughing and didn't stop for a solid thirty seconds. "My god, you holy innocent. They taught you nothing, did they? Nathaniel is and was and will be uncle to all of us."

Abby, who knew quite well from her reading that Nathaniel was Grandfather's first cousin through his mother's side, kept quiet.

"He's bringing eternal life," Briggs said, as though he were reciting in church, going by what Abby had seen of church, which was not so much. But it had that solemn empty rote sound. "No more hopping body to body, eternal life in one form, perfected, and total power over all humankind."

"And that's so great?" Abby said lightly, as though it weren't blasphemous.

They both opened up to her then, their energy spilling out like they didn't know it was leaving. "Hard-water Waites couldn't understand, hard-water Waites don't know a thing about power," Briggs said, while Enoch said "what is WRONG with you," as though that explained anything.

She'd confused them. As proof, she was drawing down on their emotion like they were a couple of teenagers she'd tricked into arguing about politics. She didn't let on, though. She acted impressed by their sudden loudness, oblivious to their underlying fear.

In the driver's seat, the cop twitched. You couldn't hold someone like that down for so long by main force, though you could fool her a lot longer. They'd overestimated themselves that way too, even before they got distracted, and now they were barely trying. No need to draw their attention to it. Quite the opposite.

"We must be getting close to Shepherdstown," she said, though they'd only been going a bit above the speed limit and they should have been forty minutes out or more. She just wanted to sound dumb and in the dark about what awaited them, keep the confusion going. But Enoch tilted his head again and said, "Yes. Just a few more minutes."

Abby caught herself before she glared at Martha. They wouldn't know anything about Martha's powers, Grandma's powers, which were from the rocky hills and barely-fertile farms of inland Mass, not from the sea coast where the Waites had always remained if they could. That had been Grandfather's ace in the hole all those years, the power of last resort to protect himself if more powerful, hungrier cousins came calling. He'd never had to use it, as things turned out. Abby had wanted to save it as an ace in the hole too, but that was all shot to shit if Martha was going off on her own recognizance while sitting right next to her.

Fine then. She'd take care of it herself, like always.

"If you're getting eternal life in one body, what do you need us for?" she asked, trying a different tack to playing dumb. "You've got a couple of strong young bodies right now. Fine-looking, too," she added in case that was the kind of sop they'd take. They should be ready to take any sop, honestly. There was no saying what kind of body Enoch had left behind to burn in Daines, but she thought of the sketch of the old man they'd found on the Bonetragers' floor and shuddered as inwardly as she could, hoping the cousins wouldn't see. It was almost enough to make her feel bad for Briggs. The thought of ending up in there, even temporarily, made her stomach feel rotted. Getting out of it, in turn… they should be pleased as two well-fed kittens right now, not as fierce and determined as they were.

Enoch glared at her, but Briggs remained reliably loquacious. "These? Feh." He gestured at #findCaiden's wiry torso. "These bodies won't last. You need bodies with the Waite blood in them to hold up to our level of power. The others go bad on you in a few years, a decade or two tops."

"Even a mixed-breed girl Waite is better than a strapping young fool like this," Enoch added. He sounded a little bitter. Abby suspected that Great-Uncle Nathaniel hadn't ended up in the body of a distaff half-Waite daughter.

She also suspected that they'd forgotten that the cop was listening entirely. Indeed, they seemed to have forgotten that the car wasn't driving itself.

It was a good few days after the pop-eyed boy died that the whole school was called together in an assembly; it might even have been the following week. Mrs. Grant seemed as surprised as anyone when she read the announcement to the class. That fact alone made the prospect exciting and worrying, knocked it out of the routine. They filed into the auditorium single-file and were herded to the front, the fashion when the assembly was for stern purposes; when it was for fun the kindergartners got these seats, because there was less chance that the fifth graders would try to escape.

The principal, Mr. Langan, came from the side of the stage to stand in the spotlight in all his balding lack of magnificence; one of Abby's favorite things, at most school assemblies where he spoke, was to watch the weird attention-waves he drew, fear and respect all braided together with contempt and near-rage and even a few strands of amused, head-pat condescension from the teachers who knew their way around him or were lucky enough to be related to his wife. Today things were different. Today even his in-laws were confused, on the wrong foot, and therefore a little fearful. Today that fear and attention, as much as a touch of extra yellow in the lights, was making him look stronger and taller than usual, and Abby was determined to pay closer attention than ever to figuring out where that energy came from and where it went.

He held a sheaf of papers in his hand, but he only glanced at it before he started speaking seemingly by heart. "I'm very disappointed to have to hold this assembly," he said, and the wave of attention shimmered and hardened, especially from the teachers, but from the oldest and the youngest of the kids as well. "I've always expected the highest levels of responsibility from every student at this school, always expected you to be good ambassadors for our community, good citizens, good Americans." There was a fringed and drooping flag by the side of the stage, as there'd always been, always ignored, but now a few strands of attention darted towards it before circling back to Mr. Langan. "And for most of my twenty years here, class after class has met my expectations."

He paused. It worked, and it annoyed Abby, even as young as she was, that it worked. People should know better. He held up the sheets of paper, and Abby was almost surprised that they didn't catch fire from the intensity they drew. She wished they would, and he would yelp and drop them and be a cartoon to everyone and this would stop.

"These are the messages I've been getting. Phone calls, faxes, even people walking in and leaving messages in person with Mrs. Barron," he said, inclining his head in the vague direction of his office where even now the matriarch secretary was probably sitting and filing mail. "Not just parents, either. Grandparents, aunts and uncles, people who live in Alden and care about you children. The whole town cares very much. As they should.

"But that means that you also have to be responsible. You can't abuse people's caring for you the way you have."

The threads of attention were growing confused, now. Whatever trouble they'd been expecting—bomb threat, bathroom vandalism, maybe even something as exotic and citified as drugs or sex—this didn't map to any of them, or anything they'd ever been told not to do before.

"I don't know how many of you went home and spread the rumor that a strange man was standing outside the playground, watching you." He paused again, but it was less effective this time, they were not waiting on his next. Abby wondered if he knew, if he could feel it in some sort of strange muted way, like a blind man feeling how he's standing a patch of sun. "Each and every one of you who did should be ashamed of yourselves."

A flare of rage from Mrs. Grant that would have gratified Abby on any other day. A similar, smaller one from Mr. Berman. A horrible miasma of stinking self-doubt from Nicole, sitting in the row ahead of her, and the same—it almost made Abby sad to see it—up in front from the kindergarten teacher who'd gone to confront the pop-eyed boy first.

"Rumor-mongering is cruel. You made the people who care about you worry for no reason, and you accused an innocent man of something awful." You would think he meant the pop-eyed boy—Abby was sure he thought he meant the pop-eyed boy. But his thoughts were all in a defensive bubble around himself. An innocent man had been accused of failing to protect the school from capital-S Strangers.

"I'm very disappointed in all of you, and there will be no outdoor recess for the rest of the quarter."

A groan went up across the hall, but there was no real energy of rebellion in it.

"Maybe next time you'll think about this before you start to cry wolf."

Looking back, it was one of the strangest things ever to happen in Abby's childhood—at least, one of the things that confused her most. For years and years, even into adulthood whenever she happened to remember it, she'd wonder—had Mom somehow had a hand in it, had she gone in and pushed a few more minds to make sure no one would ever again compare notes about the pop-eyed boy and his sudden appearance and disappearance? Had she known that being told they had lied would make most of the kids think it was a lie, the thing they'd really seen? Or had it all just been a particularly weird working-out of Mr. Langan's wounded duck-person pride against the weight of the era's fear?

CHAPTER TWENTY

They pulled up to a rest stop on an outcropping with a scenic view before she could think much further, and rolled into the parking spot furthest away from the interpretive sign. She didn't have to be told twice to get out of the car, step onto the blacktop. She could feel the power below the tree-sprigged bluff and the river, deep in the bedrock. It wasn't as good as Minnesota, no, but she understood why this was what they'd looked for, understood as well or better than they had themselves. She drew as much strength from it as they did. Or at least she hoped she did.

They were all out now, Abby and Martha, Enoch and Briggs, the cop. Enoch and Briggs both looked taller than they'd been when they got into the car, longer-limbed, less firmly jointed together. No wonder bodies don't last for them, Abby thought, if the idiots run them ragged like that.

Briggs grabbed Abby by the upper arm, fingers pinching into flesh. "Get the other one," he told the cop, and Martha's flinch actually seemed to steady the other woman under Briggs' control. Abby thought of school, and the weird ways that thinking they had power worked on the duck people.

She didn't have long to think about it, though, because Briggs started shoving. He was pushing her towards the guardrail, the cop and Martha close behind him and then Enoch covering the whole lot with his damn gun. When they came to the wooden fence, waist-high and painted a red a bit too bright and eye-catching to be a real wood tone, he kept pushing. For one heady moment Abby grew dizzy and tensed to struggle before she realized that throwing her down the slope into the river couldn't possibly be part of their plan. They'd need her whole.

Nevertheless, once she stepped over the guardrail it took a moment to gather her nerve back up. A person didn't have to fall off a cliff on purpose to die at the bottom. She had no idea what the cop's balance was like, Briggs and Enoch were in bodies they had only days or hours of familiarity with, and Martha was terrified. There was ledge enough to walk, here, and path enough to navigate down a little way on, but it would only take one round stone or turned ankle and they were clustered enough that they'd all go down together—or rather, Enoch would be left alone and thwarted looking at a crumpled mess of limbs below.

She was being dramatic, she told herself. It wasn't that much of a cliff, wasn't even that much of a river.

"It's not much of a river," Enoch said as he caught up to them and for a horrible moment she thought he could read her mind outright, but his attention wasn't on her at all; he was just legitimately disappointed in the glistening band below them. "Why couldn't we get closer to the sea?"

"And do the rite at the edge of the waves? Without Nathaniel's explicit permission? That would turn into the biggest family reunion since Halifax." Briggs shook his head. "We need privacy for this." He jabbed at Abby's shoulder with his free hand, driving her towards the path that led down towards the water. She concentrated on her feet and didn't allow the tendril shadows that came too far out from beneath the scrubby trees to distract her.

Her eyes were still down when a hawk screeched above and she was too late bringing them up to see either man's reaction. She'd just assumed, in the first rush of fear, that she'd been mistaken about the hawks earlier, that the birds were the tools of this pair the same as the cop, but the more she made herself think calmly the less likely it seemed. They couldn't both have been in the hawks— Briggs at least would have been busy occupying #findCaiden— and it didn't make sense. Not if they were following the shoggoth, which stayed under and alongside and in shadow and in secret. A soaring bird above the treetops could never trace it.

Besides which, the hawk she'd killed had wanted to hurt them, not possess them.

One problem at a time, she told herself. They were at the foot of the bluff now, on a nice paved new bike trail, the kind of thing that hopeful towns made out of abandoned railbeds and old rights-of-way. Further ahead, trees closed over the path into an arch that would suit the shoggoth far too well and didn't suit Abby at all.

Martha recognized the danger too, and slowed despite the cop's shoving. This seemed to amuse Enoch.

"Briggs," he said, "I think our little cousin is afraid of the dark."

"She's only right to be," Briggs replied with a chuckle. "The dark woods aren't safe for little girls. There might be a big bad wolf. Good thing you have two big strong Waite boys to protect you."

You cringe before an old man who pretends to be a prophet, Abby thought, a man who sends his own sons to bring him little girls or die trying. Even my mother alone was stronger than your whole soft-water family.

The gestures Enoch made as they passed under the shadow of the trees were constrained, and he muttered words instead of yelling them. But the shadows shrank back instead of reaching for the group of soft vulnerable humans. So maybe that was one point for him over Mom after all.

They came through the trees quickly, and Abby wasn't sorry—
even knowing the thing was constrained it was hard not to look for
it in every moving leaf and ripple. Now the blacktop veered away—
it didn't track the main body of the river but an oddly straight
tributary. An old canal, Abby guessed.

It wasn't easy to guess how far they walked, or how long it took,
especially not with Martha as freaked out as she was. Certainly
there was no more conversation, and though she considered herself
to be in good shape she was tired and a little sweaty when they
reached the cave. It was just a slot in the rock, vaguely and raggedly
keyhole-shaped, nothing to draw attention to it as it sat near a bend
in the path a bit beyond a cluster of picnic tables. Once Briggs and
Abby were inside, he let go of her arm. There was no need to do
anything to control her but let Enoch keep covering the entrance.

When they got out of this, Abby thought, and they would get out
of this, she was going to take that gun and carry it goddamn everywhere with her. She couldn't possibly be as stupid with it as Enoch.

"I told you this would work," Briggs said to Enoch, in the tone
of an old argument only continued because it must be; he wasn't
expecting a reply.

But Enoch had too much pride to take it with good humor.
"Hurrah, yes, lovely, we get to be a couple of rather stupid girls for
the next devil knows how many decades."

"It hardly matters that they're stupid *now,*" Briggs said airily.
"And just imagine how popular you'll be back at home!"

Abby put a hand on Martha's arm to steady her, and faked an
aghast look to match her sister's real one. And that, a stupid gross
remark that might or might not have been a rape joke, was what finally broke Briggs' hold on the cop. Abby saw the break and leaped
in, not controlling the cop but channeling her, pushing her away
from her natural inclination to see them all as bad guys now and
forcing her to realize what her duck-brain had been avoiding, that

she'd pulled a gun on a pair of innocents and committed a blatant kidnapping.

This only enraged her at Briggs and Enoch more—she seemed to sense that they were to blame, though she didn't know how.

Briggs pushed back, of course, in moments and as hard as he could. But he wasn't expecting Abby's strength. The cop's weapon cleared holster before Enoch even realized what was going on, and he went down with a bullet in his leg before he knew he was in danger.

The noise in that enclosed space nearly deafened Abby and as much as Enoch's pain delighted her, she couldn't have any more gun play—the risk of a ricochet just seemed too great. She grabbed the cop and, mentally, pinned her wings as you would a flapping bird, soothing and restraining her. It would have worked, too, except for goddamn Enoch. His mind, outraged by both the pain and the fact that this being he'd been thinking of as his servant a moment ago had caused it, seemed to forget all about ricochets and for that matter the horrible noise they'd all just been subjected to. He barely aimed the gun before he shot.

Of course he didn't hit his target and of course the damn bullet ricocheted straight into Martha's arm, Abby saw her fall to her knees and dropped down beside her to make sure she didn't get stepped on in what was now as near to mass confusion as you could achieve with five people, the sounds of the shots still ringing in the rock and the cop clearly shouting but completely inaudible, drawing another bead on Enoch—who, at this point, could get shot all he wanted as far as Abby was concerned. Briggs was shouting too and between lip-reading and watching his mind she could see that he didn't know who to be outraged at first, the cop for opposing his will or his nephew for damaging one of their precious new bodies.

She also noticed what no one else could be bothered with—the shadow that briefly braved full sunlight just outside the cave to get to its now-distracted targets, the men who'd been keeping it at bay. She couldn't have shouted a warning if she'd wanted to, and she wasn't sure she wanted to until it was too late and a dark tentacle thick with toothed mouths latched itself to Enoch's leg. The cave suddenly smelled exactly like their basement back home—a smell that Abby had always chalked up to the damp but now saw was something else entirely.

Briggs lunged towards Enoch, still shouting inaudibly, and the cop, not understanding what she was seeing, assumed that he was going for Enoch's gun and lunged towards him. Abby grabbed Martha's hand, which was weak to clasp but still warm, and hoped that they would kill each other quickly, without any more stray bullets. If they did she could take care of the rest. She remembered the words.

Martha made a strange strangled sound and Abby looked away from the fight to her sister, the enormous patch of blood now sheeting her arm and staining the edge of her sleeve, but she wasn't hit in the center mass and certainly not in the lung, that would be impossible and so freaking unfair now when they needed each other so much...

Of course, Abby didn't just think about her social life and the weird dramas of the duck-people while all this was going on. She tried to figure out what Mom did with the bodies, too. She wasn't made of stone.

She had some ideas, naturally. Grandfather's notebooks were full of important tips on how to put someone down so that they couldn't come back up again on their own—it was one of the first techniques he'd had to perfect, of necessity. It wasn't so hard with one of the duck-people, of course. Even if another Waite, or someone with similar powers, found a nice fresh dead duck-person body, they couldn't get it out if it was buried in the right kind of earth and the spot was marked with the right kind of symbols—the kind of symbols that confused archaeologists down the years, carved in marble or granite, or seemed to disappear when scratched in soft earth or scribbled on paper and yet left a residue of power hanging in the air.

With Waite bodies it was a bit trickier. Someone like Grandfather or the pop-eyed boy—or for that matter, someone like Abby herself—wouldn't give up even when weakened to the point of death. Death just sort of seemed to irritate the Waites, offended them, pissed them off. They'd try anything to stave it off, even jumping back out of the grave a time or two before they rotted. Keeping another Waite dead was therefore an important skill for any Waite who wanted, themselves, to stay alive.

The cleaver was the first tool you needed, Abby didn't really have to be told that. Hard to jump out of the grave when your feet were someplace miles away from your head. It also made the holes you had to dig much smaller, and the body easier to transport, which was helpful when you needed to travel to find that right kind of earth. You also needed a shovel to dig in that earth, and salt for the grave—table salt was good, rock salt was better—and the strength to oppose a pissed-off, desperate Waite. Nothing hard to get, except the last one. And you needed a couple nice patches of that right kind of earth.

The farm itself wasn't, technically, the right kind of earth. When Grandfather had first come here, new-married and trying to evade his family, he'd needed someplace cheap and obscure and fast. He'd bought the first farm available that was even sort of right, and he'd sunk power into making it a place where he could live. The search for the cabin in Minnesota came later. In a way it had been the right decision, because no one had ever thought to look for them here until he'd let the shoggoth out in his fit of pride and anger.

But that meant that Grandfather and the pop-eyed boy weren't buried anyplace convenient. The earth here wouldn't hold them down. Grandfather himself had proved that with what Abby now thought of, with a bit of a sneer, as his final experiment.

"Where did you go?" she asked Martha one Saturday, trying to sound casual. She succeeded too well, because Martha just looked at her stupidly.

"When Grandfather was in your body. You could tell when he was coming back. Could you tell how far he went, or in what direction?"

At first it seemed like she'd veered from too casual to too direct, and that Martha was upset and would refuse to talk about it. She tried to act nonchalant, to preserve the idea that it hadn't been weird to ask so she could try again later.

Then Martha relented, or maybe she just remembered something she actually wanted to share. "A couple of times I could see, just for a second, what he was looking at with my eyes. Or however it worked." She shuddered. "It wasn't anything I recognized, much. A dead tree, or a creek or a swamp. One time he was driving and I saw a road sign for Wyoming County and I freaked out thinking I was actually driving and I was gonna crash."

Abby wondered how he'd thought he'd get away with it, how he didn't expect to be pulled over as a nine-year-old girl driving his stupid giant Buick. And yet he had gotten away with it.

But that was all Martha had—trees and water and driving away out into the sticks—and it was obviously useless to ask Mom. After a while she'd had to give up. Only, she told herself, until she herself could drive.

CHAPTER TWENTY-ONE

Of course there was no real town to be found and they had to settle for Subway. Buddy started whining after about fifty miles. "Maybe he has to pee," Martha suggested. That seemed plausible. Might actually be the first helpful thing she'd said since she got out of jail—although Abby had a vague recollection that she'd done something pretty clutch.

Oh yeah, that. She was going to have to work to remember it, and that knowledge irritated Abby half to death.

They pulled over and let him out. It wasn't as muggy as Abby would have predicted, but still too hot for her liking. The grass exploded with brown grasshoppers that flew away on black-and-yellow wings as Buddy nosed around, wagging vigorously. "We should have saved the sandwiches," Martha said. "We could have had a picnic." Abby just nodded, thinking of how fast Martha had inhaled a foot-long, a bag of chips, the big chocolate cookie, the large soda. She thought of the grasshoppers leaping into their hair if they sat on the ground, of Buddy trying to snorfle up their food.

Abby half expected the dog to run off through the fields, abandoning them to undertake some kind of Incredible Journey human-interest story trek back to Daines. That was what dogs did, wasn't it? But he marked a telephone post and hopped back up into the truck obediently when Martha patted the seat.

Martha crooned over him then, rubbing his ears and telling him what a good boy he was, and though it made Abby want to roll her eyes she had to admit she was a little pleased too. She snapped a picture of him and tagged it #dogsofinstagram and it was an instant hit, almost a head rush. With that under her belt Abby decided that the best plan was to just drive as long as she could and then find a Holiday Inn or something. She obviously couldn't let Martha drive again. Not and make her explain at the same time.

"So," she said, leaving the opening as ambiguous as she could as she pulled back onto the road. "What was that all about?"

Martha had the brass ones to look blandly confused for a moment, as though she was trying to figure out which 'that' Abby was referring to. Or maybe she couldn't remember clearly any more than Abby could, and they'd never know—which raised horrible questions about everything Abby did remember, and for a moment she wanted to pull back over and sit still until she wasn't dizzied by it. But then Martha straightened and said, "Oh! Of course." She smiled; her cheerful pride was a palpable thing, the pride of a small child holding a large fish.

"I mean obviously," Abby said, hazarding a guess that wouldn't run her too much risk of being wrong, "obviously you went far enough back to fix…"

"I made sure you didn't let that thing out," Martha said with just a tiny gloat in her voice. She thought Abby was trying to avoid admitting an old mistake, not avoid making a new one. "So none of that ever happened. Ryan's fine—except that we have his dog and truck, I guess. Daines isn't blown up, no one got murdered back at home, we didn't get arrested or shot at. All gone."

"And you can hold all that, and the fold that got you out of prison early. All at once, indefinitely."

"Well, no, that would be nuts. No one could do that. I could barely even do the fold in the first place, when my arm hurt so bad."

"So…" Abby looked around her, at the road that could be any-place, at the sky. "How long do we have? Will we know when it's about to unfold?"

"It won't, I tied it off." Martha was downright enjoying being the one who got to explain things for once, Abby could tell. It was irritating, but worth it to know what the hell was going on. "Grandma taught me but she said it was only for emergencies. You don't just fold, you make a knot, and then it never unfolds and you can never go back past that point and fold it or change anything again."

Abby nodded, although she was only mostly sure she really understood.

"That moment you closed the door, and everything before it—that's permanent now. I can never go back there again. Not that we'd want to."

Abby nodded again. She'd closed the door, all right. One of the two main possibilities for fixing this shit had always been asking Martha to take them both back far enough that she could get diagnosed earlier, treated earlier—but that meant asking Martha to put herself back in prison, which seemed awkward. And now it was too late to ask. Which left only one possibility that Abby could see.

Martha had no idea of any of this—it was irrational to be angry, it was Abby's own fault she hadn't opened the wine and had the conversation—but still, seeing her so pleased with herself over it was almost unbearable. Abby forced her face into a grin.

"Of course now I have the world's worst headache. And I'll probably nap all day." Martha had already settled back and down in her seat, leaning her head to one side. "But still. No one chasing us. No more of those stupid hawks."

Her eyes were already closed, and she couldn't see what Abby saw—the dark rounded form on the telephone pole ahead, rising and soaring out to pace them.

The time that Abby thinks of as "when we were normal"—the time after grandfather and after the pop-eyed boy, the time when Mom had a job, a few work friends who would drop by or take her out for drinks, when besides reading and re-reading that handful of saved notebooks Abby spent her afternoons eating microwave burritos and watching TV and playing Duck Hunt with Martha—is in her mind a short historical aberration. But when she tries to put her finger on it, things didn't get fucked up again in any specific way until they were fifteen, nearly sixteen.

By that time she would have been popular if she'd been in a different school, around people who didn't know that she and Martha were creepy by definition. But of course by sophomore year there were a few kids who desperately wanted to be as creepy as they thought she was, kids who had discovered Nine Inch Nails and Manic Panic. A girl named Kristen who scribbled poetry in a notebook with a black velvet cover during math class. Electric Carl, now Kristen's boyfriend—still supposedly the smartest kid in school by the IQ tests and final exams, but he wanted nothing in life but to sneak sips of vodka out of a Snapple bottle and avoid going home to his prison guard dad. Duane, who was a senior and had been held back a year and mostly just read comics and stared at the world through uncomfortably thick glasses. A clique, a gang, friends of a sort although Abby found them irritating half the time.

It was Duane who caused the trouble. Being a senior, he decided to ask Martha to the prom.

For once, the forces of the student body and the school administration aligned; both were appalled by the idea. There was already a rule, in fact, that only juniors and seniors could attend the prom, although no one could remember the fiasco that had led to this (rumors assigned blame to one of Paula Piechowski's older cousins, the one with all the babies). Duane should have known, it had been explained to all the seniors in some kind of handout, along with the dress code and the fact that you couldn't bring a date from another school. Abby suspected that the handout hadn't included enough pictures for Duane to bother reading it.

That explanation wasn't good enough for the school, though. Somehow it had to be Martha's fault, or at least Martha's fault too, and that in turn meant that somehow it had to be Abby's fault, and that meant they were sitting in the counselor's office together again.

"What you have to understand, girls, is that at your age you start to have a lot of power." Abby had tuned out everything Mrs. DeAngelo had said up until now, concentrating on soaking up the edges of her fluttering concern, but the mention of power caught her attention.

"Boys can't help what they are," the woman said nervously. "If you get them too wound up, they can't handle themselves. It's not fair to ask them to break the rules for you."

"But I didn't…" Martha had been explaining this for a week, and if anyone was going to believe her Abby assumed they would have started by now.

"And you can get hurt," Mrs. DeAngelo said firmly over Martha's protest. Her knobbed fingers, just a few years shy of arthritis and retirement, curled slightly—not a clench but the ghost of one.

"You don't get hurt when you have power!" Abby was surprised at how offended she felt by the notion. "You get hurt when you don't have enough power."

Mrs. DeAngelo frowned. It was the first time Abby had spoken during the meeting, and it took the counselor a moment to put together her response.

"You both," she said, emphasizing the word both, "need to think very hard about the path you're on. I know you think you're very smart at this age, but acting out for attention isn't going to get you anywhere good in the long run." Then she dismissed them, and math class wasn't even over yet.

So that was annoying. But the worst of it was at home. The same day, after school, Mom walked into Abby's bedroom without knocking, and sat on the bed.

"So tell me about this Duane kid," Mom said. She seemed to be aiming for curious, maybe gossipy, the way she talked to her girl-friends while they drank wine, but she sounded annoyed.

"He's no big deal," Abby said, annoyed herself. "He's a lump. He hates everything except Batman and Rush."

"And Martha, apparently."

"I guess."

"You guess? Mrs. DeAngelo said they're together constantly, that he cuts gym class to go sit with her in the newspaper office."

"Well, yeah, but that's because everyone's there. Kristen and Carl and whoever."

"But he didn't ask Kristen to the prom."

"Carl would probably kill him." Carl spent hours of his days coming up with elaborate scenarios for killing people, and lists of potential victims. It was easy to get on the list and as far as Abby could tell no one had ever gotten off. Mrs. Grant was on the list, that was why Abby and Carl were friends, even though he'd been getting less electric for years and was barely any more use than anyone else now.

"And he didn't ask you."

As gross as Duane was, Abby could tell Mom thought this was an insult, and that made it prickle. "That's because he's stupid, Mom! Martha doesn't even like him!"

"Oh, she's got so many boys after her that she can afford to be picky, now?"

"No!"

"Don't raise your voice to me, young lady. I asked you a simple question."

"And I answered it. Now leave me alone. I need to do homework."

"Homework?" Mom snorted. "That's a first." But she left.

Obviously she didn't need to do homework. She always had Martha stretch a study hall so she didn't have to carry books home, and copied off of Carl if even that wasn't enough. What was actually happening was that she'd been inspired by the combination of Kristen's poetry and the memories of Grandfather's notebooks to start writing down everything she could think of about drawing power from people. Sure, she'd stumbled on the whole thing by accident but that didn't mean that writing it down might not somehow help her get better.

The problem was, she'd plateaued. After the first breakthrough, after Grandfather died, it had seemed for a while that she could just keep on harvesting more and more energy. Besides the reliably electric few, she'd discovered that most people flickered on and off, giving her a jolt sometimes and other times just lying dead.

It had something to do with whether they were paying attention. Just because they were looking at her or talking to her didn't always mean she could use them, but when they were ignoring her it was no good, no matter what she did.

At least they could never manage to ignore her for very long. She didn't even need to do anything particularly flamboyant, no matter what Mrs. DeAngelo said. Once every few weeks it would occur to some classmate that she was a bad person and something needed to be done. Sometimes it would go too far—they'd tossed her library books into a puddle once, and she'd had to pay a fine, and another time one of the girls from Bush Gardens had decided to fight her in the parking lot after school for reasons that no one could quite explain and she'd ended up with a fat lip and a torn shirt that she hid in the bottom of the closet so Mom couldn't complain about having to buy her a new one. But usually someone just insulted her or prayed at her and she'd gotten pretty good at handling that. She harvested the energy from them then, if she could. If she could do it every time, she'd be doing great.

But she couldn't. There was still more power out there for the taking. There was a way to get it. There had to be. If she wrote down everything she knew, maybe she could figure it out. It had worked for Grandfather.

But in five minutes she was frustrated. Everything she was writing was vague, and sounded dumb even to her. She went by instinct, by feeling, far more than by the techniques Mom and Grandfather had taught her. The techniques she only half-remembered, and the feelings were a bunch of bullshit when she wrote them down—the ones she could put into words at all. She sensed something big and pure and not bullshit at all, inside of her brain somewhere. But she couldn't get it out on the page.

Maybe if she tried again later, when she wasn't irritated at Mom and school and the big fat hairy deal everyone was making about Martha and stupid Duane. The attention didn't do Martha any good, she couldn't use it. She didn't even like attention. Abby shop-lifted plenty of black lipstick and eyeliner for everyone on their bi-weekly expeditions to the Walden Galleria, but Martha never wore hers; instead she let her hair fall down over her face and mumbled on the rare occasions that teachers bothered to call on her.

Downstairs, the phone rang and Abby listened hopefully for Mom or Martha to call her name. Nothing.

She closed the notebook and stuffed it between her mattress and bedspring. Flipped on the TV, intending to tune in to Tribes, but Sally Jesse Raphael was on and something about the line-up of guests caught her eye.

Three sets of twins, all teens, all girls. The levels of sullenness and defiance varied, but none of them looked happy to be there. One set was gothed up, far more extreme than anything Abby had ever attempted to get past the doors of Alden Central School. The second set, who looked Mexican she thought, were severe and scowling in tank tops, their hair cropped short and spiky. One of them had a tattoo on her bicep, some kind of bird. The third set of twins looked far too tame for the show, sad, wispy, almost Martha-like although they were short, round-cheeked redheads. Sally was grilling one of the redheads now, and the girl was so hunched over and folded-in that she could as easily have been twelve, or ten, as the sixteen that the banner at the bottom of the screen claimed. Evidently she and her sister had tried to poison another girl at their school by putting antifreeze into a Snapple.

"You say she was plotting against you," Sally said. Her red glasses struck Abby suddenly as though they'd been painted on the screen, a trick of the light. That wasn't a real person, with those glasses and a name like that. It was a messenger.

"She was." The hunched redhead sounded certain, despite her miserable pose. "It was her or us."

Sally drew up with that air that adults used to dispense their most dubious wisdom, but Abby leaned in anyway. "She had her own problems. Everyone in high school does. She wasn't plotting against you, she wasn't even thinking about you."

"She'd stare at us. All the time. Give us mean looks."

"Don't be so stuck on yourself. Most people aren't thinking about you, even when they're looking right at you."

Just then, when Abby thought she'd almost seen through the whole issue, there was a knock on the door. "Can I come in?" Martha's voice. Sad, helpless. The voice that went with the girl on the screen.

The camera had switched focus to the Hispanic twins. Abby

sighed and said, "Come in," in as pained a tone as she could muster.

Martha opened the door, which had started to whine on its hinges—Abby had thought about getting oil for it but frankly if people were going to barge in they deserved the awful noise—and, almost in one motion, threw herself down on the bed. Abby hesitated just long enough to make her point and muted the TV.

"Just make Duane stop," Martha said, sounding close to tears. "Everyone hates me since he started acting like this, and he won't leave me alone, and I don't want to date him! He's weird and he's ugly and he's not even nice to me."

"He asked you to the prom," Abby said without turning from the screen. "That was pretty nice." The banner at the bottom now was saying something about the boot camp the twins were going to be sent to. The insight she thought she'd had was gone.

"No, it wasn't! Not when I don't want to go to the prom! You won't be there, and everyone will pick on me. Anyway, I told him to stop calling here and he called again and every time he does, Mom looks at me like I'm doing it on purpose!"

"Fine. I'll make him knock it off." Abby turned the sound back up. One of the goth girls was crying, eyeliner creeping thickly onto her white cheeks. Martha settled in beside her to watch, and Abby didn't make her leave. Sometimes, although she'd never admit it, she missed sharing a room.

CHAPTER TWENTY-TWO

That night they ended up at a La Quinta near Madison. It was a good choice even if it wasn't the cheapest—not a hole, and no extra fee for pets.

Abby updated her Twitter feed with a note about how much better she was feeling, her Instagram with a picture of the nondescript pizzeria salad she ended up eating from what they ordered in. That wasn't enough so she followed it up with another picture of Buddy, eating canned chicken and rice from the new pawprint bowl Martha insisted they buy for him. The likes were warming, which was helpful, because whoever had the room last turned the AC far too high.

Then she sat down to fiddle with the GPS unit she took from Ryan's truck. No more wandering off course. The GPS came with half a dozen voices—Han Solo, a clipped British aristocrat, a movie mobster. Abby couldn't imagine not being annoyed by any of them after five turns or so. She let it return to the default, the nondescript woman with the same carefully enunciated accent that Abby once trained herself to use. In fact, it could almost be Abby's voice, except that Abby knew when to get louder, when to sound like she was having fun or was genuinely upset.

"Go to State Route 19," the woman said, when Abby entered their destination. "Turn left."

Martha picked up the remote and started flipping through the channels. Buddy jumped onto the bed between them and began licking Abby's shoulder.

"Hey!" She pushed his nose away. "You're getting me damp!"

He drooped his head and then looked up at her, mimicking shame very convincingly. But as soon as she went back to her phone, he started again.

He was licking the mole. She remembered when that story about cancer-detecting dogs came out. She thought they had to be trained, though.

Martha put her arm around Buddy, pulled him away. "Don't piss her off, Buddy. You wouldn't like her when she's angry."

"He's okay," Abby said. She was too unnerved to be offended by the implication that she was some kind of dog-abusing monster. She almost hadn't thought about the mole, this past day, and that seemed impossible when really it was the point of the whole exercise.

Was now a good time to tell Martha that she was dying? They could open the Moscato, finally, have the difficult conversation. Martha would feel bad, because… Martha would feel bad for her.

Abby turned and almost opened her mouth, but the sight of Martha stroking Buddy's head changed her mind. Martha was happy right now, and a happy Martha was a cooperative Martha, while a distressed one tended to screw everything up in new and exciting ways.

Somehow, she drifted off to sleep without noticing. That was the only way it could happen that the voice of the GPS woke her up.

It was calm, pleasant, precise. It was reciting the words of that goddamned song.

She laid her back against a thorn, it said. *All alone and so lonely-*

oh. And there she had two pretty babes born, down by the greenwood side-o.

Buddy was tense beside her, and when she put her hand on his back she could feel the hair of his ruff prickling up.

She took her penknife long and sharp, all alone and so lonely-oh, and with it pierced their tender hearts, down by the greenwood side-o.

Martha moaned quietly, a noise between sleeping and awake. Abby knew that she needed to get up and make the chanting stop before Martha heard it, but she just lay there, that first move not so much too hard as simply in a different universe.

Buddy began to growl.

As she came to her father's hall, all alone and so lonely-oh, she saw two pretty babes playing at ball, down by the greenwood side-o.

"Abby?" Martha's voice was quiet, but the fear came through. "Are you saying something?"

"The GPS is malfunctioning, is all. Don't worry about it."

Oh mother, oh mother, we once were thine, all alone and so lonely-oh. You didn't dress us in scarlet fine, down by the greenwood side-o.

Abby absently wondered whether it was creepier without the music, or if it was just being jarred out of sleep that made her feel that way. The repetitive nonsense that glided by in a folk song now seemed intentional, demented.

Martha whimpered—too late now to stop her realizing what was going on. Buddy responded by increasing the volume of his growls a notch. Now that Abby's eyes had adjusted she could see that his ears were swiveled forward and his teeth were bared. Too bad this wasn't a problem that could be solved by biting.

Oh babes, oh babes, what have I to do, all alone and so lonely-oh, for the cruel thing that I did to you? Down by the greenwood side-o.

"It's still after us. It's one of them after all, isn't it?"

That was enough. "He can't actually hurt us, not like Enoch and Briggs could," she said. "Or he'd do that, instead of throwing birds at us and making our gadgets act up."

"Are you sure?"

Abby wasn't. But then she felt a tingle around the edge of her mind. Weak, pointless, easily swatted away, but he was trying to break in. Her words pissed him off, probably.

Good.

"Which of them do you think it is?" Martha asked in a low monotone.

"How am I supposed to answer that? They never had names." But they were different, she knew that. One hungrier and stronger than the other. She remembered. And she'd bet this was the hungry one.

"You know how. Mine or yours."

She tried to feel. Was it the hungry one? Or the other? She mustn't underestimate the other just because she'd be the hungry one in their shoes.

She couldn't tell. It was too tangled. It wasn't like a person at all after all this time. It had barely been like a person at all to begin with.

They saw Duane every morning on the bus; he was so bad at being a senior that he had neither a car of his own nor a friend close enough to give him a ride to school, though his brother Charlie, who had graduated the year before, gave him rides home sometimes when his work schedule lined up right. It was the work of half a minute to tell him to lay off Martha; she barely even had to push, once he heard her tone of voice. He just looked at her with his over-sized stuffed animal eyes and nodded.

She'd thought about snagging Duane and his invitations for herself, after Mom's digs and especially after he'd offered to buy Martha a dress on his wages from Arby's if that was her problem. But Martha was right, he was weird and ugly. There was nothing electric about him, and when he looked at Martha his attention didn't even reach her, it swirled around and dived back in on itself. Somehow, Abby knew he would be useless.

Duane, despite his nods, called again that night, and every night for the rest of the week. And every night, Mom either teased Martha or yelled at her until she cried. They were getting impossible to live with.

Every morning Abby got on the bus and pushed him harder. The problem was, it didn't stick. Like Martha's folds in time, it came undone, sooner if she was distracted and later if she was determined, but always by the end of the day in the face of what was looking more and more like a straight-up obsession on Duane's part. So she would push him again on the bus home, if he was there, and a few hours later he'd be on the phone.

Martha spent every daylight hour outside that weekend, pretending that she could pretend not to hear Mom yelling that the phone was for her. Abby propped the phone just off the hook or unplugged it, but Mom kept noticing and putting it back. "People might need to call me, you know," she told Abby with a tone of sarcasm that didn't even fit her words. "I might pick up an extra shift or two. It costs a lot of money to support a pair of social butterflies." At least, Abby thought it was sarcasm. But on Sunday, Mom actually did go to work, although not for as long as a shift usually lasted, and not because she got a call on the phone.

And then, the following Monday, she walked into the newspaper office and found Martha and Duane holding hands. Kristen was there too, and it wasn't a good time to start yelling, so Abby just walked back out. And kept walking. She was prepared to tie anyone who tried to stop her into a mental pretzel, but no one did, so she left the building and headed to McDonald's.

"Shouldn't you be in school?" Duane's brother Charlie was behind the counter, which was just what her mood needed. "Anyway you can't be in here during school hours."

"Screw you, Charlie," she said, and pushed him, and then ordered a Big Mac she didn't really want and ate it as slowly as she could.

Too slowly, she realized when a yellow bus chugged by. Now she was going to have to walk home. Pain in the ass, more than two miles and mostly no sidewalks, muddy ditches, stinking roadkill. Maybe she could find a pay phone and call Mom, but it wouldn't be worth the yelling even if she did agree to drive into town.

She could go back to school and see if anyone trapped late in detention could be pushed into giving her a ride home. She'd have a headache afterward and it would probably be one of the pain-in-the-ass stoner kids, but maybe that was better than raccoon guts on her shoes.

As she stood up to go, Martha and Duane walked in. They were still holding hands, fingers knit together at the knuckles, and in a flash of irritation Abby imagined that they hadn't let go of each other all day, had shrugged on their jackets and shouldered their backpacks while awkwardly conjoined.

"Hi, Abby!" If Martha was surprised to see her, she covered it far more smoothly than seemed Martha-like. "Charlie can give you a ride home too, if you like."

Charlie opened his mouth but then closed it again without saying a word. The girl working the drive-through window shot him a sympathetic glance.

She wanted, badly, to refuse. Sitting in a car with Charlie and Duane and her traitor sister even for the five minutes it would take to get home sounded excruciating. But she couldn't—well, what if she was walking home and they drove by. That would be worse.

She nodded and in two minutes Charlie had clocked out and they were in the car.

Mom wasn't as good at concealing her activities as Grandfather had been, or maybe she thought that Abby wouldn't care. Either way, it only took the car ride home for Abby to figure out that something was up. Martha wasn't just all over Duane, she was bubbling and chatting to the world in general. She made an actual double entendre when Charlie complained about his battered Toyota shifting hard. Duane, over the course of five minutes, went from rolling his eyes back with delight to sort of terrified.

Abby didn't say a word the entire ride. Had Martha—Mom—pushed her? Was that what it felt like? It had been so long she barely remembered. Or maybe she was so used to it she didn't notice most of the time. Maybe it had taken something this out of character and weird to catch on. *Ugh.*

At home the breakfast dishes were still on the table and Mom, at least her body, was asleep on the couch. A bottle of pills and a half-full glass of water sat on the coffee table; Martha frowned and grabbed them both, darting the edge of a glance at Abby. Abby acted like she hadn't noticed and went upstairs. Everything on TV was boring and she couldn't even look at her notebook, and when Martha finally crept up the stairs and into her room, Abby only let her stay long enough to see that it was really Martha before she threw a stuffed bear at her and told her to get lost.

During dinner the phone didn't ring and Martha didn't cry and Mom just smirked. Somehow it was even worse this way. Once Mom and Martha were both in bed, Abby went to the bathroom and checked the medicine cabinet. There was the bottle of Seconal on the middle shelf, not even half-assedly concealed behind the Tums.

She picked the bottle up and rattled it, just a little, enough to tell that it was nearly full. She could steal it, sure. That might hold Mom up for a day or two, but she'd get more. There was nothing to burn down.

She hadn't looked at Grandfather's notebooks again since she'd realized she was doing things he'd never even bothered to try, but there was no use beating herself up for that now. She'd just have to start again.

CHAPTER TWENTY-THREE

Abby found herself awake in the gray before dawn, unable to go back to sleep. It was stupid, especially with how little rest she'd gotten, but there was nothing she could do to will herself back under, to forget that her shoulder still felt damp (even though that was absurd, it had been hours since Buddy licked her).

It had been so long since she'd been back to the cabin. Why did she never go before, these years when no one could have stopped her? Just because she didn't need to, she supposed. She didn't need Grandfather's power or Grandfather's wisdom or even Grandfather's tricks for getting money. The Internet and the life she had built for herself were enough. Why try any rites as risky as what she was going to have to do now?

She should have worked faster. She'd thought she'd have so much more time. *I will have more time.* She needed to calm down. She needed to go back to sleep.

Outside, there was a shadow at the windowsill and she knew before she even turned her head that it was going to be a goddamn hawk, staring in through the curtain gap at them.

She turned her head and grinned at it. It didn't move, and it was still dark enough out there that she could only see a mossy, cobwebby lump of form. It probably couldn't see her either, so her mockery was wasted. She could get up and chase it off, but what would be the point?

People were waking up on the east coast. A few were checking Facebook before work or school and seeing her picture of a cute puppy. She could feel it buoying her. After a few deeps breaths she fell back to sleep.

The room was full of sunlight when she was awakened by the shift and thump of Buddy jumping off the bed. To her surprise, Martha was already up and dressed, standing by the mirrored closet door fastening the necklace at her nape. She turned and gestured to Buddy to get back on the bed but he ignored her, wiggling his tail and pressing against her legs.

"I think he needs a walk," Martha said when she saw that Abby was awake. "I can take him." Abby could tell she didn't want to, she knew the birds were out there, but she felt like she had to offer.

"Looks like. Where were you headed so early?"

"They have a breakfast buffet."

"You go ahead down and eat," Abby said, trying to sound matchingly generous. "I'll shower and then take this guy out to the truck."

"Do you think he'll be okay by himself?"

"It can't be that hot out yet."

And, in fact, it wasn't. The birdless sky was clear and it was downright chilly again, enough to make her unhappy that she'd come outside with her hair still wet. Weird for July—she remembered waking up those mornings in the cabin and running out barefoot to the first of the sun, splashing into the creek without flinching.

But there was nothing less attractive than moping about the good old days. She'd seen it happen over and over again, someone with a decent online presence turned thirty-five, or in the worst cases thirty. They started with a little thing—they complained about Christmas decorations up too early, or linked to some listicle about

25 Signs That You're a Child of the 90s, or they just refused to make the jump from LiveJournal to WordPress, Facebook to Tumblr, and then they were gone, trapped on an island with a tiny irrelevant handful of fans and followers they already had, sinking slowly beneath the rising tide of new in-jokes and outrages. The only way that Abby's plans could work—the only way that her life could work—was if she never, never, never let that happen to her. She couldn't look back.

Sometimes it made her laugh to think how, if Grandfather had actually succeeded, he would have been destroyed anyway by his pride and his absolute refusal to pay attention. He thought his brain was so special that it needed no input. A person Mom's age with Grandfather's attitudes would be marginalized, chalked up as having one of those fancy new autism spectrum disorders or just written off as an asshole, depending. One more generation, leaping into Martha, and he'd have been institutionalized flat out, no matter how young and healthy the body he'd managed to get hold of.

He thought he was so much smarter than us. Just girls, so our brains couldn't possibly be as big as his. He was going to be so mad.

Her laugh made Buddy glance up from the tree he was sniffing, alarmed.

Back inside, she found Martha perched alone at the end of a long table with a fat blond family of five at the other end. "They have a waffle bar!" she said cheerfully, holding up a fork with a few crumbs clinging to it and a strawberry speared on the end, covered in whipped cream. Abby felt a little ill.

They had fruit salad too, though, and yogurt, and she made herself take a couple of hard-boiled eggs as well since she already knew they wouldn't be stopping for lunch. She sat next to Martha and looked up at the screens playing Fox, trying to see something she could tweet a snarky remark about, but they were doing the weather right now. She'd expected a fire or something, a big explosion.

Oh, right.

"Is that all you're eating?" Martha frowned, and stabbed another strawberry from the sludge of whipped cream and syrup on her plate.

"I'm not very hungry."

Martha frowned harder, and held the strawberry in a wavery middle ground between them for a moment as though she was thinking of offering it to Abby before she popped it in her own mouth.

"Are you sick?" she asked after chewing for a moment.

"No." The answer came so quickly from instinct that it took Abby a moment to realize that she'd actually lied.

Over the weekend Duane kept Martha on the phone for two hours each night. Mom gloated. Abby knew gloating now, when she saw it.

The gloating appeared on Martha's face on Monday morning and Abby knew. It looked like a deformity, it was that foreign to the real Martha. It was disgusting to watch, but Abby didn't have to see it for long. At lunch Duane and Martha weren't in the newspaper office, or the library, or even against all odds in the cafeteria. They were ditching.

When Martha found out, she was going to be horrified. Not only was Duane way too stupid to pull this off without getting caught, she had Art today, the one class she actually liked.

When Abby got home, Mom was already awake.

"Since when did Duane not have a car?" Mom asked Abby snidely as she searched through the cupboards for an after-school snack.

"Since he rides the school bus every day?" Abby didn't add a "duh" but she couldn't keep it out of her voice. Mom slapped her across the back of the head.

"You didn't tell me your sister was dating a loser."

"She wasn't dating him until you... nagged her into it." Abby stood up straighter. She hadn't realized up to this minute how close she was to Mom's height now. Mom seemed on the verge of slapping her again but instead she was pushing her—the feeling was not hard to recognize, now that she'd noticed it once, an idea that popped up out of nowhere, a sense of 'well why not?' that slowly heated up until it felt irresistible.

She wasn't going to forget about this, though, no matter what Mom pushed. She had already written down what happened in school today, she carried a notebook everywhere now.

She'd even wondered if that was how Grandfather got into the habit, if there were earlier notebooks he'd lost along the way somewhere that documented a line of ancestors all pulling this same shit on each other, ancestors he'd left Rhode Island to avoid the same as he left Mass to get away from Grandma's people. It was easier to push and hold your own blood than anyone else, she knew even then, but she still didn't like thinking that there were people out there somewhere who could try to push Grandfather. People who could push Grandfather, and succeed, even when he wasn't already dying or dead. It would make sense, then, why they might think that sending a weak boy to deal with Mom was a worthwhile plan.

But compared to those mysterious people Mom didn't seem so scary. Abby turned and let Mom think she'd won and went upstairs. Martha's room was silent but the door was closed, so Abby knocked on it. After a minute she knocked again, louder. A minute later Martha finally opened up.

Despite the silence, it was clear from Martha's eyes that she'd been crying, or trying very hard not to.

"What's the matter?"

"I don't know. I just… I feel sick. Like something bad happened while Mom had my body. Was I acting weird in school?"

"You weren't even there this afternoon. You and Duane disappeared somewhere."

"Oh god." Martha sounded so broken over this news that it couldn't just be her art class, but she didn't say anything else.

"The good news is, I think Mom has gone off Duane. Apparently she didn't even know that he doesn't have a car."

Martha made a strange noise that seemed like it was meant to be a laugh.

At dinner, Mom was still sulky and hostile. Martha sat with her head bent low, ignored her green beans even though she usually loved green beans, and worked at not making eye contact with anyone.

It didn't save her.

"Is there something wrong with the food?" Mom didn't even bother trying to sound normal. "Or are you being a stubborn, picky bitch about that too?"

Abby, startled by the apparent reversal in Mom's opinion, made the fatal mistake of looking up.

"Don't give me that look. You're spoiled rotten, the both of you."

That was a song and dance Abby was used to. Ever since Mom had gone back to work she expected Abby and Martha to be grateful for every single breath they drew, like she was making some big sacrifice for them. The urge to defend herself flared briefly in Abby's chest, but she was able to tamp it down to an eye-roll and an aggressive forking of her stroganoff.

Mom's rant didn't go on the usual rails this time, though.

"When I was your age," she said fiercely, and that was enough to make both Abby and Martha look up again, "your grandfather had big plans for who your father was going to be. The idea of letting me be a normal girl, go with the local boys, have fun, that was never on his agenda, oh no. Oh no. It's only thanks to me that you weren't both born with gills and tails."

Abby set her fork down as quietly as she could. Was Mom... could she be drunk? They didn't talk about this.

"And what thanks do I get? I bust my ass to let you two have normal lives, and you throw it back in my face! Being the town weirdoes! Dating losers! Thinking you're too good to date at all!"

Martha was crying again. Abby wondered if crying too much could actually hurt her. Give her an eye infection or something.

"If I'd let your grandfather have his way, maybe I'd at least have kids who were smarter!" Mom stood up, abandoning her plate—but taking her glass, Abby noticed—and left in a rush. A moment later the front door slammed and the porch swing began to creak, too fast for the old chains.

Martha began to clear the table, and after a few minutes of trying to force down more stroganoff Abby joined her. They retreated upstairs to the sound of the porch swing still creaking.

"You can hang out in my room if you want," Abby said when Martha hesitated at her door. "We can watch some TV or something. The Simpsons is on."

By the time Abby heard Mom's bedroom door slam, hours later, Martha was asleep across the foot of the bed. Abby wasn't even tired—she was furious. She'd read enough in Grandfather's notes to have assumed that his plans for their birth had gone forward, that she was sure to become as powerful as she could dream of, that it was in her blood. All she could think about now was that Mom had had a chance to make them half-gods, and instead their father was some hick kid from Alden.

Fuck it, she thought, I'm not going to let that stop me.

CHAPTER TWENTY-FOUR

They arrived at the cabin well after sundown, with Martha in a silent sulk because they hadn't stopped for dinner and Buddy whimpering with the need to pee again. Abby hadn't had a chance to to update anything all day and she felt harassed, headachey. She threw the GPS in the dumpster back at the hotel and bought a map, which yes, had led to an illegal U-turn and a bunch of lost time on top of whatever Martha had done in her misery. Worth it to not hear that goddamn song again.

Buddy leapt over the seat and down from the truck as soon as Abby opened the door, and rushed to douse a tree by the edge of the driveway. Martha, on the other hand, continued to sit silently, not even undoing her seatbelt.

Abby stared at her for a moment, and then noticed that the moon had moved.

"Knock it off. Get out of the car and help me get shit inside."

Martha slouched off to the porch, Buddy at her heels. But she wasn't about to be the first one through the door, any more than she would be at home; and so after a minute's pointed staring and not moving on Abby's part, she slouched back down to the truck again.

"Here." Abby handed her the heaviest bag and gathered up the rest. "Now we only have to make one trip."

The property management company sent someone to check up on the cabin every so often when it wasn't rental season, to keep it from falling apart under the stern uncaring hands of weather and rot. Like Bonetrager back home, but Abby didn't know this man, not well enough to hate him the way she had Bonetrager. Still hated Bonetrager, she thought, when did she imagine she'd stopped hating Bonetrager?

This guy in Minnesota, though, he seemed to have done his job well enough that she wouldn't need to start hating him either. The lock turned smoothly to her key, the door opened without squealing. She had to set down two of the bags in the mudroom to fumble for the pull string for the overhead light, but it came on when she tugged and didn't flicker.

"Leave the bag here," she said to Martha, who was close behind her, crowded by a curious Buddy. "I'll get all this crap sorted out in the morning."

Martha dropped the bag with a thud. "Where's my stuff? If we're not having dinner then I want to go to sleep."

If she was sleeping, she wasn't sulking. Abby glanced at the bags and picked up the one that seemed to have the most Martha clothes showing at the top. "Here."

Martha left without another word, although the overloud sound of her footsteps was comment enough. It was easy to hear that she'd taken their old childhood room, which was good—it would be tedious to have to fight her for the master bedroom. 'Master' was a bit of a stretch, it wasn't like it had its own bathroom or anything, but it was the biggest and Abby was going to need the space.

Buddy looked up at her, the white showing at the edges of his eyes.

"Go on, go with her," Abby said, and he did. She picked up

two of the bags. She didn't feel like sleeping, she might as well get started.

There was a tiny thrill of transgression in stepping into the room that Grandfather always claimed. The cabin didn't have the dark, seething power of their childhood home—in fact, as Abby switched on the light she heard the rustle of a mouse in the walls, proof positive that Grandfather's aura never sank in here. But this didn't worry her. She had power enough of her own now. Any old shadows would just be distractions. This was a better place than home for a fresh start.

Over the years, the cabin had been updated a bit to appeal to hunters and fishermen, as first Mom and then Abby agreed to lease it out short-term to more traditional Minnesota vacationers. There was nothing here that an unknowing idiot could damage, and relatively little that they could be damaged by—at least, not in a way that would make people wonder or whisper. Plus, it had delighted Mom and Abby both to think how much the presence of ruddy-cheeked, camouflaged men would annoy Grandfather if he could see it, drinking beers by the fireplace and cooking steaks on the old-fashioned stove.

So now the master bedroom, which Grandfather always kept spartan, had a dark green throw rug made of knotted rags covering the pine floor in the space between the bed and the window. The bedspread and curtains were also green, not quite a perfect match. There was a large print just above the bed, a fisherman wrestling a man-sized fish, bear-hugging it as they stood on the water, the sun going down in the mountains behind them. Abby rather liked it, but it was what would pass for weird among the ruddy-cheeked men; she couldn't help but wonder why the property manager chose it. She leaned in to see the artist's name but spotted the title first: "Dancing Trout".

Dancing. She stepped back from the picture, a little disgusted.

They were being cute.

Still, she had to admit that the room was more comfortable than it used to be. There was an armchair in the corner, deep blue and forest green woven together in a nubbly fabric, with a convenient lamp at its shoulder. She set the bags near the chair and went back for the rest.

Once all the bags were retrieved she shuffled the clothes into the old maple dresser—a few of the clothes were Martha's but they could sort that out later—and discovered to her delight that the last renter left a bottle of Jack Daniel's in a drawer, a quarter full. She went to the bathroom and stole the glass from beside the sink, only because the kitchen was whole steps farther, then returned and settled into the chair. It was perfect for reading—comfortable, but firm and straight-backed. The lamp could be brighter, she was going to have to squint at Grandfather's handwriting, but it would do for now. She'd buy new bulbs in the morning when they went grocery shopping.

The first sip of whiskey burned bright, then raced straight from her stomach up her arteries to her head. It erased hunger, erased the nighttime slump. It even erased what little sleepiness she'd managed to build up.

She flipped through a notebook—it wasn't the one she needed. Neither were any of the three others in the bag she pulled it from.

She was only irritated as she pulled a notebook out of the second bag, but by the time she reached the bottom of the last bag her stomach had hardened into a knot of denial. She couldn't have left the most important notebook behind. She knew she'd packed it. She remembered, specifically, picking it up, flipping open the pages until she saw a date, letting it fall closed and sliding it into the shopping bag. Unless… but no, she'd have some trace if Martha had changed that too, and also, why would Martha do that? What would make her think she needed to?

Which bag she'd slipped it into, though, that she was not sure of. It had the natural mistiness of something that didn't seem important at the time. And they've shuffled things around so much, and… Jesus, it could have slid out in the accident, gotten lost under a seat. She checked, she thought, but she was in a hurry too. If it was still in the rental car, with those fucking yokels poking around with nothing to distract or destroy them, that was as bad as if she'd left it behind completely. Worse.

It could be in the bag she gave Martha. That was the answer—it had to be. But Abby didn't get out of the chair, even though she could go knock on Martha's bedroom door and get the bag back. If it wasn't there, she didn't want to know until daylight. She couldn't start driving back in the dark, without sleep, with a half-gut of whiskey, and she would if it wasn't there, even though it wouldn't help. And, too, she didn't want to knock on Martha's door like a supplicant.

Instead she took Grandfather's skull from the bottom of the bag where he'd lain concealed and carried it across to the dresser where she could watch it from the corner of her eye as she read. She had the Hutchinson-Orne book, and Grandfather's notes on that. They should be enough to keep her occupied until she got tired.

It seemed like tired would never happen now, though. She sipped more whiskey, hoping it would tip her over, but it didn't help. Every time she tried to lean back, relax and settle her body into drowsiness some note in the margins caught her eye and she went flipping through the heavy book for another reference to some key point of Orne's or another of Grandfather's annotations. Eventually she thought she had it all, even without the notebook.

The cell phone said it was three in the morning. She should have felt drained. In fact, she knew she did, but the feeling hadn't reached the front of her brain to tell her eyes to stop and close. If she got into bed, she knew her mind wouldn't shut off, it would search for the missing notebook all night, or worse, pick over the past and try to find the hole, or go start the kind of Twitter fight that would cost her more in the long run than she'd gained right now. At least sitting up she was doing something productive.

The ritual was simple, really, for something they made such a big deal of. But so cool. And it needed to happen soon. She could do it right now, middle of the night and all. Why not?

She should only need a little bit of Grandfather. His notes said an ounce was enough, but Orne and Hutchinson insisted that more is always better. They used to have to use whole bodies, got weird subhuman gibbering things if parts were missing. Hard to imagine how they got anything done that way. Dig up a guy who's been dead for centuries, some mage or alchemist who supposedly knew the secrets of the ages, how were parts not going to be missing? Plus the chanting for hours at the top of your lungs, Hebrew, Latin, Greek and the whole nine yards, and nothing could save you if you mispronounced something or fucking stuttered. It all belonged in the era with leeches for medicine and horse shit in the streets.

No, Abby had a plan, and there was nothing in Orne and Hutchinson to say the plan wouldn't work. Part of it was based on Grandfather's own experiments, so it served him right. She giggled at that like she was in fifth grade again.

She sipped, and realized that half the whiskey was gone. She poured more, three fingers this time instead of two, since she was in it for the long haul now. Then she Instagrammed the glass. That was always popular with the late-night crowd.

It was warm in here. Much warmer than it should be, in the middle of the night with the furnace not on. She couldn't work like this; she went back to the dresser, pulled out a sun dress, and abandoned her jeans and blouse on the floor. The dress felt looser than she remembered. At least the road food wasn't getting to her.

Okay. To work.

She retrieved a knife from the kitchen. It wasn't silver. It wasn't even iron—stainless steel didn't count, for reasons she'd never really understood and Grandfather had given up trying to explain. It would do anyway.

The voice recorder app on her phone was simple, and she could turn it on and off without thinking; a good thing, since she needed to get the words she was recording just right. Only a few lines at a time, though, and all the elocution practice stood her in good stead. She set it beside the glass and let it get going as she made the rest of the preparations.

She'd have to go outside in the dark to get firewood, but the flame of a candle would do, and there were candles stashed in every room against the power outages that came with the summer thunderstorms and the winter ice. She had matches. She was all set.

Now for Grandfather. He'd never taken very good care of himself to begin with and now his dirt-caked teeth were loose. A molar pried out easily. She just needed to smash it up somehow. It was doubtful that there was a mortar and pestle in here.

The edge of the socket that the tooth was in, though… that was crumbling on its own. She could break enough of that up with her fingers, maybe. It hurt, the bits were pointy, but she needed to just keep at it.

Abby tried the obvious first, faking sick for three days straight so she could stay at home. It didn't work—she couldn't find a thing in the notebooks or inside her own mind to tell her what to do about this. All she could do was watch terrible TV and wonder what the hell Mom was even up to. Why did she want to be Martha and mooch around in Alden Central High School all day? Abby couldn't wait to get out of this place, that was one thing she agreed with Carl on. When Grandfather did it, it had made sense, he was getting weaker and must have seen death getting ready to take its shot at him, he needed a body that could still do things. But Mom seemed fine. She liked her job. She had friends who took her out to dinner or drank with her sometimes, and for a while a guy had come around, although Abby didn't like him and had pushed him away and Mom hadn't liked him enough to stop her.

It probably didn't matter why. It just had to stop, was all. Martha had to be rescued.

By the time Abby went back to school, Duane + Martha was an established social fact. Nicole even said something catty in chorus class about wasn't it a surprise that Abby was the single one.

Abby did manage to find Martha alone in the newspaper office, eventually, while Duane had math. It was Martha, too. Not only was she alone, she was picking at the price sticker on the back of her notebook and not looking at anything in particular.

"What are you doing?"

Martha looked startled. "Nothing. I mean, what do you mean?"

"All of the sudden you're just fine with dating Duane? When I've been busting my butt to keep him away from you like you asked?"

"No! It's not like that, I…"

"So you guys aren't dating."

"We are. But I don't want to be. He put…" Martha glanced around the empty room. "He took my hand and put it in his lap under the table on Thursday. With Carl and Kristen sitting right there and everything. It was weird. He's not acting like before. It's like he thinks he can do whatever."

"And you're just going along with it?"

"That's what people do when they're dating? I can't just dump him if he didn't do anything wrong."

"I'm pretty sure you can. Tell him you're dumping him and he's dumped."

"I'm not you, Abby. I can't just make people do what I want."

Abby stared at Martha while she peeled the price sticker the rest of the way off. "He's not going to let me dump him when he's this happy to have a girlfriend at all."

"Okay," Abby said in disgust. "Have fun at prom, then."

She wasn't actually going to give up and let Duane have her. Or Mom. She never meant that. She was just mad at Martha, and sometimes she said things she didn't mean when she was mad. Martha should have known that.

CHAPTER TWENTY-FIVE

Abby woke up on top of the comforter, still wearing the sun dress. A little bit of morning light had managed to sneak through the drapes and was trying to stab out her eyes; her stomach wobbled as she turned over and covered her head with a pillow.

The old college program to check up on herself ran without actual thought. She was in an otherwise empty bed, good. She was dressed, good. She just had to find her shoes, and make sure she still had her wallet, her keys, her phone…

Her phone. *Shit.* She sat up and lurched across the room in such a pure state of panic that she was at the dresser before the dizziness hit her and she sank down onto the rug.

But at some point during the night, after the liquor knocked her down, the battery on the chanting iPhone ran out. No way to know exactly when, but… if it hadn't, she probably wouldn't have woken up in the first place. Stupid, stupid. Careless. And not like her, even without dinner.

God damn it. And now today was going to be half wasted on recovering. Martha was going to want to go to the store—and she wasn't wrong, Abby had a dim awareness that she'd want food again someday herself. What a mess.

As if on cue, she heard the front door creak open and Buddy's toenails clicking on the floor. Martha came in behind him, and she probably wasn't really stomping as loud as she could on purpose but Abby was in no position to tell.

She pushed herself to her feet and dug through the bags until she found the phone charger, plugged it in. A few tweets about hangovers should help. Although "Don't pass out in the middle of necromancy" was probably a bit too on the nose even for her audience.

Martha was in the bathroom now; Abby heard the shower running. She braced herself and looked out the window. A beautiful day. Driving east to the nearest town with a grocery store was going to be hell.

As she stood at the window, she heard a motor far off. So far off that for a little while she wasn't sure whether it was approaching or driving away, but of course it was approaching. Of course it was, when she felt like she could barely stand up herself, let alone push anything or anyone else.

And how? Had Martha's work come undone, despite her promises? Did they have another way to follow? Was she all wrong about the hawks after all?

The truck pulled into the driveway just a bit before the moment that she reached the door, having poured and slammed down a glass of water in the hope that it would help. Unfortunately, the water only seemed to have started the whiskey circulating again, making her brave and stupid and maybe just desperate to get it over with and stop hurting.

She opened the door before they were even all out of the truck, hoping to wrong-foot them just a little. It worked. All three looked startled. And then, suddenly, hope bubbled dull and distant to the surface of her hangover, because these were just men, not Waites at all. Just common, ordinary duck-men, turning up here by coincidence. If she hadn't been in so much pain she would have laughed out loud.

"Ma'am?" The driver, a man of about forty with a brown cap and a flannel shirt, stopped with his hand still on the fishing rod he'd been unpacking and looked up. "Are you all right?"

Abby took a deep breath, made sure her feet were set so that she was steady, ignored the more unpleasant implications of the 'ma'am'. "I'm fine. What can I do for you gentlemen?"

"Well, we've rented this cabin, here, for the next week or so. There must have been a mix-up."

The other two men, both younger than the driver, were out and staring at her now. She was surprised at how hostile they felt. She must have looked like a wreck, and the bubble of hope had popped into swamp gas. She needed these guys out of here, now, even if they weren't Waites. And she needed not to have them complaining later or comparing notes with the rental agent, and how the hell was she going to do that?

She felt Buddy slide past her legs and the men grew even more tense, though the dog wasn't being aggressive, just sniffing around in friendly Lab fashion. She called him back anyway, just to be safe. But he ignored her and trotted towards the interlopers, head up, utterly confident of his reception—he'd no doubt spent hundreds of happy hours with men like these.

One of the younger men drew a gun. His hand was shaking but his jaw was set. Abby forgot whatever subtle charming plan she'd been starting to form and grasped his will in her own so hard she was almost hurting herself.

"Buddy!" Abby flinched and twisted, Martha's voice stinging her ear from right behind her. She'd never known Martha could yell that loud. She caught the stranger's intent and got hold of him again just in time to relax his finger from the tight edge of pulling the trigger. Buddy galloped by her and back into the house, almost knocking her off balance, and she loosed the man on purpose this

time—it was a risk, but now he had to lower the gun or look stupid anyway. His companions were staring at him, a little shocked.
Behind her, Martha was sobbing, from the sound of it crouched
down, probably caressing Buddy and putting on a good show of
being helpless, harmless, the pair of them.

A smile wouldn't be quite right now, but if there was one thing
local news in Buffalo ever gave her it was a thorough schooling on
how to look serious, even sad, and attractive at the same time.

"Could everyone just please calm down," she said, wobbling
her voice enough to not sound like a ballbuster. "I'm sorry Buddy
scared you, but he's harmless."

"I apologize, ma'am," the driver said. "Mitch gets nervous around
dogs." He turned a little and glared at Mitch. "And you surprised
us. There've been some cabin break-ins lately. You never know who
you could run into."

Jesus Christ, did they take her for a meth cook or something?
Could three days on the road and one bender have messed her up
that badly?

"Well, I apologize for the mix-up. You see, I own the cabin and I
was told no one was booked for this week, so…"

She hadn't even thought to check, actually, both because that
would have given their location away back when she'd thought this
would be a real jail-break and because she just hadn't thought—fall
was when hunting accidents popped up in the news and she didn't
know anything about fishing.

And who was to say these men were telling the truth? Who was
to say they were not the meth cooks, meth cooks with fishing rods?

She was distracted by all this at the moment the hawk screamed
out of the air from over the cabin, straight into the driver. He
screamed in turn and twisted away from the impact but he was
bleeding like crazy and Mitch whipped the gun up in one startled
movement and managed to shoot his buddy in the face while only

knocking a few feathers from the bird. The third man, the quiet one, yelled something incoherent now and jumped on Mitch.

Abby backed through the door, crowding Martha and Buddy to safety behind her. "Get down," she said. "Stay away from the windows." For herself, she ignored her own advice and peered around the edge of a curtain.

Blood was sluicing down the driver's face but he was still on his feet, barely, leaning against the truck while the other two men wrestled on the ground. The fight might have been about possession of the gun only seconds ago, but now they just wanted to hurt each other in their fury and confusion. The gun was knocked to one side, no one's mind on it.

And then the driver's mind moved. His attention, a moment ago clustered and roiling around his own head, his own pain, reached for the gun. Then his hand did.

Beyond the truck, the hawk landed heavily on the ground and blinked as though it was confused.

The driver leaned too far and stumbled to the ground belly-first, but he didn't flinch or try to catch himself. Instead, he grabbed the gun with one hand, propped himself up with the other, and fired the gun at the still-grappling men three times. The repeated noise started Buddy howling. Great. A Lab that didn't like guns. A genetic defect.

However good a hunter this man once was, the mind controlling him now couldn't access his abilities, so couldn't aim; or maybe he was blinded by the blood gushing from his former face. His targets were still alive, although in one case Abby could only tell because of the tiny flicker of will that remained, a flame that would snuff out on its own in a second in the cool damp of the morning. The other one, Mitch, couldn't seem to get up but he was yelling his lungs out. There was no one to hear him. Grandfather bought enough land to make sure of that.

The driver's body scrambled to its feet, then turned towards the cabin and raised the gun to point at the window. Abby, energized by the energy the men had poured into her moments before when she was all they had to worry about, didn't flinch.

The driver's body didn't have intent, now, so much as a murky wad of hunger and rage. She wasn't sure if that was because his grip was weak, or if that was the way he existed all the time, forever a wailing infant. It didn't matter why though, only what.

"Get in the pantry, lock the door, put a chair against it or something." It was the only place in the cabin with no windows. Martha grabbed Buddy by the collar and his howls crescendoed as she dragged him away. Abby waited until they were out of sight around the corner before she reached for the doorknob. Mitch's screams had died away to whimpers. The driver kept shuffling in her direction.

She'd thought right, he couldn't see. He didn't even raise the gun before she was on him, and no wonder, one eye was basically gone and the other was completely shrouded in blood from the gash the hawk had left on his brow.

Behind her, there was a dull rustling thump. She risked a glance backwards but it was just the hawk, with whatever remained of the driver's consciousness now shunted inside, trying to figure out how its wings worked. A farce that wouldn't last long, a pity she wouldn't be able to enjoy it.

First thing was to get the gun, but this body was strong. She pushed at the incoherent hungry mind and threw it into confusion while she grabbed his thumb and bent it back sharply, an old self-defense class trick from college, and it worked, for a moment. Until something lurched into her from behind.

She was so confused and shocked that it took a moment for her to realize that the body attacking her was the third man, the one who'd flickered and died just a moment ago. He was just as incoherent and clumsy as the driver, but together the two bodies were stronger than she was and besides that she was sick and besides that she was stunned. How could he be managing two bodies at once?

He couldn't manage them well, though. Slippery with blood, she wrenched out of the third man's grip, and the two bodies clawed at each other for a moment as they all dropped to the ground. The third man knocked the gun from the driver's grasp. She kicked it backwards towards the cabin, and now it was just a matter of forcing him out of the body. Bodies. She had the advantage there. A dead form was easier to take over but it was harder to hold against any opposition, with the physical structure of the brain already broken.

She head-butted the driver's body—she was going to be covered in blood no matter what she did, she already was though she hadn't had time to notice yet, there was no sense in being squeamish. As he reeled from that she turned to the third man and kneed him in the groin, and then twice for good measure. He jerked backwards and fell, and she pinned him to the ground. The blinded driver groped in the wrong direction.

After that it was a piece of cake. Keep the body confused and in pain and work on the mind until it loses control. As soon as the body started to slacken, she dropped it and turned for the gun.

Too late. The driver went limp on his own and the hawk took off.

At least she had a gun now. Among other things, she could put Mitch out of his misery.

Leaving campus and stomping down to McDonald's wasn't an option anymore. Luckily, she found Carl and Kristen in the library. It was never hard to find a good excuse to be in the library, and Mrs. Warren was too nice to bother checking hall passes much anyway.

They shot the shit a little as though things were normal. It wasn't hard. Carl had discovered the works of Dean Koontz a few months back, and he loved describing the plots to any available audience. He almost turned electric again when he did.

Abby didn't mind listening. He wasn't paying any attention to her when he spoke, of course, but as far as she could tell Carl barely paid attention to anybody any more, even himself. Certainly not Kristen, which kept Abby from getting jealous or feeling like she should try to grab Carl for herself. He just cared about books and lists, worlds that didn't exist yet or never would or never could together. When he got to college was a big one. And when he got revenge.

And it wasn't like she had to put any effort into what he was saying about the latest book, either, until he got to what he'd inevitably describe as "the really kickass part" where the monster or the serial killer or whatever cut someone up. Then he'd get so excited that his energy would just spill all over the place. It was almost obscene. Tapping into that, somehow, the energy that people spent on their obsessions, making that into energy they focused on her, that was the key.

As if she had any idea how to do it.

But in the meantime, free of the need to be alert, soothed by the flow of words from Carl's mouth and the familiarity of Kristen's company, she could worry about her own problems.

Such as, what was Mom even doing? And how could Abby pry her off of Martha, and Martha off of Duane, for good?

"You know," she said once Carl was out of mayhem to recount. "Duane's being weird with Martha. Have you noticed?"

Carl frowned, and she pushed, and in a moment it was his own idea. Kristen even helped, chipping in. "He is totally weird with her. It's not right. I can tell it's freaking her out."

"He can't be one of us if he's not behaving honorably towards Martha." Carl was big on honor, although what that meant in practical terms was always nebulous. Pissing off the rest of the group was generally dishonorable, though, unless Carl was the one doing it.

"So what should we do?"

She wanted to hear that he'd go on the list, that he wouldn't be around at lunch or in the newspaper room anymore, that she wouldn't have to deal with this and could just concentrate on the Mom problem. She pushed too hard. Carl's thoughts, that she'd thought she had well in hand just a moment ago, shied from her question like crayfish darting backwards. "I'll talk to him. Girls make him nervous."

"I've noticed," she said wryly, and then Carl went back to the book. She didn't know what she'd expected. Of course other people were useless.

CHAPTER TWENTY-SIX

Three bodies were two more than a person should try to bury with a hangover and no breakfast, using a little camping shovel not much bigger than a hand trowel, but there wasn't much choice. Leaving them out in the open was just begging for the hawk to recoup its strength and come back for another shot. Shot, haha. And Abby didn't know how to reload the gun, although Martha had already uncovered a box of ammo in the course of raiding the newcomers' truck for the food and cooking gear they brought along.

At least that took a trip into town for food off the to-do list. And Martha seemed to have forgiven Abby for whatever was eating her last night; Abby had felt the shift when she saved Buddy, and now it was fully set like concrete or a stain.

Still, letting Martha occupy herself with the dead men's groceries was better than making her help with the burial and unsettling what was set, or worse having her screw it up, either with sulking and time-folding or just through sheer ignorance. Abby was the only person left alive who'd read enough of Grandfather's notebooks to know what happened with some of his early, misguided experiments in burying people on this land. There were some things you didn't want the coyotes to dig up.

At least she was able to find a good-enough vacant spot near the house, overlooked by Grandfather's ambition to always have the best. Dragging all this mess through the woods, with brush and little creeks and changes in elevation every few yards, would have been almost impossible right then. As it was, she'd only managed to dig the first hole halfway deep enough, and the sun dress already wrinkled with drunken sleep and grimed with blood was now soaked with sweat as well. A nagging thought kept telling her that she'd be better off eating breakfast, as quickly as possible of course, and then returning to finish the job with some strength. She suspected that thought was a push from outside, though, and ignored it. Besides, after she ate she'd still have a rotten stomach and a pounding head.

If Martha was any kind of decent sister, though, she'd at least have thought to bring Abby a cup of coffee by now.

What if she just buried them all in one hole? There was nothing in Grandfather's notes about that; it was rare he'd get three in a summer, let alone a day. But that would mean a hole three times as deep, into the hard-packed foundations of the earth.

Or three times as long, along the direction of the ley line. More of a trench. Yes, that could work. She could do that.

Buddy, who'd been sticking close to Martha ever since the gun went off the first time, had recovered enough to trot cautiously around the truck a few yards from where Abby was working. The smell of blood-soaked earth seemed to have him stuck, the good-dog part of his brain fearful and the wolf underneath intrigued. He avoided the bodies themselves, but he wouldn't stop sniffing and pawing.

The inspiration hit Abby all at once. Why not? He ought to be good for something besides entertaining Martha.

She picked a shallow spot between two tree roots and sat down, arranging herself for stability and comfort.

"C'mere." She patted the ground next to her feet and Buddy looked up from his smells. "Come."

The good-dog brain took over at once and he trotted up to her. "Sit." He did. Good. "Stay."

He curled at her feet like a lamb on an old tombstone, without her pushing at all.

Swapping was harder than pushing, even with a compliant-minded creature. She was tired, and for a flickering moment she and Buddy were both inside the dog body and his intentions, though not visible through these eyes, gave the strong sense that they were cocking their head at her. Or that was just the way she pictured it, because then the physical head did cock, and she got vertigo, and forced Buddy all the way out so she could take control.

A quick few steps to make sure she could use the unfamiliar legs—muscle memory did stay with the body when you did this after all, no matter what Martha said, and four legs didn't prove that much harder than two—and then she bounded to the weak beginning she'd made of the trench and started digging, sending dirt flying into the air behind her with an abandon that a camping shovel could never match. She felt incredible, elated, though she suspected that most of that was being out from under the hangover and the rest was pleasure at her own cleverness. Her tail started to wag on its own authority. Maybe being a Labrador retriever was just a naturally happy state.

It was a bit harder to judge the length of the trench from this close to the ground, but not very. Anyway, the digging was now so easy she'd have kept doing it for hours just for the sense of accomplishment. But the most important work was yet to come.

She approached the first corpse, the driver, and yes, the blood smell was a strange thing in these nostrils. Repugnant but living at the border of appetizing, like a scent she'd caught in certain airport bathrooms that was a bit too close to the smell of strawberry yogurt. And the training not to put her mouth on a human, even a dead human, was strong in her borrowed mind. But her own mind was stronger, and did what needed to be done, dragging the bodies to the trench and lugging them in, then kicking the dirt back over the top of them until they were good and deep.

The last step was too delicate for paws, so she returned to her own body. Buddy had almost managed to stay, although he'd flopped the body over on its side in his confusion.

The whimpering noise coming from what should be her mouth was disturbing. She wondered how Grandfather ever got used to it. And… my god, she stank. It was definitely shower time when she was done.

The switch back was easier, as always. Buddy, back in his own body, tucked his tail between his legs and retreated to the truck before he remembered he was still supposed to stay; he sank to his belly and watched her with upraised eyes.

"Goddamnit." In standing up, she found that Buddy went and wet himself while she left him in her body. She pulled the damp panties down and off of her ankles and flung them into the trees. Not a pair she liked anyway.

Despite that, she tried to make reassuring noises to the dog as she searched for the right stick for her next task. He'd served his purpose well. By the time she found a stick of the right diameter and convenient length, Buddy had perked up enough to thump his tail on the ground a couple of times and then lower his head to sleep.

The symbols she drew in the dirt over the trench—three times, just to be safe—weren't so elaborate. A stranger might think they were natural, if he didn't look very close, the scratches and footprints of some foraging bird perhaps. But they did need to be precise, or they wouldn't work. She couldn't get cocky like Grandfather did, and she couldn't allow her exhausted, uncaffeinated hand to shake as she drew. So it was slow going, and she was sweaty again when she was done.

Definitely shower time. The last thing she did was look around until she'd spotted a good sturdy hand-sized rock to take inside with her.

Back in the house, Martha was just spooning Folger's crystals into two cups. Of course those assholes wouldn't have brought real coffee. Abby was glad she didn't waste time digging separate graves for the cheap bastards. Still, it was better than nothing once it was in her hands, under her nose, and then down her throat to her bloodstream.

"That was fast," Martha said. She was wearing the necklace again, Abby noticed.

"It's not as hard as it looks. Did you find anything good?"

"They had the biggest log of summer sausage I've ever seen," Martha said, and smirked just enough to let Abby know that she'd done it on purpose, that she wasn't freaked out anymore, that she was going to try to jolly things back to normal. "And all the usual camping stuff. Eggs, bacon, potatoes, cheese. Looks like they were planning to make fajitas one night."

"Nice." Abby slurped the coffee again, and it was already gone. She left the mug on the table and headed for the bathroom, with a detour to drop the rock off in her bedroom.

The dress was a total loss, and she stripped it off as fast as she could, though it caught around the shoulders and seemed not to want to leave her. Maybe it felt a kinship because she looked like a total loss right now herself—exhausted and low on power, no makeup, a day and a half since she washed her hair, sweat streaks in grave dirt. Wrists and hips and shoulder-blades sticking out all exaggerated like one of those awful thinspiration girls. Maybe, she thought, she should Instagram this. Get everyone worked up thinking she was sick.

And then she remembered again, duh, she was sick. Only because out of habit, she twisted around to check how she looked from the rear. Near the biopsy site another mole that the doctor had called out as suspicious has grown to the size of her thumb-pad and it was streaked and raised and lumpy like one of those carnival squash. That's what the dress had snagged on.

It was growing much faster than she expected. She couldn't waste any more time.

Carl seemed to forget all about Duane and honor every other day or so, after talking a good game about how he was going to tell the older boy what was what and get him to act right, and then snubbing him and acting uncomfortable and doing everything but telling him. Kristen was a different story. She was indignant. She didn't even have to be pushed, she was there on her own. Abby suspected she had some kind of old anger at Duane, so easily did her intentions snap into the exact right channels.

It should have been enough to push Duane away with their combined indignation. Martha's own actions should have been enough, for that matter. When she was herself she was as repulsed by Duane as ever, and when Mom took over she now pursued more popular boys with a no-holds-barred alacrity that seemed to alarm even the coolest. But somehow, Duane refused to notice any of these changes for long, his attention remained focused on something that was in the same space as Martha but had barely anything to do with her. Whatever role he was playing in his own head, it had only the most tangential relationship to Martha's actions. It required him to sit by her side whenever he could, bring her presents of mall kiosk jewelry and supermarket flowers, and occasionally try to draw her into a fight about her 'infidelities.' Mom would respond by pointing out that there was nothing to be unfaithful to, since Duane was definitely, one hundred percent not her boyfriend. The real Martha would cry and stammer, which was apparently all the encouragement Duane needed.

The talk was non-stop and brutal, and even if Abby hadn't wanted to shut it down for Martha's sake it would have driven her crazy
to see all that good energy wasted on someone who couldn't use it.
As soon as Abby blocked one stream it sluiced over into another.
Mom seemed to love it, though it didn't make her any stronger. She
just… enjoyed it emotionally somehow. But when Martha was in
her own body the constant barrage of whispered "sluts" and hissed
"psychos" and book-scattering shoulder-slams in the hallways kept
her pretty much pinned down in the newspaper office. It was no
surprise to Abby when the days started speeding up.

Abby had tried to hide her renewed interest in Grandfather's
notebooks, but it was harder now than when she was a little kid and
no one thought her capable of even understanding the handwriting, let alone the substance. Now that she'd learned to watch out
for and resist Mom's pushing, Mom seemed to have settled on her
as an enemy—coming down like a bird of prey on any perceived
insolence or insubordination. And she couldn't feel safe when she
caught Martha in the corner of her eye, either, until she'd looked
long enough to be sure of her gait and her mannerisms. That was
way too long.

The long and short of it was that finally Mom caught her in the
master bedroom, reading through the old notebooks, and grabbed
her by the hair and ripped her backwards so hard that Abby heard,
as well as felt, a crunching between her vertebrae. The chair half-
spun and spilled her out.

It was impossible to be dignified with her belly on the floor, with
her mother crouched over her still holding her hair. This, more
than the pain, made her furious.

"What the hell, Mom," she said as best she could, though she
knew it would mean another yank and it did. Her jaw was clenched
over the words. She was not going to cry.

"What the hell? What the hell do you think you're doing?"

There was nothing to do but go full forward. "I was reading." She gestured with her elbow to the notebook that had tumbled to the floor beside her and tried for the cool sarcasm of a kid on a sitcom. "It's pretty interesting, you know. Family history and all that."

"Who told you you could read those?"

"No one. I didn't know we were living in Soviet Russia, I figured I could read what I liked." Abby tried to get up, if not to her feet then at least to her knees, but Mom crouched lower over her.

"You know good and well those are dangerous. You haven't got any right to jump ahead of what you've been taught—you could kill us all, like your grandfather nearly did."

"You haven't taught me a single new thing since he died!" And that was when the bastard tears spilled out, when she wasn't actually in pain at all. "You think I can just go along with a few little-kid tricks forever? Everything at school's a mess—" and she managed not to say, it's all your fault, "—I need to be able to handle it. I need to know this stuff."

Mom stood up then. There was a strange smirk on her face, as though the tears had satisfied her. Abby scrambled to her feet as well.

"That's your problem," Mom pronounced. "You just want everything handed to you. Do you think anyone taught me anything? Who? Your grandfather or his stupid notebooks? I had to figure it out all on my own. Read the damn notebooks all you want, if you think they're just going to spoon-feed you what you need to know, you have another think coming. I doubt you even can get far enough to kill yourself with it, if that's your attitude."

As she walked away, Abby picked up the notebook and righted the chair. Mom obviously thought she'd won some kind of battle. But if she was underestimating what Abby could get out of the notebooks, that other think was coming to her, not Abby.

The very next day, Martha cut school again. Duane was in the newspaper office, though, moping.

If this was Mom dumping him and going out with someone cooler, it was a golden opportunity. And at least she was wearing good walking shoes this time. And the next period was gym. Fifty percent chance that Mr. Dolan was drunk and wouldn't miss her, and if he did Kristen would cover for her.

She got home to find Mom's body sprawled on the couch again, the pill bottle nearby. A slight snore rasped out of her nose and parted lips. It felt disrespectful and weird to leave Martha that way—she always slept bundled and curled up, and she definitely didn't snore—and Abby went upstairs to look for a blanket even though the weather was still warm.

She was pulling a crocheted pink and orange afghan from the closet when the phone began to ring, a blat in the empty house that made her flinch even though they'd all had to get used to it since Duane had started sniffing around. Before that, they'd never gotten calls. There was no answering machine. The ringing just went on and on while Abby carried the blanket downstairs and covered as much of her mother's body as she could. Finally, while she was carrying the pills into the bathroom, it stopped.

It started again as she was assembling the notebooks in her backpack. They were a hell of a load, but she could get them back to school in one trip, and they'd fit in her locker. She was tempted to wait and get them in on the bus in the morning, but Mom finding her here at home would make it all for nothing.

She was standing with her hand on the doorknob, ready to head back into town, when she heard footsteps on the porch. She thought to run but she'd be visible through the windows, it was no good. She braced for another fight.

But instead of opening the door, whoever was out there knocked. Which was impossible. No one came here to knock.

Now what? If she moved straight backward, silently, she could maybe get to the side door without being seen. It would be tough, though. And no good if they actually leaned to one side and looked through the window at an angle.

The knock again. "Genesee County sheriff's department. Open up."

Behind Abby, Mom's body stirred a little, but the dose must have been too high; she hadn't anticipated needing to get back into her own body earlier than planned.

Abby opened the door and saw two men there, with Martha's body gripped by the shoulders between them; the classic after-school special pose. The look on Martha's face left no doubt that Mom was in there, it was venomous, teeth clenched, brows down; the same look she'd worn the other night when she'd caught Abby.

Mom was pushing the officers with all her might but there were two of them and as soon as she got one of them almost where she wanted him the other would break free. She's no better at this than I am, Abby realized. Maybe not as good.

It was easy enough for Abby to apply the little bit of extra pressure, like a finger in the middle of a tricky knot, and put Mom in control. At the same time she tried to put the right degree of concern into her smile and her voice and said, "Hello? What's the matter?"

"Zillah Waite?"

Mom, Martha, grimaced and nodded at her, so she nodded along.

"Yes, Officer… what's wrong?"

"Is this your daughter Martha?"

Well, isn't that a long story, she was tempted to say. Instead she nodded and let her concerned smile fade to a concerned frown. "What did she do?" She wasn't quite sure that she was hitting the right motherly note, but the cops were softening, Mom had them pretty much under control now.

"We caught her out joy-riding. Is that your car?" He nodded over his shoulder to the stupid five-year-old LeBaron Mom had treated herself to last summer, promising she'd teach the girls to drive it.

She craned up, made a show of looking. Then, as she pulled back, she grabbed Mom by the ear and twisted.

"You little... Officer, I am so embarrassed. I hope she didn't cause too much trouble for you."

The cops looked at each other, checking their sudden impulse to let this go in the mirrors of each other's shades.

"Well, ma'am," one of them said, "you'd best make sure she stays in school from now on. There's a fine if you don't."

"Oh, I'll see to it," Abby said, and pulled her brows down in a way that she hoped looked like Mom glaring.

"Thank you, ma'am. We're sorry to disturb you like this."

As their boots sounded away down the porch steps, Abby let go of Martha's ear and flinched back. The moment of revenge had been sweet, but poorly thought out. She was going to get it now.

Instead, Martha burst into tears like the real Martha. And before Abby could step back or turn, Mom came up behind her and grabbed her, ruffled her hair, squeezed.

"There's my girl!" The grin in her voice was obvious and it overlaid, overpowered Abby's doubts and anger. "Good work. You should be an actress or something!"

CHAPTER TWENTY-SEVEN

Abby emerged from the shower with her plan all mapped out, wrapped a towel around herself, and headed for the bedroom that Martha had claimed. No more dilly-dallying.

As so often happened when she'd procrastinated on something, it didn't take as long as she expected. The notebooks were on the bedside table, which was not at all what Abby would have expected Martha to do if she'd found them while unpacking; she'd leave them outside Abby's bedroom door, or hide them in a dresser drawer out of sight, or just shove them back to the bottom of the bag. But keep them beside her as she slept? Weird.

The main thing, though, was that they hadn't been left along the way and now Abby had them. A quick flip through confirmed that the contents were what she remembered.

Then she scooped the books up and carried them back to her own room. She dropped the towel on the floor and put on the first clothes she saw that were mostly clean. Her head and stomach felt close to normal now, the hangover sweated away: but she was beyond thirsty, in the sort of place where Gatorade would start to taste good. No chance those yahoos brought Gatorade, she supposed. But maybe at least orange juice, or lemonade, something with some sugar and strength in it.

Back in the kitchen Martha was scrambling eggs; there was a big bottle of Tropicana on the table, sweating onto a yellow and green plastic tablecloth, an oasis. Abby took a slug from the bottle.

"What are you, twelve?" Martha wrinkled her nose as she turned from the stove. "There are glasses in the cupboard right of the sink. Our jam jars even. Strawberry Shortcake."

"Don't worry," Abby said, wiping a stray trickle from the edge of her mouth. "I don't have cooties."

"Yes you do." Abby stuck her tongue out, the correct traditional response. Martha turned back to the eggs. "These are going to be done in a minute. Hope you like Cajun seasoning, it's the only spice they brought."

Abby put the juice down and started poking through the cupboards for plates. No point in arguing with Martha now; it would blow over. And it was easy to see that the cooties crack was only because she was mad that Abby lied about being sick. She couldn't have missed the mole. Tumor. It must count as a tumor now.

"Got any plans for the afternoon?" Abby asked, as though she hadn't noticed Martha's mood. "It might be nice to take Buddy for a walk. I think all the excitement this morning upset him."

"It upset me too," Martha said. "I just want to spend a day sitting still, and doing whatever I want. Finally."

Abby kept facing the cupboard, because she was tired and her frustration would show. Dealing with Grandfather would be too noisy and obvious with Martha in the next room and wide awake. Maybe she'd decide what she wanted to do was go outside anyway. Or take a nap.

But after lunch, Martha stayed in the kitchen, still puttering with the bags and boxes that the dead men brought.

"You don't have to do that," Abby tried. "None of that stuff needs to be refrigerated. You can leave it for right now." She felt like it came out right, gracious but casual. But Martha ignored her, stayed focused on the boxes.

"You don't know that. They would have been just the kind of idiots to leave a jar of mayo at the bottom, under the cereal and everything."

"Let me help, then."

Martha didn't say no, but the mood around her darkened just a shade. Abby ignored that and moved in, plucking a box of Ritz crackers from a grocery sack.

"It's okay," Martha said, her voice tight. "I've got it. I want to do it, really."

Abby considered whether keeping this up would drive Martha out of the cabin, but it didn't seem likely—she was more apt to go to her room and sulk—and the truth was that Abby didn't want to sort food and fiddle with shelving arrangements, not really. She dropped the crackers on the table and left without another word, taking the bottle of orange juice with her.

This was how it was going to end, she thought, with us sour at each other.

Abby must have tried to teach Martha how to resist Mom's pressure a thousand times. Or at least ten; she remembered sitting in Martha's room at night for more than a week giving instructions that Martha would listen to, nod earnestly at, and fail to follow.

"It won't work when you're freaking out," she said for the thousandth, or the tenth, time. "Can you for Christ's sake just try to breath from your diaphragm and stop sniffling?"

"I am trying!" Martha gulped air and stifled a sob into a hiccup. It didn't help Abby's mood—or Martha's either, from what Abby could see.

Abby felt her voice come out hotter and harsher than would help. "Then stop trying and just do it like I said. There's nothing to even be upset about, not right now!"

"I hate feeling that way though. Like I'm just a passenger in my body and whatever someone else decides is going to happen to me. It's scary." She was getting more worked up. Her mind was visibly scattered and roiled. If Abby was any judge, Martha couldn't even tell herself what she wanted or was going to do at this minute. It was no different than someone else controlling her anyway.

Abby was the one who had to be in control, so she took it. When she pushed Martha it was because she wanted to, yeah, and because she could get away with it. But also because it would work. And sure enough she was gentle and Martha didn't even notice. Her breathing slowed and evened out.

"Good girl." Abby patted Martha's arm, just above the wrist, which was as far as she could reach across the bed now that Martha was sitting up straight instead of slumping and miserable.

"Now. Make sure you're comfortable, and just... fill up with yourself."

"That doesn't make any more sense than it did the first ten times you said it." Martha was annoyed, started to slump again. Abby adjusted her pressure accordingly.

"You know yourself, don't you? You know who you are."

"Of course I do!"

"Well, be that all the way out to the edge of your brain, so there's no room for anyone else."

Martha, in spite of Abby's efforts, sank back down in her chair and folded her arms in. "You sound like some kind of insane supervillain Oprah."

"What if I just show you?"

Martha frowned, suspicious. "How?"

"I'll push you to do something. Something harmless, obvious. And you can recognize how it feels and fight it."

"No!" She scuttled back across the bed, out of Abby's reach, as though that would help. "Never push me. Never. It's bad enough that Mom does it."

"It's different when Mom does it. This will help."

"I don't want you to. Even to help." Martha lurched up and off the bed entirely. "You know how much I hate it."

"Okay," Abby said, and gave one last little calming press. "But you've got to yell for me if anything happens again."

"You know I can't." Martha should have been distracted enough by that little bit of meanness to not care or notice the change when Abby walked out. But then, before she was quite through the door, Martha yelled something that wasn't quite a word, and what sounded like a paperback book hit the wall to her left.

If it was anyone else she wouldn't have turned around, it would have looked too much like fear or obedience. And Martha looked surprised when she did turn around.

"I'm trying to help you!" Abby wanted to slap her sister, but she remembered how small Mom had seemed after pulling her hair. "You need to get stronger!"

"If being pushed around made me stronger I'd be stronger than all of you by now," Martha said, now crying again for real. Abby was so sick of that. *If Martha won't work for it, then fine,* she decided.

"What do you want? Do you want me to promise that I'm not going to push you, or something?" Abby honestly couldn't tell if she was being sarcastic or not.

Martha jumped on the words like she was sincere. "Never. Promise me you're not like Mom and Grandfather. Promise me you're at least going to treat me like a real person."

What does that even mean? Abby thought. *Do you think there are people who don't get treated this way?* But she nodded. "I'm never going to push you just to push you, only if we really need…"

"No," Martha cut her off. "Never. Push everyone else around if you want but we're supposed to be best friends. Sisters."

"Oh!" Thinking of it as like a friendship bracelet, or like those promise rings that the saddest and most annoying girls got from their boyfriends, that made more sense. Of course Martha wanted to feel special to someone, with Mom and Duane treating her like a piece of meat all the time. "Okay, look. If it means that much to you then yes. I promise I will never, ever push you for anything."

She wasn't sure if she was going to keep the promise, but as she left the room she intended to try at least for a while.

CHAPTER TWENTY-EIGHT

Back in the master bedroom, Abby checked the notebook against the Orne and Hutchinson to make doubly sure her plan would work, lit the candles, drew the curtains, threw the still-damp towel over the mirror on the dresser, turned the stupid fish painting to the wall. Probably unnecessary, but as careless as she had been last night she felt like an abundance of caution would help balance the accounts now.

Most everything was still in place, aside from the phone. The rock she pocketed from the grave would do for the mortar she lacked last night. It wasn't like she was dealing with Lowell or Longfellow or Holmes, for god's sake, irreplaceable, with a demand out of all proportion to the inevitable limits of the supply. She'd have what she needed with plenty of Grandfather to spare.

If Mom had had any foresight at all, she would have just cremated the old guy and then she could have had a pinch of him whenever she needed him, like baking powder, and kept him hidden from Abby with no rite more complicated than a tin in her desk at work, or if she was really paranoid a safe deposit box.

Well, it wasn't Abby's problem when other people were stupid, unless they made it her problem, and Mom couldn't do that anymore.

A tooth was too much, in the sober light of... sobriety. Really, why had she thought to try this drunk? She was lucky she hadn't caused a zombie apocalypse or set off the Yellowstone supervolcano. She pried loose a narrow, rattling remnant of cartilage from inside Grandfather's nasal cavity, careful this time as she should have been before not to slice or jab her fingers. Once it came away she set it apart and hit it with the rock a few times, not even very hard because she didn't want to mar the finish of the dresser too badly—though why not? She couldn't say, it wasn't like she'd ever use this dresser again. The cartilage crumbled quickly under her attack. A little coarse, but it should do.

She adjusted the phone's volume carefully—too quiet and the ritual would be sapped of power, too loud and she'd upset Martha.

She wished she dared to snap a photo of this for Instagram, or tweet about it; she could have used the boost. Her followers would see it as a bit of witchy play-acting, or better yet some kind of conspiracy-theory fodder, the kind that made you nine days wonder and sent idiots with guns storming around. But you could only post so many human skulls before even the dullest police had to take notice.

At first she tried to keep half an ear free to listen for Martha but she soon gave it up. She couldn't do anything about anything she heard short of aborting the ritual entirely, and she wasn't going to do that unless the cabin was on fire. Anyway, it was useless to try to divide her attention, as she should have known from the beginning. Not because the spell was so hard, though it would be, for most people. Because it was so interesting, the power flowing out of the words and flooding the bones, her power everywhere, saturating the air and the furniture, the walls, the waves peaking and resonating in time with the little shreds of old power left there by Grandfather, by strangers before him, and most deeply with the much greater power in the lines and fissures of the earth beneath her. She'd have missed all of this, or forgotten, if she'd done it drunk, and that would have been a shame because she saw the whole pattern for a moment. Distorted reflections of things she once saw Grandfather do in the dark appeared before her. A woman in a high-collared dress shouted at the flames, a Native man with a stone blade stood over the body of a creature that was, perhaps, half a bear. If she concentrated she didn't just see, she could almost understand the whole history of power and terror that happened right here. This was why she had to cover the mirrors, though they were so far from the sea, though the doors were closed back at home—because other things besides herself could watch, and learn, and such things were everywhere. Some of them had nothing to do with the Waites at all, except the same hungers.

Also, because a small distraction like a moving shadow could keep her from cutting her own hand or snuffing the flame at the right moment.

As it was, of course, she executed the ritual flawlessly. Which made it all the more irritating when Grandfather rose from the dying smoke already laughing at her. She hadn't expected distress or fear—those were the reactions of conventional, pious people to being raised from the dead by someone other than their expected deity—but it would have been nice if he'd at least looked impressed.

"Girl," he said, his voice a dry crackle, "wasn't the first thing I taught you not to raise what you can't put down?"

"I didn't," Abby said, flatly. Anything more elaborately menacing and he'd take it as fearful bluster and get onto it like a dog on a scent. She didn't have time or inclination to second guess every word she said right now.

"Well," he said, still grinning like a jackass, "I guess you inherited the family's big brass ones. But now you've called me up, so you still need dear old Grandfather for something, don't you?"

In the books, the dead didn't play these games. They pleaded or they cursed or they just gave in right away and did whatever you asked, but they didn't get sarcastic with you and try to push your buttons the way only the people who installed them could, as she'd read on some sarcastic gif once.

She didn't have time for it, she told herself firmly when she felt herself wanting to argue. "We're at the cabin. There's a spot some-where near here that's good for fixing the transition, but you never wrote it down. I want," she almost said 'need', but you couldn't say that to Grandfather, "to know where it is."

"Too lazy to do the math on your own?"

'The math' involved charting the stars for years, to say nothing of the time with her face in the books, decoding and translating. But you couldn't admit urgency, either. Especially not now.

"Maybe I am. Or maybe I'm efficient."

"You'll never get anywhere depending on other people to do things for you." That was actually one of Mom's taunts, when she'd call them spoiled, but good for him for remembering it.

"I will if I can make them. And I can make you. You should know that better than anyone." He flinched, or more accurately wavered, a little. Good for him for remembering that, too. Sometimes they came back not knowing all the things they should, which would be disastrous now, but that was mostly a problem with the ones who had been in the ground for a century or who got torn up and scattered.

"You're awfully well-preserved, if you're looking like that and of an age to need the spot," he said.

"Better to know it before I need it than need it before I know it." She made a mental note not to turn her back on him, even once she was outside the circle, even in this top that covered her shoulders. He might be able to sense the thing, sense her weakness.

"When'd you start planning ahead? You hit your head or some-thing?" He pulled a mocking face. "You sure you're actually my little Abihail, and not an impostor?"

"I just want to know." She held up her cut hand, which hadn't yet scabbed, where he could see it clearly but not get near. "So tell me, and stop babbling like a lonely old grandpa in a nursing home."

He was trying to pretend to be indifferent to the blood, glancing at it and then away, leaning toward it like a candle-flame in a draft and then forcing himself to correct and stand upright. Abby curled her fingers in to hide the cut, then unfolded them slowly. Flirting with him. Demonstrating control.

"You head due south from the front door of the cabin," he said after a moment, conversationally, as if he'd merely decided there was no harm in doing her a favor. "Cross the creek. Veer left fifteen degrees at the first standing stone. You'll know the table rock when you see it, unless you're even lazier than I remember."

The little dig made her curl her fingers in again.

"That's it, that's all the directions. You have to give it to me now," he said, a look of seriousness and demand on his face that still intimidated her though he was largely impotent in this form. "You owe me."

"I know exactly what I owe you. Have you told me everything I need to know?"

"Worried I left a little surprise under the stone?" He grinned. "I did. But it won't be triggered if it's a hard-water Waite using it."

She let the silence go long enough that he couldn't claim later he'd been meaning to tell more when she cut him off.

"You owe me," he said again.

She almost turned to the bed, then remembered and reached backwards to pick up the stained sun dress. "I know exactly what I owe you," she repeated, "and that's exactly what you're going to get. No more." She tossed the dress to him.

He caught it with surprising ease for a disincorporated old man. Sniffed. Frowned. "Muddy. This isn't yours."

"You get what you get."

He couldn't argue with that, though he stared at her for a long moment as though he was going to try. She stared back, stared him down. She was the one who was still alive, she was the one who got to tell him what was what now. Finally, sooner than she expected, he quavered and pressed the fabric to his face. There was a sound that was oddly disgusting for how quiet and dry it was, and Abby looked down at the carpet. It was still her dress, even if it was ruined, and it angered her a bit on that level.

Still, it was a good move, giving him the dress. Much better than having to concoct some kind of story to tell Martha about how Buddy got a cut on his neck. And much, much better than giving Grandfather her own blood and triggering the spell he recorded in the notebooks he never expected her to read or understand, the spell that would give him another doorway back into the world through her, one last shot at his old plan.

After as long with the sound as she could stand, she snapped her fingers just so and said the word. Grandfather wavered again, grimaced, tried to hold on for a moment and then dissipated back into smoke. She'd put down things that fought harder.

Abby uncovered a window, wincing in the sudden stab of light, and opened it wide. Spoke another word to break the power, which was always the hardest part—more like sobering up than sobering up felt, all the anger and sadness, the sheer resentment that it had to end. Only when the haze was gone did she step into the circle and pick up the dress.

It was already ruined, she told herself, poking a finger through the holes in the fabric, not tears so much as worn-away places, as though the fabric had been rubbed and washed for years. I can get another, I can get ten others just like it. There was no reason to be so upset.

Abby tried one of the pills one night, just to see what was so great about it, but it didn't do anything but make her sleepy and dumb, and around one in the morning she was seized with a terrible fear that she'd throw up and choke to death even though she knew that was mostly D.A.R.E. bullshit.

Kristen liked them well enough, though, and paid Abby for the ones she stole and brought to school. The money didn't matter much—Abby found ways to make people give her what she wanted usually, these days—but Kristen's rapt attention and gratitude did. When it was almost time for another deal, she was the most important thing in Kristen's world, way more important than Carl or her hatred of Duane or anything.

That said, it was important not to skim too much. She didn't want Mom running out, didn't want to deal with the unpredictable anger and sarcasm that sometimes still gave her claws. It seemed like Abby was always misjudging, though, and most of the time she could do nothing right, was the bane of Mom's existence. Most of the time. Sometimes Mom would whipsaw around and be chummy again and that was almost as unpleasant for Abby, trying not to let her disgust at the obvious fakeness leak through and slam shut the short window when she could actually get rides, favors, a moment to breathe.

Running out of pills might be the only thing that would stop Mom's ride down the rollercoaster now. She seemed almost as addicted to Martha and the life she led in her body as she was to the chemicals. Somehow, Mom/Martha was popular. Luke Bowman, one of the wrestlers, had even shaken Duane loose from her at last by threatening to beat him up. And though Abby knew that none of this was Martha's fault exactly—she was weak and whiny and incompetent and so unable to protect herself that how would anyone on earth not want to take advantage?—it was boring trying to protect her now that there were other people who looked at Abby with grateful eyes. Like Kristen. So the pills had to keep coming, and Mom could make do, or steal more herself.

For all of that she knew, in one deliberately-ignored corner of her mind, that a confrontation might come. So when Martha slipped into her room without permission one night near eleven and said, "You have to stop," she assumed that this was it. She braced herself, turned, and got ready to try and push someone who as far as she knew couldn't be pushed.

The instant yielding was the first clue that she was wrong, and the tears in Martha's eyes were the second. She stopped herself as fast as she could. She'd break Martha using the kind of power she'd need to make a dent in Mom.

"What? Why?" If she'd thought about it, she'd have said she was doing Martha a favor too.

"It isn't helping. The only way out of this is to go through it, Abby. She can't keep it up forever."

Abby sat up and swung her feet to the floor. "You think she's going to quit?"

"She'll have to, eventually."

How could she think that anyone would give it up? She didn't know anything. "That's not a plan."

"Yes it is." Martha sped up, and Abby began to see a hint of brittle anger behind the fear, something that reminded her of Grandma. "You didn't do anything so I'm doing something. And the more pills she takes, the sooner she'll get too sick to hold on to me."

Abby didn't push, even then, but she took a minute just to stare and pretend to be shocked. It was a pretty good idea. She should have thought of it. Since there was no barn to burn down this time.

"You're trying to kill Mom." Maybe it was stupid to say it out loud but she wanted to punish Martha, a little, for being bolder than Abby and thinking of it first.

"No! She won't die!" Martha looked legitimately upset at the thought, which sealed the deal that it was really Martha; if it had been Mom she would have tried to egg Abby on into saying that she'd help, or something else incriminating. "She'll just get too sick to keep grabbing me. I can feel her getting weaker already."

"Can you."

"Yeah. The amount of folding I've been doing, she can't possibly keep it up much longer, she keeps having to take more and more to keep me asleep."

"What the hell," Abby said, because she couldn't think of anything else to say. She hadn't thought of this, that Martha would be willing to fold her own life away, that she'd do it all on her own. She wasn't even sure if she was angry with her sister or not. "I guess it's worth a try." She picked up the remote—if what Martha was doing was working, Mom probably wouldn't hear them turn on the television at this time of night. Then she thought of something. "But be careful. Leave enough time for me to do what I need to do." Martha might think she meant homework but she was still sure she could learn enough, gain enough power, to stop Mom on her own.

Martha looked at the ground, at the blank gray face of the television. "Okay. I can leave you more time. If you'll stop stealing the pills."

And Abby meant to, until the first time Kristen asked for more, and then she decided Martha's plan wasn't going to work anyway.

CHAPTER TWENTY-NINE

Abby cleared away every trace of the ritual with more care than she'd devoted to cleaning anything in five years of living in her old apartment. Stepping in a bit of stray ash probably wouldn't do any harm, but why risk it now, when she was so close? She tried to take the mirror off the dresser, too, in an abundance of caution, but it was bolted firmly to the dresser and the entire piece of furniture was too heavy to move on her own, too close to the wall to come at with a screwdriver. She just left the towel over it. The skull she put back in a shopping bag, the shopping bag she put in the closet.

Time for lunch. Past time. She felt herself weakening and losing will from hunger. It was no good.

She didn't want to leave the room and look at Martha. That was a hell of a thing to get hung up on, after she'd done all this work. So close to the end.

If only she could use someone else, anyone. But she'd thought it over and over and the things that Briggs and Enoch had said (but hadn't said, now, but she'd still heard them) were true. Holding onto someone who wasn't family, who she didn't know with her own blood, it wouldn't stick or it would fall apart. That was why Grandfather and Mom both kept coming at Martha, instead of picking on one of the duck-people who would have been easier, unprepared, undefended, with no Abbys in their lives. That was what the notebooks claimed, and in the notebooks Grandfather only lied to himself. It might be true that Grandfather wanted the power to bend time as well—and would she still have that, in Martha's body? That would be pretty cool, she had to admit—but Mom didn't care, Abby was almost sure of that. Mom just wanted to have the teenage years back, with Grandfather dead and gone. And Martha was her only opportunity for those years.

Abby tried to convince herself that it was anything else, that she didn't feel guilty, that she wouldn't even enjoy being anyone else—and she wouldn't, that was true—and most of all that she was not afraid. But she was. If she failed now, for love of Martha or any other reason, she was never any better than Grandfather or Mom. She would die like they did, but even younger, and all that would be left was Martha. And it wouldn't even do Martha any good because without Abby, Martha would be easy pickings and end up in that hawk in the woods, just like the damn song said.

So it wouldn't be a kindness to Martha, to sacrifice herself, would it.

If she failed now, she was nothing. Oh, she'd jump out of the grave once or twice, if anyone wandered by, because Martha wouldn't think to pour salt on her and wouldn't know the words to scratch in the dirt. But she'd end up falling back. Eventually no one would even remember her, someone else would repost one of her pithy tweets perhaps and get the credit or someone would find a picture of a dead hawk and wonder why it was taken and then there'd be a slow long nothing. She felt heavy-legged, tired. She could go to the kitchen and get lunch, but she just wanted to rest here for a moment.

She should have understood. She should have been paying attention, should have figured it out. But she didn't until the night when she turned off the television at midnight and heard a thin scream, almost more a gasp, from outside. It sounded like it came from the back yard on the flat of grass between the house and the burned pit of the barn. She would have sworn it wasn't three months later.

It happened only once and she tried to ignore it for maybe an hour or so, following the cue of Mom, who didn't even stir to it. Mom was full of pills a lot of the time now even when she wasn't in Martha. But Abby couldn't sleep and Martha didn't come back inside and eventually she couldn't tell herself it was a rabbit or a neighbor. So finally she went out.

Martha was in the back yard, at the foot of the old maple tree, her jeans discarded in a bloody damp mess by her side. The first one had been born by the time Abby got there, in another bloody damp mess in the grass, and Martha was holding her hand over its mouth and nose. Her own mouth looked as though she were biting off her lips from the inside, she was so determined not to make another sound.

"Martha!"

Martha looked at her but her eyes were a dog's eyes for all they had in them. The spark in the infant faded as Abby watched but Martha didn't move her hand even as her teeth clenched and her body cramped and she pressed her back against the tree.

"Why didn't you tell me? We could have fixed this."

Martha shook her head and Abby couldn't argue with the message, "What would you have done?" But still. She hadn't even been given a chance.

She turned to walk away and Martha finally opened her mouth to whisper, "Don't leave me." But she did leave, just as far as the kitchen, to take a carving knife from the drawer and leave the light on as she came back outside.

The second one was born as she crossed back to the maple in the light from the window. She bent down by the thing. It was bloody and pink and wrinkled and covered with a sort of wax; there was nothing going on with its face that looked human, and its intentions were all inward, towards hunger, endless need, a gigantic sucking vortex not much different than the tentacles and mouths in the shadows. She was careful not to touch it. The intentions were enormous. It would be powerful if it was allowed. No wonder the first one had scared Martha so badly.

"Fuck you," she said, holding the steel point to pink flesh. "Fuck you for hurting my sister." And she pressed down. She was surprised how satisfying it felt to pierce the skin.

When Martha stopped sobbing and shuddering, Abby sent her inside to take a shower and rest. She buried the mess in the yard herself. Maybe that was the last really kind thing she could remember doing for her sister. But she hadn't known the lines to draw then, and she'd screwed it up. She hadn't brought salt. She didn't know.

CHAPTER THIRTY

It didn't feel like she slept—it didn't feel like she was sleepy, just tired in a sore, sick way. But when she opened her eyes again, it was dark.

Her first thought was *goddammit Martha*. But getting antagonistic wouldn't help. Instead she sat up, got her feet to the floor, made it to a standing position. Christ, she couldn't have actually slept. She still felt like she'd had her marrow sucked out.

Through the curtains, a sharp sliver of light, then a crack and roll of noise. Abby flinched involuntarily, but she also thought, not Martha then. Good. Just a storm. Just a normal summer storm and nothing to do with anything, anyone in their family, dead or alive, because she really couldn't deal with that right now. Warm front, cold front, something for the weather guy to worry about and not her.

Just to be sure she peered through the curtains. The rain was pounding, bending the branches—she thought she saw small pellets of hail but it was hard to tell in the maelstrom. The light was greenish-black. The graves, well, the grave singular with the three bodies, was carved with rivulets, the symbols completely washed away no doubt but if she did it right it shouldn't matter now. So long as enough dirt didn't erode away to actually expose the corpses.

Abby dropped the curtain and made her way back across the room, half by feel. The lightning flashed twice more as she did so, the second time with thunder so close at its tail that they might have been the same animal. It was hard not to be afraid when it was that close, though she knew the cabin was perfectly safe.

Martha always used to freak out during storms. She should go and check in on her. Do something nice. Take care of her, at least, until the last.

Martha wasn't in her room, or the bedroom that had once been Mom's, and she wasn't in the kitchen. Not in the bathroom. Abby headed down into the last room then. It was a sunken living room, or that's what they'd called it; with hindsight it was more like a den. At any rate it was a place they'd never spent much time because Grandfather liked to spread his books out there and work in the glow from the fireplace, even on hot days. Sometimes in the evenings Mom would corral them all together and insist on a few rounds of cards or a board game, or once an abortive attempt to make S'mores that ended with shouting and tears and chocolate stains and scorch marks on the rug. Abby always thought it was because Mom didn't want to feel stupid for having packed those things in the first place, camouflage meant to convince herself and nonexistent observers that they were having a normal vacation.

The scorched carpet was long replaced but the living room still felt half-forbidden, and even more dangerous in the darkness with the rain pinging off the windows. Abby found it thrilling to enter, understood at once why Grandfather had claimed it, but she would be surprised if Martha would take refuge here.

She was even more surprised, though, to find the living room empty but for Buddy. He was crouched low to the floor between sofa and coffee table, not even whimpering but panting so fast and shallow that it was like a rabbit's breath, a mouse's.

"Martha?" Raising her voice felt risky, in this light and in this place, but there was nowhere left to look. There was no reply. God-damn, but the rain was loud. She wasn't sure she'd hear an answer in Martha's voice if it came.

Abby made her way back to the kitchen, though you couldn't miss a grown woman in a kitchen that size. Maybe Martha stepped into the pantry for... some reason. Maybe she'd lost it completely and Abby would find her crouched down behind the island, pant-ing with fear like Buddy, or crawled and curled into a cupboard. Maybe she was sick and passed out on the floor, or she was also overcome by that strange sleepiness.

Or maybe something far worse had gone wrong. Maybe, despite Mom's and Abby's confidence that the place could take care of itself and bear the steps of outsiders, something on this land was left too long untended. Maybe something had been too recently disturbed. Maybe by drawing her adversary here she'd empowered him, as much as herself. Maybe the power was in the air as well as the earth, and even a hawk could find it.

This was what she must not do. Lose confidence. Start dwelling on all the things that could go wrong and she'd never surface again, no one would, the mind can't hold so many possibilities and stay able. Confidence, pride, knowing that she was strong even when she wasn't, that was all that held the world in the correct shape. She would find Martha and whatever was wrong with Martha, keeping Martha from answering her, she'd fix, and move on with her plan. That was the only problem to think about right now. Then she'd worry about everything else.

The lightning and thunder came again all at once. Abby, tense and focused as she was, noticed the flash where it shouldn't be, and then the shadows moving slightly as the wind gusted and fell. The front door was wide open.

Outside, Martha had made it about halfway across the lawn. The hawk strutted ahead of her like a big angry chicken. It was a slow process, and Martha was shuffling in the soaked grass not to overtake the bird, but it looked too soaked and matted to fly.

Idiot, Abby thought. If it wasn't someone easy like Martha he could blow it just by looking that ridiculous. He should have waited until the rain let up, and soared around being magnificent—but he wanted to move while Abby was asleep, probably.

Abby hesitated, just for an instant, trying to judge if the rain was turning to hail again. It wasn't, or she hoped it wasn't. She was soaked the instant she stepped out from under the roof of the porch, straight to the socks and underwear.

At least now it didn't matter what she did next, she'd be wet regardless. So she ran across the lawn, the grass squishing and streaming like a sponge underneath her, and grabbed Martha by the shoulder at the same moment that she grabbed the focus of Martha's attention and wrenched it away from the bedraggled hawk. Martha turned, frowning at first, but when she recognized Abby she hugged her tight and buried her face against her sister's soaked left shoulder.

The hawk shrieked and beat its wings, but there was nothing he could do. It couldn't even take off. It sort of marched towards them, rolling from side to side, but a harsh stare from Abby was enough to remind him of how helpless he was in that soaked body, what happened last time he tried to take her on physically.

After minutes, when her shoulder felt like it was beginning to steam with Martha's breath and she was almost headachy from staring down the hawk, Abby shrugged Martha off. Before her sister could interpret that as rejection, she grabbed her hand, lacing their fingers together.

Something struck her hard on the back, with a sharp burning pain, and she and Martha fell heavily together onto the grass. Abby managed to stay on her knees but Martha was flat on her face for a

moment before she scrambled and rolled and screamed and pointed. Abby turned to see a fresher, drier hawk circling down for a second blow and threw her hand up only just in time. Talons slashed
deep into the meat of her forearm.

He was in two separate birds, holding one in reserve someplace
sheltered… No, she realized. *They* were in two separate birds. There
was a separation that one mind could never achieve no matter how
sophisticated or how maddened. They both survived, they both
still existed somehow.

The one on the ground was the weaker of the two so she grabbed
at his intentions blindly and sent him fluttering. As she hoped, this
distracted the flying bird and he turned his attention from her and
Martha for a moment. She pulled her sister to her feet and they
lurched back towards the door, but the hawk in the air was too
fast for them and came down in front, trying to drive them back
towards its twin, towards the graves, towards the woods… which?
Or all of those things?

She tried to reach for both of them at once but that was too
much, she lost her hold on the grounded bird and couldn't catch
the other. Martha started to let go of her hand so Abby clenched
her fingers tighter to keep her sister from panicking and bolting.
They both backed up a step instinctively, away from the beating
wings and grasping claws of the swooping bird, towards whatever
it was that the hawks wanted them to go towards. That was the first
mistake, to do what they wanted for any reason was a crack they
could pry at, she'd done it herself. She felt the push of the stronger
one, finally realizing that getting at her was the key to getting at
Martha, telling her to just let her sister go and save herself.

Little fools didn't realize that she couldn't save herself without
Martha. They'd stuck together themselves down the years, from
some kind of instinct or simply not to be alone, but they couldn't
reason, so they couldn't apply their own behavior to others. Maybe

they took after Grandfather at that, Abby thought spitefully, using sarcasm and contempt to close off the soft spot in her mind from their pressure.

She had to do this. She knew she could. They were both focused on her now, not on Martha, and though they were strong and fast they were not smart, not canny, not experienced, still babies really. And most of all, they didn't know what they actually wanted. To kill, to possess, to keep alive and suffering, they wanted it all and there was no way they could have it so they weren't acting in unison, not really. She drew deep, pulling strength from them while they focused on her unguarded, and they didn't realize she was doing it until it was too late for them and she could throw her mind over both of them like a net. The flying bird tumbled to the ground just before he could reach them. The other let out a weak scream.

She didn't dare let go of Martha's hand so she stepped on the bird at her feet, one foot on its wing and then the other deliberately and firmly on its neck. The spine was stronger than she thought it would be—they were supposed to be hollow, weren't they? The bones. It wasn't this hard when she was hitting it with the wine bottle. She leaned forward with all her weight and there was a crunch. The other bird beat its wings but still couldn't get off the ground.

"Come on," Abby said, lifting her foot, tugging Martha towards the door. "They'll find new birds as soon as the rain stops. We have to get under cover."

Martha, before they'd walked more than three steps, began to cry. That was okay, though. It wouldn't get them any wetter.

Mom said nothing for days, pretending not to notice as Abby tried to keep Martha out of sight, tried to keep her eyes or her mind from resting on the little patch of disturbed soil behind the maple. Maybe she really didn't notice, at first—the pills and the wine and all—or maybe she'd been planning to bring the hammer down in some elaborate, unbalancing way. Abby could never have asked her, after, and if she had asked she could never have trusted her answer.

It was a week, maybe, that they all lived like that, like they were inside a bag of broken glass trying not to move or rub up against each other. Abby and Martha went to school and they came home, they ate dinner and they washed dishes, and Abby had just enough time to go from *This is finally it, finally now we'll have to fight her head-on* to *Even this changes nothing, even this wasn't that big a deal.* If Martha felt sad or sick or scared of what Mom might do, she didn't show it any more than usual.

Then one night while Abby was finishing up the dishes flashing lights broke up the darkness of the road outside and sirens wailed in from the west. Even that didn't seem so odd until the police cars pulled into their driveway. Mom slammed a book shut in the living room and swore, rattling off to the bathroom to hide her pills. Abby ran for Martha's room, but Martha wasn't there. She wasn't in Abby's room either. When Abby found her she was downstairs opening the door to two police officers with thoughts much darker and harder than the ones who'd brought Mom home in her body.

Abby's only excuse for not doing more was that she simply could not understand what she was seeing. Martha was Martha and Mom was just emerging from the bathroom, smiling and trying to placate, by the time Martha led the officers out the back door and to the foot of the tree and undid all Abby's handiwork. Dark hard thoughts, dark hard nods, another man came forward with a shovel. What they found was nothing so awful, not for someone who'd seen the last of Grandfather, but it upset the duck-people into a frenzy. And for a moment Abby froze and wanted to scream as the police looked at her and Mom and asked, "Did they know?"

But Martha said no without pushing or so much as a scowl from either of them.

The police questioned Abby anyway, of course, and that was

giddy, terrifying fun, being the subject of so much focus. But after a while all the questions were about Martha—had she acted weird before? After? Had she done anything else wrong? Oh, cutting a lot of school and running around with older boys? Was she on drugs? Abby thought about narcing on Mom for a moment, she deserved it, but getting put in foster care seemed like more trouble than it was worth. And then the questions ended but she still wasn't allowed to go up to bed, just had to sit in the living room with Mom, both of them staring at the floor while strangers bagged their kitchen knives and Martha's bedsheets and dug up more of the yard than they needed to.

Even after they left, long after midnight, Mom didn't say anything to Abby. She didn't say anything about it in the days that followed, nothing specific or incriminating, just long wine-fueled rants about how Martha had always been weak and ungrateful between ever-increasing dozes. She was getting weaker and Abby—more stared at than ever and learning how to use that better every day—was getting stronger and they could both feel the balance of power tipping. Mom even made noises about keeping Abby out of school, as though that would be a favor, and the guidance counselor called the house and suggested the same thing. Abby was able to bat both of them down.

If she'd thought she knew what attention felt like before that had been nothing. Every emotion in the world was in the stares that she got now—fear so deep it felt like nausea, genuinely murderous hatred, but also fascination and in more than a few eyes a weird sort of respect. She was part of something they had to care about. No one could ignore her now.

Then, slowly, the yellow tape around the maple tattered and rattled in the wind. People stopped driving by just to yell vulgarities at the house, and the attention at school stopped being quite so lightning-hot. Abby waited to feel weaker again but she didn't.

She'd leveled up somehow, in some way she didn't fully understand. She'd become an adult, maybe. Now all she had to do was go un-fuck her sister's mistakes and things could be better than they'd ever been. She and Martha could do anything they wanted now. They could be happy.

When she finally pushed Mom into sobering up long enough to drive her to visit Martha, she had her plan all ready.

"I can fix it," she said, not in a whisper—that would be suspicious, and she was already pushing the guards to ignore them—but quietly enough. "All I have to do is be in the room when the jury goes out to deliberate, and it'll be fine. I'll just nudge each of them a little bit. Doubt's not that hard, right?" She was projecting more bravado than she felt, since she couldn't be in the room with them during deliberations—she'd tried to think of a way but even if she pushed everyone at court, some lawyer would realize what she'd done later. But she wanted to cheer Martha up, and herself too; the sight of her twin drowning in a too-big orange shirt was depressing.

Instead, Martha looked disgusted. "No. There won't be a trial. I'm going to plead guilty, you won't even get to testify." She said it fast, like she was afraid the defiance in her voice would just fall out and leave her with nothing. "I know that probably breaks your heart. No one will be looking at you."

"What?"

"Abby, I'm not stupid. What do you think I planned to have happen when I called the cops and confessed? Why would I do that and then plead innocent?"

"You confessed?" Abby inhaled deeply. "What *did* you plan? Why the hell *would* you do that?"

Martha looked over Abby's shoulder for a moment to where Mom was waiting, and then back into her sister's eyes. "I figured I'd be safer in here."

CHAPTER THIRTY-ONE

A mosquito landed on her arm as she changed into dry clothes and as she squashed it she realized that the door was still open. That was no good with the hawk, a forest full of hawks, still out there. She needed to focus. She took a picture of the mosquito bite, captioned it "Tiny vampires everywhere!"

Wait, now it was night again. The moon was smaller, eaten away by a sliver. Goddamn Martha and her sulking. She needed more time, not less. And Martha should want more time, not less.

She blinked. It was light, the light of morning.

She blinked. The sun was slanted the other way.

Goddammit, Martha. There was no way she could be doing this by accident, in a sulk. And here Abby was feeling sorry for her.

Abby stuck her phone out the window and took a photo of whatever trees were in her way, filtered it blue and purple to make it eye-catching. No wonder the surges of power were falling off. If days were getting folded away and she wasn't posting...

She lifted herself to her feet—she felt so dizzy, fragile, she was sure she wasn't dead yet but she wasn't sure how she could be so sure—and went to confront her sister.

"You will not," Mom said. "I forbid it." She was doing a good job of trying to imitate the person she once was, the person who could forbid things. She was sober and upright and dressed in actual clothes, not sweats or pajamas. Abby could barely remember the last time this had been true—maybe at Martha's sentencing.

None of it was going to do her any good, though. Abby wondered what Mom saw, was it the kindergartner with the birthday party invitation? The kid who had, though neither of them ever did admit it out loud to each other, burned down the barn to save her sister and set the process in motion that rid them all of Grandfather for good? The teenager who could walk through the mall and come out of every store with an armload of goodies if she chose, smiling at checkout clerks and security guards as she passed them? Or did she just see her natural prey?

"I can and I will. I already filled out the paperwork."

"With what money?" The answer was obvious—with Mom's money, Grandfather's money that should have been Martha's and the income from the cabin in Minnesota. Abby had put herself to the task of imitating Mom's handwriting well enough to sign checks, and it had come easily enough—which was fortunate, since the bills hardly would have gotten paid otherwise. And what worked for checks worked for credit card applications as well when they arrived in the mail.

"I got a scholarship."

"To NYU? With your grades?"

"On account of my sparkling personality." All of this was, technically, true. The scholarship was only a partial and she'd pushed hard for it, but it was real.

"And if you leave, who's going to look out for your sister?"

Abby actually had to choke back a laugh at this line of attack—look out for Martha? Even at the sentencing, Martha's hard leave-me-alone stare had dissuaded Abby from trying to fix the judge's mind on mercy. All she'd been able to do was shut him up half-finished from his long-planned speech on the depravity of today's youth, and she hadn't done that for Martha, but because he was annoying the shit out of her, Abby. She'd written letters to no reply, she wasn't sure if they even made it through, and then she gave up. What she did for Martha was make sure her commissary account never went dry, and she could do that as easily from Manhattan as from Alden.

Mom hadn't even done those few things, so anything she had to say about looking out for Martha could go and curdle the wind.

"You're just going to leave me here all alone." Mom's few remaining work friends had abandoned her, naturally, after the case hit the papers and she lost her job. The only outside humans she talked to now were a few easily-influenced pharmacists in a handful of locations far apart from each other—one in Batavia, one in Attica, one in Depew. Every so often one would get fired and she'd have to drive all over and find a new one. It had gotten depressing to watch.

Abby had lost most of her friends too. Kristen's parents had put her in rehab after they found her incoherent in the bathroom one night, and Carl blamed Abby for that, and Duane—well, Duane wasn't a functional friend to begin with, and he'd graduated, barely, under a steady stream of taunts about being the father of dead babies. For some reason Luke hadn't gotten any of those, but then again, no one but Abby knew why doing the regular kind of math didn't solve this problem, and she wasn't going to defend stupid Duane. After a year moping around at home he'd gone off to one of the sadder SUNY schools to start over. He'd called Abby once, just after midnight and so drunk she knew instantly that someone had put him up to the drinking and he'd only dialed their number from the instincts in his fingers. She hung up on him and he was finally gone.

None of that mattered, though, because people still stared at her and warmed her, whispered and fed her, sneered or struggled not to ask an awkward question and gave her strength—more than any friend ever could. And she had a plan now too, inspired by the news coverage of Martha's case. She was going to study journalism and be a TV anchor and people would never stop looking at her. She'd be damn near invincible. She might never die, she might achieve Grandfather's dream for her own self and in a way he was too limited to imagine.

Thinking of it made her feel stronger even now, and she quickly detected the signs of Mom pushing at the edges now that she saw Abby was serious, looking to force her. "You will be alone," Abby said evenly. "You didn't exactly do anything to make me want to stay with you, and you put Martha where she is now. I don't see how you can complain."

Mom stood up at that, but when she raised her hand to slap Abby—who now stood well over her—Abby caught her mind and her wrist both. She squeezed, just a little. Mom sat down again with a sob.

"You stupid, spoiled little brat," she said through clenched-back tears. "I hope that when you have children, they salt your grave." And that was how Abby learned the last key to keeping her relatives dead. She looked it up later in the Orne to be sure, and there it was, if you knew what you were looking for.

In the moment, she simply filed the fact away and turned for the door. The car was already loaded and the tank was full; she'd known better than to tell Mom one minute earlier than that. It was the last time Abby saw her mother before she poured salt over her face, and then dirt.

CHAPTER THIRTY-TWO

Martha was still sitting in the kitchen and it was not clear from her eyes or the swirl of her intentions just what was going on. Did she know Grandfather had been here? Did she realize that there were two minds pursuing her as hawks and not just one? She didn't say a word as Abby pulled the summer sausage from the refrigerator and a crayon-yellow squeeze bottle of mustard to go with it. She was wearing that locket Grandmother left her. Abby thought, I should have recognized that before. After the moment on the cliff, the tying of the knot, I should have known. I wasn't paying attention.

"Where's the bread?" Abby asked when the silence got too annoying.

"Where it always is."

And it was, in the same drawer that Mom used to file it in when they'd come out here.

Half a sandwich later Abby finally decided that confronting Martha probably meant actually having a confrontation, not just hoping she'd fold without pushing or talk. It felt obscene, but she was supposed to be the one who lived in a world where privacy was obsolete, right? Not being able to actually talk to her sister was just ridiculous, a hangover from the way Mom and Grandfather raised them, never able to tell anyone the truth about anything.

"You're trying to kill me," Martha said while Abby was thinking and her mouth was full.

There was only so fast a person could swallow, and Abby didn't rush it, refused to choke and sputter like she was in some kind of sitcom. She chewed until she was done.

"I'm not. You're the one who started it with the killing people, anyway." Martha stared at her. She took another bite of the sandwich and chewed neither faster nor slower than she had before.

"You want to take over my body," Martha said. Speaking was costing her, the way she had to force her will to focus on Abby. She found this conversation hard too. That comforted Abby in a weird way. "And your body is dying. I saw you were sick as soon as you picked me up. So if you're in my body and I'm in yours, I'll be the one who dies."

"You'll die anyway, without anyone to protect you from what's out there."

"I might not. I just want a chance. You're not giving me a chance."

"You think they'll turn sentimental on you?"

Martha shook her head. "They're family. They're just like you."

"And you. You're no different."

"You can't be... you can't be mad at me for that. You can't be surprised at what I'll do to survive." Martha was the one who seemed to be having a hard time swallowing, even though Abby's throat was the one that was dry with crappy Wonder bread and sodium-packed sausage.

She was about to say, "I'm only surprised that you think you'll win," and just let it be, finally, that they were blown apart into open war, like everyone in their family had to be when the truth was out. Then the hawks screamed outside the window. It will be those little bastards winning, she thought, and that made her angrier. They'd only got one brain between them and it was a bird brain. Wait. One brain between them. And they were not, were never, any better than her, for all that they had raw power.

"I'm only surprised that you don't trust me," she said. "I wasn't going to put you into my body."

"You weren't going to let yourself die! You just said so!" She sounded offended, but her mind was turning to Abby a bit more hopefully now.

"Of course not, that would be stupid. But I don't need your whole body, Martha. We can share."

"That's…"

"I mean of course Mom and Grandfather never even tried! Mom and Grandfather were selfish bastards!" Something they could agree on together, to get their minds in alignment without pushing. "But look at those two out there—" she nodded towards the window. "It's both of them, even when it's only one hawk."

"You're lying." That was a fair thought, Abby couldn't be mad at her for thinking that, even now she was finally not lying at all. And it wasn't like Martha could see for herself.

Except she did. "No, think about it. Outside, in the rain just now. Or however long ago it really was. You saw that two separate birds attacked us. Two separate birds, two separate minds."

"Mom was able to control two bodies at once."

"Only when she needed two bodies doing the exact same thing. And only when they were really close together, practically touching. This is both of them, sharing a body, and if they can we can."

Martha's mind settled like a bird onto a nest, back to the place where Abby was her protector—the earliest place. She wanted to believe. She knew she couldn't win, and it was cold comfort fighting to lose. But she was still scared, too. She breathed hard, as though all this had been a physical exertion. "But what if we don't want to do the same things?"

"We'll do what we've always done. Argue about it." Abby grinned like a sister on a sitcom or in one of Martha's book club books and didn't point out that she'd do what she'd always done, and win.

"What if I want to… I don't know, do something you'd never do? What if I want to eat waffles for breakfast, or get another dog, or move to Montana?"

"We'll work it out." Abby tried to think of what a nice person would say. "Compromise or something. I promise you'll get some of the things you want, sometimes."

"What if I want to have more kids? You can't compromise on that."

Abby started to say *Are you crazy* but of course she'd, they'd, have to unless she wanted to be just this screwed again in sixty years. Or worse, as screwed as Enoch and Briggs.

"We'll figure something out, there'll be plenty of time to make a plan."

Martha wanted to believe her. And that was not the same as pushing to Martha to give Abby what she wanted, even if the tendrils of Martha's mind wavered and clutched in the same way. But Martha kept looking away, she always did when she thought she might be pushed, as though that would protect her.

"You're just telling me what I want to hear, and then you'll be in my body and I'll be stuck."

"Listen." Abby leaned in. She didn't push even now, Martha was waiting for that and it would ruin everything, but she used every other trick she knew. "I'm your sister. I was always on your side. I would have saved you from all of it if I could. I burned down the goddamn barn for you." Abby squeezed the sandwich for emphasis. Mustard on her hands, a thing some people might do as a sincere mistake. Martha was going to notice even in her peripheral vision. She didn't really want the rest anyway.

Martha shook her head.

"Come on," Abby said. She stood up, licked her fingers. "Take a walk with me, huh?"

Martha followed.

Out the door into the golden light. Past where Grandfather stood to frighten the bear. Past where the bear was. The creek was high for summer, but it did just rain. Abby splashed through, not caring any more about wet socks and hems, just wanting to take the direct path.

"Why are you doing that?" Martha asked. "I don't want to get muddy."

"You can jump across." Abby held out her hands. There was still a yellow smear on one. "Come on."

"No, let's just go the other way."

Abby thought again about pushing, it would be so easy, but she wouldn't. There was no magic in promises but there was a weird kind of magic in someone knowing they'd been broken or kept. They headed away west instead, along the creek, towards the little waterfall where they once saw the garter snakes mate. At some point Buddy started bounding after them, and now he'd caught up. Martha ruffled his ears.

A hawk circled above them but it didn't stoop or cry out. It might have been just a hawk. There were plenty of hawks in the woods.

Martha had changed her mind about getting wet, it seemed. She walked the rocks half in the water, bent to trail her fingers in the stream as Buddy splashed and snapped at minnows. "Do you remember how we used to hunt crayfish here?"

Abby nodded. The crayfish would run away backwards. They didn't hurt them. Just caught them and let them go. Tried not to get pinched. A way to kill time.

Leaves were floating. Brown and yellow. Abby caught one, the water cold around her fingers. Oak. Fallen too soon.

Martha stared at her until Abby said, "What, are you going to push me in?"

"Jesus, Abby. No, I'm just thinking, okay?"

"Thinking about what?"

"About when we were kids."

"It wasn't that great," Abby said, feeling defensive without knowing why.

"It was when we were here, though, wasn't it? No one messed with us when we were here."

Abby nodded slowly. No one messed with them when they were here. A long time ago, she'd enjoyed that time to herself, when no one was paying attention. A long time ago, she'd been a child.

She could do this. She'd always been able to do what she set her mind to, and she could do this, and save her sister and herself too.

Dark fell before they got to the standing stone. As she stepped into the clearing, her feet crunched on frost in the grass.

"Martha. Jesus."

"I'm..." Martha visibly gathered her strength. She was really scared, Abby realized with dismay. "I'm not doing that. I think they can do it too. It would only make sense, right?"

Abby wanted to laugh out loud. If he'd been kinder, more interested in persuading, Grandfather could have gotten his wish in one more generation.

Martha kept trying to unfold what they'd folded, but then they pushed her and Abby could see her face go blank and her work undone. They jumped hot to cold, light to dark. If this spot wasn't as strong as Grandfather claimed, if Abby needed to wait for the stars to be right, she'd be screwed.

At least they didn't have the technique to knot off time, yet. You had to be taught.

"Okay," she said, and pressed a hand to Martha's chest to lean her back onto the stone. On her shoulder the tumor was the size of a cabbage rose and restricted her movements, and it felt for a breath like Martha was going to to change her mind at the last moment and fight. Abby almost despaired, almost pushed.

Buddy growled. She was pretty sure it was at the hawk that had landed awkwardly in the only tree to dare to throw a branch out over the clearing. Pretty sure she was still not Grandfather. She didn't push Martha, just to prove to herself that she was doing the right thing, and also because Martha stopped fighting at the sight of the hawk.

She was at the last of her strength. She flashed back and forth. Facing down, facing up. A healthy body. A body wracked by something she'd barely noticed growing.

She threw herself completely into her sister at the same moment the infants riding the hawks flung themselves downward and tried to do the same, but they didn't know what they were doing, they never had the chance to learn.

The starving inchoate creatures bore down on her but she and her sister didn't have to give in. She said the words, yelled them really. She sat up. The near-skeletal form was across her lap. *Damn, I look like hell*, she thought, and then caught herself. It was not her and it was important not to think of it as her. It was it, empty and rotting like a house or a barn. The tumor was huge on its shoulder.

Then it was no longer an it, but a them. The body with the tumor screamed, high pitched, wordless because they never learned language, nothing but the urge to take and take and take around their head. The scream itself was what taxed the body over the edge. She rolled them away, lurched to her feet, let them fall to the forest floor to break physical contact. The scream didn't cut off, instead it died away and echoed down the forest. Every living creature for miles could hear what happened, most could smell it too. The rocks and earth absorbed it. Sometimes patches of woods like these stayed cold and shadowed and avoided for generations, with stories about ghosts or strange apes around them. All the better. This would be part of the lore that someone might see here if anyone else ever dared try for a ritual in the cabin.

Bare toes burned in the snow. Why didn't Martha put on shoes? *You didn't give me time.* A whimper. She touched the locket around her neck, and Martha seemed to calm down.

Her old body twitched in the leaf litter and died, the hunger with it. No strength left for them to make a return trip, not after the last desperate plunge and the scream. A hawk plummeted out of the tree beside them and Buddy started to run in to sniff it, then shied away with his ruff raised.

Now she just needed to bury them. No need to use Buddy for it; they wouldn't stir for a while and Martha should be able to bring time to a spring thaw by the time she'd, they'd, driven to town to buy a shovel and a cleaver and more salt. The ceremony would be simple and they'd stay down, like Mom did. She felt so much stronger now.

Abby started the walk back to the cabin, striding, swinging her arms, barely feeling the cold. She felt all-powerful, that she pulled that off.

In the back of her head she still heard a whimper from Martha. She wondered how long it would be before she would get over it, what she could do to cheer her sister up. "Listen," she said, jolly, like she planned it this way all along. "We can have that wine now."

ACKNOWLEDGMENTS

I'd like to thank my editor Ross Lockhart at Word Horde and my fantastic agent Stephen Barbara. Paul Tremblay and John Langan were big parts of making this happen as well.

Thanks to those who read all or part of this in manuscript form and offered valuable feedback, support, and the occasional 'fuck yeah'—Myrrah Dubey, Cara Hoffman, Janice Laben, Leah Laben, Robert Levy, Kaylen Mallard, Nick Mamatas, Andrew May, and James Nokes.

Thanks to the MacDowell Colony and the Anne LaBastille Memorial Writers Residency for offering me the gift of time and space and community and feeling like a real writer.

Thanks to the University of Montana MFA crew—especially Jon Bachmann, Zoey Barnes, Kim Bell, Alice Bolin, Nick Bosworth, Mackenzie Cole, Ariana Del Negro, Sam Duncan, Josh Foman, Elizabeth Geier, Molly Laich, Rosemary Madero, Emma Pfieffer, Brian Pillion, Jordan Rossen, Julie Rouse, Asta So, B.J. Soloy, Jamie Stathis, Emma Torzs, Keema Waterfield, Diana Xin, Khaty Xiong, Nathan Yrizarry, and all those who joined me in Debra Magpie Earling's witchy workshops (and of course Debra herself). Love to my advisor Judy Blunt, even if I've strayed from the path of truth and light known as creative nonfiction! And to the Nut House girls + co. (including but not limited to Megan 'Little Bee' Bland, Megan 'Biscuit' Cleinmark, Deana DeWire, Elena Evans, Colleen Fitzpatrick, Shane Glidewell, Connie and Julian McCune, Karin Riley, Alan Swanson, Aaron Fleisch, Jenn Estrada, and Boluda) and persons affiliated with the 503 and Butterfly Herbs (again ibnlt River Aloia, Charlie Darling, Ingrid Malesich, Jeff Rummel, Skunk Sanner, and Kris Van Whye), without whom I'd have starved or frozen to death.

Besides the above, thanks to S.J. Bagley, Laird Barron, Steve Berman, Daniel Braum, Jenn Brissett, Michael Cisco, Neil Clarke, Ellen Datlow, Erik den Breejen, Andy Duncan, Andrea Elliott, John Foster, Amy Gall, Janie Geiser, Molly Grattan, Karen Heuler, Judy Hoffman, Amanda Huynh, Gabino Iglesias, Juleen Johnson, Laura Kammermeier, Nick Kaufmann, David James Keaton, Gwendolyn Kiste, Matthew Kressel, Sarah Langan, Victor LaValle, J. Robert Lennon, Marc Lepson, Casey Llewellyn, Greg Marshall, Tara Mateik, Justin Maxwell, Koji Nakano, Marc Ohrem-Leclef, Ekaterina Sedia, Chandler Klang Smith, Farah Rose Smith, Haruko Tanaka, Morgan Thorson, Genevieve Valentine, Sean Wallace, Michael Wehunt, and Joyce Zonana.

Speaking of not freezing to death, maximum thanks to Charles "Chuk" Radder, who probably did not think when he let me move in that he'd end up bankrolling the writing of a novel.

ABOUT THE AUTHOR

Carrie Laben grew up in western New York. She earned her BS at Cornell and later her MFA at the University of Montana. She now lives in Queens, where she spends a lot of time staring at birds.

Her work has appeared in such venues as *Birding*, *Clarkesworld*, *The Dark*, *Indiana Review*, *Okey-Panky*, and *Outlook Springs*. In 2017 she won the Shirley Jackson Award in Short Fiction for her story "Postcards from Natalie" and Duke University's Documentary Essay Prize for the essay "The Wrong Place". In 2015 she was selected for the Anne LaBastille Memorial Writer's Residency, in 2018 she was a MacDowell Fellow, and in 2019 she was a resident at Brush Creek.

This is her first novel. She is currently at work on a book of essays about urban environmentalism.

CPSIA information can be obtained
at www.ICGtesting.com
Printed in the USA
FSHW012229090319
56154FS